Agent of Artifice

By

S. Evan Townsend

World Castle Publishing
http://www.worldcastlepublishing.com

S. EVAN TOWNSEND

This is a work of fiction. Names, characters, places, and incidents are products of the author's imagination or are used fictitiously and are not to be construed as real. Any resemblance to actual events, locations, organizations, or person, living or dead, is entirely coincidental.

World Castle Publishing
Pensacola, Florida

Copyright © S. Evan Townsend 2011
ISBN: 9781937593186
Library of Congress Catalogue Number 2011937349

First Edition World Castle Publishing November 15, 2011
http://www.worldcastlepublishing.com

Licensing Notes

All rights reserved. No part of this book may be used or reproduced in any manner whatsoever without written permission, except in the case of brief quotations embodied in articles and reviews.

Cover: Karen Fuller
Editor: Maxine Bringenberg

AGENT OF ARTIFICE

DEDICATION

Dedicated to Orlando Zapata Tamayo and all the victims of Cuban repression.

S. EVAN TOWNSEND

CHAPTER ONE
Miami, November 25, 1963

"You know why I really hated the *bastard*?" Gomez said loudly, sloshing his drink in the general direction of the bar's TV. The brown liquid almost spilled out, which wasn't a completely bad thing; Gomez hadn't always been such a cheap drunk. Judging by the bar he'd dragged me into, his habits had changed perhaps as his fortunes had diminished, even though his waistline had grown in the five years since I'd known him in Havana, making the booth a tight fit for him. He had a head of thick white hair and a bushy white mustache, both of which served to offset his dark skin and make him appear swarthier than he actually was. He'd probably been a handsome youth but he was pushing 60, according to his dossier. Age — or the whiskey and cigars he so loved — wasn't being kind to the old Cuban.

A few of the other patrons, most sitting on stools at the bar, turned to glare at him. I ignored the bar flies, thinking anyone who chose to drink confined by dark greasy wood, dirty windows and acres of vinyl weren't worth my consideration.

"Cuba," Gomez, after taking a drink, continued, oblivious to the ire being cast in our direction. "The bastard lost my Cuba to the Reds."

I had nothing to say, so I stared through the thick, blue cigarette smoke at the TV hanging behind the bar. In blacks and grays was the iconic image of the flag-draped coffin on the horse-drawn caisson moving slowly through the streets of Washington D.C on its way to the Arlington Cemetery. The dead president was to be buried among war heroes, which was fitting, the TV commentators kept reminding us. JPK twice volunteered to continue flying combat missions rather than be "rotated" home. In his last mission, for which he earned the Navy Cross, he flew a B-24 bomber packed with explosives and set up for radio control. He got it into the air, flying it until a "mother" radio control plane could take over, then he and his co-pilot bailed out, still over England. The plane was to be crashed into a German V-2 rocket base in Normandy, but it exploded over the Channel. Kennedy hurt his back upon landing and it had caused him constant pain that he stoically and bravely ignored. I knew all this because it had been reported *ad nauseam* since the assassination. None of the three networks had resumed regular broadcasting yet.

There was a shot of the crowds lining the streets and Gomez grumbled.

"Yeah, the people loved him. Ol' Joe, Jr. We'll probably have a dynasty of them now, Robbie and what's-his-name."

"Edward," I said, surprised I knew it, but it, too, had probably been mentioned more than once since Friday.

Once Gomez got on his Kennedy rant it was best just to let it run its course. He could have picked a more appropriate day, though.

"Yeah, Teddy. The old bootlegger probably couldn't be more proud. Thank God Jack got himself killed driving his PT boat in front of a Jap destroyer. Man was incompetent; never should have been commissioned but his father couldn't have a 4-F son. Wouldn't look good." He guzzled his cheap Scotch and slammed the glass on the cheap oilcloth tabletop with a bang that echoed around the cheap bar. "But you know why I hated that *bastard*, Joe Jr."

Now everyone in the bar was looking at Gomez and me and hating us. I noticed the bartender (and probable owner) peering at us as if debating asking us to leave.

"Come on," I said, sliding out of the booth and hoping he'd follow, "it's too damn hot in here. Let's go outside." If I wanted to stay, I could. But I didn't.

Reluctantly Gomez stood, gave the television one last angry glance, and shuffled to the door.

"Cuba," Gomez said as I pulled him out onto the street and into the bright sunshine that seemed especially dazzling after the dark, dingy tavern. The bar hadn't been that warm; it was just an excuse to get him out of there. But, outside in November, it was much more pleasant.

Gomez and I walked a ways. The streets were unusually quiet, even for a Monday. Or maybe it was just quieter compared to the South Miami Beach neighborhood where I'd been living. However, the murder of the young president had sobered the nation. It didn't seem to matter now about the voting irregularities in Chicago, that his father, the "old bootlegger," had bragged that he'd bought the presidency for his oldest son, that he'd put his brother, Robert, in his cabinet, or that the man's political leadership was marginal at best. He was dead now and he was a martyr. Gomez kept up his anti-Kennedy rant for about five blocks. Finally he shut up enough I could get a word in.

"Why did you want to see me? It wasn't to complain about Joe Jr."

Gomez stopped walking, smiled, and patted my arm in a paternal style I resented. "No, no. Who knew they were gonna kill him?"

"They?"

Gomez got that look. I'd seen it many times since working for the government. The look that meant, "I've said too much."

"Oswald, you know. The guy's a pinko."

"You think the Communists killed Joe Kennedy?"

"Naw." He was carefully speaking casually. "Just that nut, Oswald. Although he had ties to Castro. We'll never know now, thanks to Ruby."

I gave up. I could hit him with a truth spell, but I really didn't care who killed Joe Patrick Kennedy, Jr. "Why did you ask to meet me?"

Gomez looked around then lowered his voice. "You're going to Cuba." It was a statement of fact.

I didn't say anything.

He started walking, forcing me to follow. "You don't think I have contacts in the DP?" He meant the Directorate of Plans at the Central Intelligence Agency, my current employer.

"If I am?" I wasn't giving anything away.

"Could you do me a favor?"

"How many?"

"Huh?" Gomez looked at me blankly.

"How many boxes?" Cigars, I meant.

"No, that's not it, but I'd love a box if you could get some."

"Then what is it?"

He stopped walking and looked around us. "You're checking the missile sites, right?"

I was silent.

"To make sure the nukes are gone, correct?"

Again I said nothing. "What is it?"

"When I was forced to leave Cuba, I left in a big hurry."

"I'm sure." Gomez was working for the CIA when Castro took over: not a healthy occupation.

"I left something behind. Something very dear to me."

I could see in his eyes that it was the truth. I could also see where this was going. "Yes?"

"If I give you an address in Havana, could you get it for me and bring it back?"

"What is it?"

"It won't be any trouble for someone of your talents."

"What is it?" I repeated.

Gomez held his hands out about two feet apart. "It's bigger than a bread box."

I fingered my talisman. The truth spell was not strong. "What is it?" I said in a louder voice.

"Please, you do this for me, okay?" He was avoiding the question, an excellent tactic when hit with a truth spell, at least a weak one like I was using that allowed you to avoid the question.

"Why should I?" Not that I didn't want to do the old man a favor, but this errand would involve added risk. I wasn't going to do a dangerous favor for Gomez just because we are, what, not friends — mutual exiles?

"I have connections," he said. "I could get you into a guild."

I looked at him. "Which guild?"

He didn't answer right away, as two young girls walked by, looking sad as if they'd just heard Ricky Nelson had laryngitis.

"North American," he said after they passed.

I sighed. Well, beggars can't be choosers. I knew he was telling the truth; I still had the spell on him. But I was curious. "How are you, a lesser, going to get me, a rogue adept, into the North American Guild?"

"Some of the current leadership came out of Cuba. I have information on them that would be embarrassing. They'll do me a favor."

"Have you asked them? I'm PNG in every guild." Look at me: I was using Company slang.

"They know about your past. They'll do it for me if I turn certain documents over to them for destruction."

Again, I knew it was the truth. And I desperately wanted back in a guild. When I joined the AMA, Mr. Kader, the Great One who brought the many diverse guilds in the U.S. together in the American Meta Association or AMA, was still its leader. The only exception was the North American Guild, sometimes called NAG, which was just barely strong enough to stay independent. Five years ago Kader was overthrown and the new regime thought I had supported Kader and, truth be known, in my heart, I did. But due to my bad luck they thought I had fought on his side when I hadn't. I escaped, barely, and have survived since by my wits and by selling my services to the U.S. Government, specifically the CIA. That arrangement both kept me mobile enough and supplied me with the financial resources to, almost, avoid the AMA's assassins. I was NOC (governments seem so enamored with acronyms): Non-Official Cover. I reported directly to the Deputy Director for

Plans (DD/P) Richard Helms or, sometimes, to the Director of Central Intelligence, John A. McCone, himself.

But I was, as the Company said about spies asked to leave certain countries, *persona non grata*, or PNG, with all guilds. If I could get into a guild I could stop working for lessers and would have protection from the new AMA leadership (who were still looking for me, evidenced by the occasional attempts on my life).

"Why don't they just kill you?"

"If I meet an untimely end, the papers go to those that could hurt them the most." He anticipated my next question, "And, no, they can't use a truth spell on me because I don't know where they are. I know what law firm has them, but it has offices all over the world."

It was a pretty good plan. I wondered how much I could push him—how dear was this item.

"I want to see those documents before you turn them over." They could be useful in my dealings with the North American Guild membership.

He hesitated, thought about it, and then decided: "Fine, when you get back." He started strolling down the street again.

We walked along for a while in silence. Then Gomez said, "You know why I hated that bastard, Kennedy?"

***

Getting rid of Gomez took a small persuasion spell and a taxi. I took the taxi back to my hotel, the Fontainebleau on Miami Beach. Since Joe Kennedy had been elected, the president and attorney general had decided that the CIA's super spook adept—that is me—should live a more luxurious lifestyle than a typical CIA junior officer. Apparently the Kennedy brothers were enamored with some spy novels and thought I should live like the hero. Some of the books had even been made into movies and I'd seen one: a silly farce called *Dr. No*. If the Kennedys thought that was what the intelligence business was like, they had scant understanding of it. But I didn't complain; I enjoyed the near unlimited expense account and the luxuries and women it allowed me to acquire.

The next morning I took a taxi to a wooded area owned by the University of Miami. The driver had trouble finding it and I had to guide him to the boxy wooden building with the sign "ZENITH TECHNOLOGICAL ENTERPRISES." He hadn't noticed the guards watching us from the tree line.

I told him to wait for me—enforcing it with a persuasion spell—and entered the office. I'd worked out of this building before but now I only visited when absolutely necessary.

The CIA had manifold ways to infiltrate a hostile country such as Cuba, including submarines on the coast and even up rivers letting out small rubber rafts or swimmers, small aircraft that flew in under the radar, and jumping out of larger airplanes at high altitude and opening the parachute at little more than treetop level. Some of those aircraft were at an airstrip near this property and the boats were behind a house in the ritzy Coral Gables neighborhood.

I wouldn't be using any of those.

I entered the building's foyer where a middle-aged woman greeted me from behind a nearby desk. She recognized me, of course, and for some reason never seemed happy to see me. I didn't know if it was just me, or people in general.

"I need to see Shackley," I stated without bothering with niceties.

She grumbled at me but picked up the phone on her desk. I took the chance while she was talking to Shackley to glance around the room at the "business license" from the

Great State of Florida and the phony sales charts. Beyond the reception desk was what could only be called a bustling office with typewriters beating out their staccato rhythm and men and women moving quickly carrying papers from desk to file and back again. Business was good at Zenith Technological Enterprises, apparently.

The receptionist was saying, "That NOC is here to see you, Mr. Shackley," so I looked out the window to ensure my hack had stayed. He was leaning against the car smoking a cigarette, oblivious to the armed man in the shadows of the trees watching him intently.

"He'll see you in a few minutes, you can wait in there," the woman said, pointing with a desiccated finger toward the door to his office. I turned from the window to look; there was a metal and vinyl government-issue chair next to the door.

I smiled at the woman, earning a roll of the eyes in return, and went to the chair and sat in it. It was uncomfortable but it did afford me a view of most of the office with those ubiquitous metal desks, large typewriters that must have weighed so much that the strong metal desks were required to hold them, and rows and rows of filing cabinets, each with a combination lock in the top drawer.

A blonde woman, slender and tall, was flipping through papers in the top drawer of one of the cabinets, obviously looking for a file.

I discreetly pointed my finger at her and she turned around, looking toward me, giving me a view of her lovely face and the rest of her svelte figure.

I smiled at her and she smiled back, looking bewildered. She didn't know why she'd turned around. The persuasion spell I'd used was subtle.

The door to Shackley's office burst open and he growled at me, "Get in here, Jackson."

I stood slowly and walked in, closing the door behind me.

"What do you want?" Shackley asked as if annoyed at me. He adjusted his horn-rim glasses and sat down behind his metal desk. He was not interested in anything that was not functional, I noticed. His office didn't even contain a family picture or other personal mementos. His blond hair was short and slicked back with some sort of pomade, which made it appear almost brown except when the overhead fluorescents hit it just right.

I sat in another metal and vinyl chair. "A car and driver."

He growled but I knew he'd cooperate. He had standing orders from McCone to assist me however I requested. He picked up the phone. "Send Mac in here."

"No," I said. "I want the blonde in the red dress."

Shackley looked at me. "Who?"

"I don't know her name. She's working in the office, blonde, red dress."

"Harper?"

"If that's her name."

"She's an analyst, not a field agent."

"Doesn't matter as long as she can drive a car."

Shackley looked at me as if trying to figure out what I wanted with her. "For how long?"

"Five days—a week at the most."

The door opened and Mac walked in, a young guy in the uniform of the day: white shirt, narrow tie, black slacks.

"Listen, Jackson," Shackley grumbled at me. "The FBI is all over us to get all we have on Oswald's connections to Castro. I don't have time to meet your every whim."

I just ignored him. "Tell her to meet me at the Fontainebleau Hotel at two this afternoon. I'll need her for five days to a week so she should bring what she needs."

"The Fontainebleau? What the hell kind of expense account do you have, Jackson?" Mac asked.

I ignored him, too.

"Why can't you use Mac?" Shackley said almost as a whine. He knew he was going to lose this argument—he lost every argument with me—but something inside him demanded he at least try.

"I'm going to...where I'm going it would look rather queer for me to arrive in the company of a man. It would blow my cover."

Shackley looked me over, looked at Mac, and said, "Fine. You may have Miss Harper."

"Thank you," I replied sincerely as I stood. I walked past Mac through the door. Miss Harper was looking at me and I noticed her blue eyes. I smiled at her again and she returned it sweetly.

***

It's about 150 miles from Miami to Key West, most of it on the Overseas Highway. The road is narrow and at times perched on top of old railroad bridges. Not on the tracks, but on the girders above the tracks. Miss Harper ("Call me Amanda, please") explained that the railroad was built first and the car road later, but that the space between the girders was too narrow for a two-lane road, so they built it on top. It looked to me as if it would have been safer to swim. Lessers and their efforts to overcome natural barriers always amazed me. They trusted their technology so much.

Key West was a sleepy little town, but was starting a thriving tourist trade. It had for years been a haven for the overly affluent, but now the loud shirt set was discovering it, too.

Amanda dropped me off in a bar and she went and checked into the Alexander Palms—so nice to travel on government money—then came back and picked me up. We discreetly went into the room (lessers are such prudes). It didn't matter if I showed up with a "Mac" or "Amanda." I simply preferred to spend time cooped up in a car in the company of a beautiful woman.

In the opulent room overlooking the ocean we waited, watching TV, which was still all about the assassination, Oswald's murder, and the new president. Johnson struck me as what my father would call "a real cotton picker." I didn't think I was going to enjoy working for him. Well, if Gomez came through, perhaps I wouldn't have to.

About midnight she drove me to the end of South Street as I requested. I stepped out of the car and walked around to the driver's window. She looked at me out the open window. She was a lovely girl with sky-blue eyes and honey-blond hair, and, like a lot of young women, dressed in such a way as to emulate Jacqueline Kennedy, the young former debutante Joe Jr. had met while in the Senate and married despite the 14-year difference in ages. But I had work to do, and fishing off the Company pier was strongly discouraged. But I had enjoyed her company.

"Now what, sir?" she asked, looking around and apparently wondering what I was going to do in an empty street in a residential neighborhood next to the ocean in the middle of the night. But she was smart enough not to ask.

"Wait for me at the hotel for five days. If I'm not back by then, report to the Miami office."

She smiled brightly and I knew why; I'd just given her a week off in a vacation paradise. "Yes, sir."

That "sir" grated on my ears. I still wasn't used to it.

"Good luck, sir," she said as she backed the car up. I watched her drive away back up South Street, the two round taillights that were supposed to be evocative of jet engines fading into red dots in the distance before she turned a corner and went out of my sight. I then walked to the sea.

There was a sign on a post with the news that this was the southernmost point in the United States. I wondered if that was still true with Hawaii having become a state about three years ago. (There was also a military base to the west that looked as if parts were further south but they were not accessible to me while still maintaining my cover.) The surf rolled in gently, bubbling and gurgling against the rocks. The sky was cloudless, which was good for my plans. The sidewalk was deserted except that over the sound of the waves I could hear laughing voices in the distance. I thought I caught the tang of wood smoke mingled with the salt air. I suspected someone was having a beach party somewhere.

I was worried about being spotted by a local looking out their window or, more likely, someone on the base on 24-hour watch duty. So I went invisible.

Then I started another spell.

It was a powerful spell and took a long time to invoke. Being invisible made it a little harder to raise. A cloud formed just above the water, bouncing up and down as the waves rolled in. It moved onshore and over me. Then it lifted me up on top of it. I took a sighting off the North Star and pointed the cloud directly south. When I was a few hundred feet off shore I let the invisibility spell dissipate. I kept it low to stay off everyone's radar. But I had to keep a keen eye out for ships. Commercial vessels were normally no problem; they were well lit and you could usually spot them a long way off. But pleasure craft tended to have only a few hard-to-see lights, and warships sometimes ran "dark," with no lights at all. But it was a big ocean, and the odds were slight.

The approximately 90-mile trip took just over an hour. But I was east of Havana and had to follow the shoreline for almost 50 miles which took nearly another hour, but at the end I was in Havana Harbor, not far from where the *Vermont* had exploded under mysterious circumstances, drawing the U.S. into war with Spain with cries of "Remember the *Vermont!*" That war led to Cuba's independence from Spain and, as some saw it, dependence on the U.S. Castro had, in the opinion of a lot of people at the CIA, simply exchanged the U.S. for the U.S.S.R.

I used an invisibility spell again so that if anyone spotted me they only saw a small bank of fog above the water. I traveled a short distance up harbor and into Old Havana. Gomez was only half correct. My mission was to Cuba but it wasn't to check out the missile sites. A U-2 equipped with a Geiger counter could do that job just fine. I had orders signed by Joe Jr. himself before Oswald spattered his brains all over Governor Connelly. I was to assassinate Castro and, if possible, his brother Raul, too.

Okay, normally I could do it while ordering a drink from the swim-up bar at the Fontainebleau Hotel on Miami Beach. After all, I knew their names: Fidel Castro Ruz and Raul Castro Ruz. But they had protection, probably a voodoo high priest judging from the power I felt on my first attempt back in Miami. I didn't think that would work; most world leaders get the most powerful adept they can afford to cast spells of protection on them. But I had to try. Maybe commies didn't believe in meta powers, I had hoped. But they do, and they believe in using powerful adepts. No, I had to find the adept, kill or at least disable him (her, them?), and then kill the Castro brothers. Once I'd accomplished the former, the latter would be as easy as winning arguments with Shackley.

But there were no guarantees I'd be able to eliminate Castro's adept.

My cloud let me off in the waterfront. Judging from the stars, it was approaching 2 A.M. The streets were deserted. Last time I had been in Havana—my god, had it really been five years ago—it had been a happening town. At two in the morning the party was just starting. There were regular flights from Miami and New York for the rich, the famous, and the powerful. I had loved Havana. The entertainment was great and the companionship warm. I'd hang around the Casino Parisien or the Tropicana and watch the shows, hobnob with movie stars, captains of industry, politicians, who were all so pleased to have an adept to introduce to their friends and bring a little intrigue and mystery to their meaningless little lives. Almost every night I could find a starlet—or a girl wishing to be a starlet—to share my hotel room, as they all wanted bragging rights about having slept with an adept. I don't think I disappointed too many of them. And when that didn't work out, there were always the warm, brown local girls.

But that was all before Kader had been deposed and Castro had come to power. Almost simultaneously I was PNG in my guild and my playground. I'd heard the Reds had kept the Tropicana open to entertain Party bosses visiting from the U.S.S.R. I didn't even want to imagine a communist version of a nightclub—some overweight Slavic matron with more facial hair than Fidel singing about her collective's glorious new tractor.

I moved through the streets, ignoring the classical Spanish Colonial architecture of old Havana. I needed to get to my contact's house by daylight. I did notice the old American cars. Since the embargo, no new cars or parts could be shipped to Cuba. I didn't see anything I recognized as a Russian-made car. But I don't know a lot about cars.

Passing out of Old Havana and into a residential neighborhood, I stuck to shadows, not even wanting to risk my shadow being cast by starlight. I remembered the city well enough that I found the house fairly easily. Like most things in Havana, it looked run-down and uncared for.

I didn't immediately approach the house. I watched it for a while — that's just tradecraft (spy, not meta). Nothing seemed to stir. The night was so quiet it was almost as if the city was abandoned. Occasionally I'd hear a vehicle moving in the distance but nothing close. Once I thought I heard gunshots.

I moved around and viewed the house from different angles. Nothing seemed out of the ordinary. But how was I to know what was ordinary now that Fidel was in charge? There was an old car parked across the street but, as I said, there were old cars everywhere.

I found myself depressed as I ended the invisibility spell and knocked on the door.

Almost immediately a male voice said, "*Hola. ¿quién es?*"

I replied, "*Es Ramon. ¿Dónde está Emil?*" to which my contact was to reply that Emil was in Miami.

The reply did not come immediately. I should have taken that for a bad sign but I was tired and, as I said, depressed. Two large men grabbed me from behind and threw me to the ground. They must have been in or behind the old car and had sneaked up on me. They painfully slapped handcuffs on me and hit me a few times and just used their considerable weight to hold me down. I couldn't teleport with these behemoths holding me. With my hands behind my back I couldn't reach my talisman and that limited the power of my spells. I didn't think going invisible would do much good. Deception was about all I had left. The spiders were big and hairy and crawled out from under me and onto the men. I felt something cold and metallic against the back of my neck. They pressed it in hard so it hurt.

"Stop the magic trick or I shoot you," one said in passable English.

The spiders dissolved.

"You think spiders scare us. I sleep with bigger spiders than that."

The door of the house opened and a man dressed in a military uniform walked out. "Pick him up but don't let go of him," he ordered the men sitting on me.

They pulled me to my feet.

"Are you hurt?" he asked me in the ancient tongue.

I was so shocked to find the adept working for Castro I spat at his feet. For that I got clubbed in the back of the head with a pistol butt—not a sensation I'd like to repeat. I had always wondered why cartoon characters saw stars when hit in the head; after that, I knew. I guess I deserved it, though. Who was I, working for the CIA, to feel superior to this man?

One of the men holding me rummaged through my pockets until he found my talisman. He handed it to the commie adept, who looked it over and smiled. "A new talisman for my collection," he said.

"Take him away, but keep him attached to something at all times," the adept said in Spanish. "You won't be harmed if you cooperate," he said to me, again using the language of the guilds.

"Screw you," I said in English (it doesn't translate well into the ancient language and I didn't feel like going to the effort to speak Spanish). It was a sign of how helpless I felt.

***

In the car they handcuffed me to an eyebolt welded to the floor, forcing me to sit on the floor behind the front seat. There was no carpet or rubber covering over the bare metal of the car's floor.

I ran a persuasion spell on one of the guards in the backseat, the one with the handcuff keys. He reached down and was about to unlock them when the other guard grabbed his hand.

"What are you doing?" he demanded.

"*El Jefe* wants him released," the guard said.

"What? What are you talking about? No he doesn't."

I did a persuasion spell on that guard.

"Oh, yeah, he does," he agreed.

The third guard, the driver, turned around in his seat. "What the hell are you two doing?" he barked. I got the feeling he was the commander.

"Castro wants us to release the prisoner," the second guard said, trying to take the keys from the first.

"You are crazy," the driver yelled. "Castro doesn't even know—"

"That's right," the one with the keys said. "We have to follow orders." My spell on him had expired because I had no talisman to strengthen it. I knew then I couldn't keep all three convinced long enough to let me go.

They drove me to what looked like a reinforced castle. I recognized it as La Cabaña fortress. Built by Spain to protect the city, it overlooked the river, the harbor, and the old city. I'd seen it before when I was in Havana, but only from the outside. And there'd been some changes since Castro took over. The outside stone wall was topped with anachronistic-looking razor wire and wooden guard towers. We entered through a modern double-gate of chain link and razor wire. The car stopped in front of the stone steps leading to the interior. They hauled me inside and took me to a small room lit by a bare bulb with crumbling white plaster walls. As two men held me, one pulled out a knife. He flashed it before my eyes with a malevolent smile showing crooked yellow teeth. Then his hand moved quickly. I took in a deep breath, waiting for the pain. It never came. He cut my shirt off so that the two guards could still hold onto me. Then he pulled off my belt and cut off my pants. A third guard held me while he removed my shoes and socks. Finally he cut off my boxers and I stood naked before them. I was a little worried; I'd seen *Lawrence of Arabia*. The guard with the knife ran his fingers through my hair, all of my hair, and checked all my major orifices. They held my legs while allowing me to put on a dirty, baggy shirt. Then they held my arms while two guards pulled over-sized dirty pants over my legs. They were so large that I had to use one hand to hold them up or they'd fall to my ankles. I suspected that was part of the plan. Finally I was allowed to put my feet in badly made tennis shoe-looking things. All during this time I was held by at least two guards, making teleportation impossible.

Then they dragged me back outside through another door, me holding up my pants with one hand. It was growing light outside, the sky a darkish purple color in the east.

We passed by a wall. I got the feeling they wanted me to see it, not the least because of the bright lights shining on the macabre scene. In front of the wall, set in a hole in the stone with concrete, was a post, about six feet high and almost a foot in diameter. The post and the wall behind it were cratered with what appeared to be thousands of bullet holes. The post, wall, and stone pavement were smeared and splattered in blood and gore and other things I didn't want to attempt to identify. One of my handlers said, "*La paredon,*" and sneered at me.

I managed to not vomit and I hoped not look as scared as I was. I'd heard of "The Wall" where "enemies of the revolution" were executed. Intel reports I'd seen at the CIA's North Building said that Ernesto "Che" Guevara had presided over the summary execution of at least a thousand people at La Cabaña.

Once past the gruesome display we entered another building. They pulled me down a hall lined with cells and put me in one of them, handcuffed one hand to an iron loop in the wall, and left me in the dark after the solid metal door closed. Being handcuffed to the wall prevented teleportation, and without a talisman I was limited in what other spells I could invoke. A single incandescent light in a wire cage far above my head flicked on, letting me see my accommodations. The cell was about three feet by six feet wide. It smelled of wet dirt and human waste. There was a hole in the floor, and from the smell coming from it I knew what its purpose was. Various insects and even scarier looking many-legged bugs, unworried about the light or my presence, were crawling on the walls. There was no bed, nor even a chair. I was sure as soon as I fell asleep my roommates would be crawling on me.

There were no windows and just a little bit of light coming under the closed door. I wondered if this was one of the La Cabaña's infamous "rat holes" I'd heard about at the CIA.

I sat down on the cold, hard floor, my one arm held above my head by the restraints, and spent a few moments in self-pity. This was certainly different from the last time I'd been in Havana.

S. EVAN TOWNSEND

CHAPTER TWO
Havana, November 29, 1958

The girl was long-limbed and a bit on the thin side. Her skin was the color of café con leche and her kisses were as sweet. I know there are people who care about skin color; I've never understood that. That she was brown made no difference to me. She was striking, with lovely black eyes, and she made love like a wild, beautiful animal. She was the cigarette girl at the Sans Souci and her English was limited pretty much to "Cigars…cigarettes." I spoke some Spanish and could use translation spells in a pinch. But we didn't need much talking for what we had in mind.

Now she was snoring, though, lying in my arms. I rolled over and picked up my watch. It was a little after two in the afternoon. I slowly pulled my arm from under her and got up quietly so as not to wake her, and walked toward the bathroom.

After the requisite morning ritual I walked to the windows and threw back the curtains. The sunlight in Havana is a marvelous thing. I know it comes from the same sun as in, say, Cleveland, but in Havana it is a bright, happy, golden light. The room filled with this radiance and the girl moaned and pulled the covers over her head. I laughed at her and looked out over the Caribbean Sea. The Hotel Nacional overlooks the ocean and, in the distance, El Morro, the sixteenth-century fortress that guarded Havana harbor from pirates and the English Navy. The blue waters of the Caribbean were reflecting that wonderful sunlight. I smiled at the sky and turned back to look at the bed.

My room was in the west wing of the hotel, with the suites for the high rollers. I wasn't a high roller *per se*, but the management liked to keep me happy. The room was luxurious, large, and a mess. The girl's dress was in a pile on the floor, my tuxedo was draped over a chair, the room service breakfast dishes from a meal we'd shared sometime in the wee hours of the morning were placed here and there in any convenient spot, and the bed had most of the covers on the floor. Only the white sheet covered the girl's naked body.

I smacked her on the butt. "Wake up!" I said playfully, forgetting she didn't speak English.

"*¿Qué hora es?*" she asked sleepily. For having been in the bed since about four A.M., we hadn't gotten much sleep.

"*Son las dos.*"

"*¡Por Dios!*" she cried out, throwing back the sheet and jumping out of the bed. "*¡Mi madre me va a matar!*"

I laughed at her again and watched her scramble around the room, finding her clothes where we'd dropped them and dressing as fast as she could, and finally standing around, looking for a high-heeled shoe.

"*¿Vives con tu madre?*" I asked.

She ignored me, still looking for the wayward shoe.

Finding it under the bed, she slipped it on and looked at me in her disheveled clothes. "*Si,*" she breathed. "*Ella me dijo que me metería en problemas si trabajaba ahí."* She sounded as if she now agreed.

"*Dale mis saludos,*" I said, laughing.

She turned and spat, "*¡Comemierda!*" at me and ran out in a fury. I shook my head, laughing. It's amazing how women change their minds about you in the harsh light of day. Not that I'm a bad-looking fellow. I guess it happens a lot as they are overcome with passion but have regrets in the morning. I rarely had to use persuasion spells. I had, but I didn't like it; it was too easy and therefore wholly unsatisfying.

Well, she was sweet and very nice. Very nice. But if you're going to dance you have to pay the fiddler, as my father was fond of saying. I was sure her mother would make sure of that.

***

I had a light late lunch in one of the hotel's many restaurants. It was an elegant room with white linen tablecloths and the bus boys wearing white jackets looking more formal than I in my suit. They looked bored, though; it wasn't very busy, which was unusual, especially considering it was Thanksgiving weekend. The revolution had really hurt the tourist business, I guessed. Being a four-day holiday for most Americans, Thanksgiving weekend was usually a very heavy tourist time in Havana. I wondered what New Year's would look like this year. It was normally a huge party but with the revolution, who knew?

I noticed that, sitting by the window overlooking the ocean, was Vinnie Scarpelli. He was with a very beautiful woman. She had lovely dark eyes that seemed to pass through my epidermis and see all of me at once. I was running short on cash, so I decided to walk over and talk to Scarpelli. I also wanted to meet this woman.

Vinnie was the manager of the casino that had been built, with mob money, about three years ago. He was a wiry guy who moved his hands a lot when talking. He had been working in Las Vegas but had to leave for some reason. I was sure he'd return when the "heat" was off. When he saw me walking toward his table, he smiled, but it wasn't a happy smile.

"Mr. Vaughan," he said in greeting. "How you doin' today?"

"I'm fine," I replied.

"Let me introduce ya to Maria Gonzalez," Vinnie said, pointing his hand, palm up, at the woman.

I turned to look into her eyes. "Hello."

She smiled sourly. "*Buenos días*," she said, brushing back a lock of her dark, curly hair.

"Miss Gonzalez is a Cuban actress," Vinnie said, seeming proud over his lunch catch.

I nodded as if I cared.

"She don't speak no English," Vinnie elaborated.

"Oh?" I said, smiling.

"*Maria*," Vinnie was saying in slow Spanish, as if he had to think of every word first, "*éste es señor Vaughan.*"

"*Gusto en conocerlo, señor Vaughan,*" she said and her voice was lovely, although I felt she didn't really mean what she was saying. Her manner was so discourteous, so dismissive of me, that I immediately forgot her looks and realized I didn't like her.

"You, too," I said, not bothering with Spanish. I turned to Scarpelli. "Any games tonight?"

He looked at me, narrow-set green eyes looking unhappy. "Yeah, nine tonight, in the room in the back. You know the one."

"Who will be there?"

"One of the Rockefeller brothers, some of his friends, others."

"Any mobbed up?"

Vinnie tried to look innocent and failed. "Hey, I run a legitimate establishment."

Yeah, I thought, and how much of the profits go back to Chicago? "No mobsters?" I pressed.

"Naw, just rich guys with more money than they knows what to do with."

"What's the buy-in?"

"Five grand."

I didn't have that much. "You spot me?"

"Yeah," he said, looking more and more miserable. I didn't know why. Our arrangement was simple: he gave me the seed money; I returned it plus twenty percent. He'd make a cool thousand tonight. And I doubted any of that went to Chicago or that his boss, Wilbur Clark, knew about our arrangement.

"I'll see you tonight," I said. I turned to the actress. *"Buenas tardes, señorita Gonzalez."* Before she could reply I walked away.

***

I spent the afternoon swimming in the hotel's kidney-shaped pool and lounging in that marvelous sunlight. The one drawback of the Hotel Nacional was that there wasn't easy access to a beach as it was on the seawall. But the pool was a passable substitute. It was surrounded by chaise lounges and upon most of them were young, lovely women. These were the girlfriends of mobsters and gamblers, or maybe the mistresses of rich industrialists, and even the singers and actresses. Maria Gonzalez was there in a white bathing suit that made her dark skin seem as if it absorbed the light. I had to admit she looked beautiful.

Snaking expertly between the closely spaced chairs were white-jacketed men bringing drinks to the women. There were a few men—mostly young and thin—perhaps the boyfriends of the mistresses. Or maybe gigolos, I mused.

I was attractive enough to garner some attention. Some knew what I was, and that intrigued them, also. Maria was looking over her sunglasses at me. When I caught her eye she looked away as if bored with gazing at my form.

The swim helped me keep my body in shape. An adept who relies solely on his powers to keep himself safe is as foolhardy as a soldier that relies on his weapon without conditioning his body. And by the pool I could ogle the girls.

After swimming some laps I was sitting on the edge of the pool drying off my torso while my legs dangled in the cool water, when a young blonde thing paddled up to me.

"Hey, my friend Constance says you're an adept. I said she's nutters. Why would an adept be here?" And she giggled. Then growing suddenly serious, she batted her large green eyes at me. "So you're not, are you?" Her voice betrayed her hope that I was. She looked maybe twenty, twenty-five.

I smiled at her. "And if I were?"

"Well, that would be just marvy!" she squealed.

I smiled at her. "Yes, I'm an adept."

Her eyes got wide and her mouth hung open. It actually looked endearing. "Can you show me something?"

I kept smiling. "I don't do parlor tricks, dear."

"Ah, come on." She was still smiling. I had a feeling she was used to getting what she wanted.

I looked around conspiratorially as if to check if the coast was clear. Then I put my finger in the water next to her body.

She smiled when she felt it. "Did you do that?"

I nodded, not taking my eyes from hers.

"What's your name?" she asked softly, paddling about in the water.

"Kookie Byrnes."

She looked at me a second, then smiled knowingly. "Oh, I get it." She swam off a ways, turned around, and said, "Maybe I'll see ya later, Kookie."

"Maybe," I replied, giving away nothing.

She went off to report to her friend, I presumed.

I loved Havana.

I noticed Maria was watching me again. I smiled at her and she acted as if she didn't notice.

I climbed out of the pool and put on my robe. I had to be careful as my fair skin burns easily and running a healing spell on it would be a nuisance.

I dismissed the boy who asked if I'd like a drink and returned to my room to dress for dinner.

***

At nine I went to the "Casino Internacional," as the hotel's gambling den was called. I was dressed in a white evening jacket with black tie. Vinnie greeted me at the entrance.

"Mr. Vaughan, good evening," he said perfunctorily. I smiled at him in his tuxedo. Reminded me of something my father used to say about putting lipstick on a pig.

I walked into the noisy casino and glanced around the room. I saw my blonde friend from the pool in a lovely strapless evening dress she was about to fall out of. She was draped on the arm of a much older man who was playing craps, which caused me to develop a low opinion of his intelligence. She saw me and smiled—a smile I felt as much as saw.

"Everything in order?" I asked Vinnie as we passed the entrance to the Starlight Terrace bar.

"Yeah."

"Chips?"

"Waiting for ya in the room."

"Good," I said and smiled at him. He didn't smile back.

"Let's go," he said, jerking his head toward the back of the casino and walking in that direction. Vinnie opened the door and walked in with me.

The room was fairly large, occupied by a round table with four leather chairs with rounded backs. The walls had dark wood wainscoting and above that red patterned wallpaper. A light hung low over the table and there were wall sconces with long curving arms and flower-like glass over the flame-shaped bulbs. I never understood why casinos had to be decorated in expensive yet loud and extremely fancy manners.

There were chips sitting in front of the chairs. Three men were smoking and talking around the table.

"Ah, this must be our fourth," one said. He was a tall man with a round face and slicked-back, thinning hair. He wasn't handsome, but carried himself like a man who was used to privilege. "I'm Winthrop Rockefeller," he said, extending his hand.

I shook it. "Mike Vaughan," I replied.

"'Vaughan'?" he repeated. "Of the Philadelphia Main Line Vaughans?"

I thought of saying, "No, of the Idaho dirt-poor farmers Vaughans," but didn't as that would tell too much of my past history, and my name wasn't Vaughan anyway. And I wasn't about to tell him, or anyone, my real name.

"No," I said simply.

He looked at me a second, perhaps expecting more of an explanation. Then he smiled and said, "Let me introduce the rest of our group." He turned to another fellow, "This is Mr. Joe Spence of Arkansas. He has some sugar interests here in Cuba."

I shook Mr. Spence's hand with a "Nice to meet you," and he replied, "You, also, Mr. Vaughan." Spence looked like a big southern boy with flaxen hair and sleepy brown eyes. I knew he had money to be in this game, probably old money, but he looked as if you took his expensive evening jacket away and put him in overalls he'd fit right in plowing the back forty.

"And," Rockefeller was saying, "this is Mr. Rosenberg of New York City."

I shook his hand and we both spoke some mechanical words of greeting. Rosenberg was a short, round man, his red curly hair going thin on top, his thick glasses hanging down too far on his nose. His smile seemed as insincere as his handshake was weak.

"And," Rockefeller continued, "this is Mr. Sanchez. He represents the establishment."

"Good evening, Mr. Vaughan," Sanchez said with a slight bow. "If you need anything, just let me know."

Vinnie gave Sanchez a look and then bid us all good night and left.

Also in the room was a young Cuban man behind a small bar and a Cuban girl in a cocktail waitress uniform that showed a nice amount of her shapely brown legs. When I caught her eye I smiled. She just looked at me—probably surprised I'd acknowledge her as more than furniture.

"Shall we, gentlemen?" Rockefeller said. "I believe those are your chips, Mr. Vaughan," he said, indicating the smallest pile on the table.

I sat behind my chips and Rockefeller opened a new pack of cards, shuffled, and started dealing. I fingered my talisman.

"Would anyone like something to drink?" Rockefeller asked. The girl came over and took our orders. I ordered mineral water and the other men looked at me. "Doctor's orders," I said. That seemed to satisfy them. It was hard work, what I was about to do, and I needed to stay focused.

I used poker to raise the funds I needed to live the lifestyle I was accustomed to. Using modified far-seeing spells, I could see the other players' cards and a few cards down into the deck. That still didn't help with luck, which is why I didn't play roulette or other games of chance. And I didn't play blackjack, baccarat, or Chemin de Fer because angering the house was not good form, especially when mobsters own the house, such as this one.

So it basically came down to money management. Bet big when I had a winning hand, bet small when I didn't. With judicious draws I was able to increase my "luck." I lost a few hands, allowed myself to be bluffed, and made my own bad fortune so as not to look too lucky. But I think I must have gotten a bit greedy, which caused the trouble that came later.

While we played, I listened to the men talk:

"If Castro's so popular, why did the national strike fail?"

"That was eight months ago; Castro's grown a lot more popular since then."

"We have nothing to worry about: Castro's just as corrupt as Batista. He's not a Red."

"Then why did he pass that 'Law Number Three' about agrarian reform?"

"Propaganda for the peasants, that's all."

"I hope you're right," Spence said. I got the feeling "agrarian reform" scared him.

"Did you catch the act last night at the Tropicana?"

"Damn, Vaughan, your luck tonight!"

"Castro can't do a thing. American corporations own this island. He'll take his bribes like Batista and be happy."

"I heard a rumor Fidel's sick or wounded. Going to go to Mexico or Venezuela to recuperate."

"And last week Raul was dead. I sometimes think there are more rumors in this revolution than fighting."

"I don't think Batista's going to be able to turn it around. And rebels are besieging Santiago. Civilians are being evacuated by airplane."

"I heard the army barracks at Moncada had fallen and the rebels had taken Santiago, not just besieging it."

"Rumors!"

"Hell, you'd think with a million dollars in military equipment from the U.S. and training by our best military minds, he could have put down this rebellion."

"Damn, how do you fight a war when your officers go over to the other side? And now the U.S. has cut off support for Batista to appear 'neutral.'"

"The man's incompetent; that's why he's losing. But Castro will be good for Cuba and for business."

"If Castro were a threat, would Lansky be building that Hotel Riviera?"

"Meyer Lansky, the mobster?"

"Yeah. I heard Ginger Rogers is headlining the casino there opening night."

"I don't know what Castro and his ilk are complaining about," Rockefeller said. "Cuba has the third highest standard of living in Latin America."

"Vaughan, you must have been born under a lucky star." That was Spence, snubbing out a cigarette. He was chain-smoking as he played, giving the room a layer of smoke just above the heads of the players.

"Yes, a little too lucky," Rosenberg snarled, eying the pile of chips in front of me and his greatly diminished stack. He was smoking too. His ashtray was fuller than Spence's and, as he spoke, a butt resting in the tray gave off malodorous fumes adding to the fog hanging from the ceiling.

I shrugged my shoulders and decided it was time to make a dignified exit. "Gentlemen, I think I'll call it a night."

"Not with fifty thousand dollars of my money," Rosenberg spat angrily, taking a drag on his cigarette.

"Sidney," Rockefeller reproved. "He was just lucky tonight. I'm out a similar amount."

I smiled. Sidney was not a good poker player and most of my winnings had come from him. Rockefeller had probably lost less than half that amount. He was trying to calm the little man down.

"He's cheating," Rosenberg said. "I don't know how, but he must be."

"I don't think so," Spence said.

I waved Sanchez over. "Yes, Mr. Vaughan?"

"Cash these in for me," I told him, keeping my voice even as if being accused of cheating didn't faze me a bit—because it didn't. "Ask Mr. Scarpelli to put the cash in the hotel safe."

"Yes, sir." He got a tray from the bar and loaded it with the chips. He started counting them.

"Now, wait just a minute, Sanchez," Rosenberg said loudly. He stood and pointed at me with two fingers, his burning cigarette wedged between them. "This man is a cheat."

Sanchez stopped counting and looked up. "Do you have evidence of that?"

"No, but nobody wins like that without cheating!" Rosenberg was close to screaming.

"Sidney, there's no need—" Rockefeller started.

"I'm not the grandson of a robber baron, Winthrop. That's real money to me."

"Then you shouldn't have bet so freely," Spence commented.

Rosenberg snarled at him and threw his cigarette on the floor. He pulled out a gun from under his dinner jacket and pointed it at me. "I don't know how you cheated, but you did."

The girl made a startled scream but choked it off as Rosenberg turned and pointed the gun at her.

"Mr. Rosenberg," Sanchez said, almost pleading. "Please."

"Shut up, you spic," Rosenberg barked and pointed the gun at him, "and go get Scarpelli."

"There's no need for this," I said. I was in a bit of a conundrum. I could easily attack Sidney Rosenberg, but that would reveal that I was an adept and had been cheating. I started to put my hand in my pocket to find my talisman. A subtle persuasion spell might do it.

"Keep your hands where I can see them!"

For some reason, at that moment, Scarpelli came in with two very large goons. I wondered if he had microphones in the room.

"Rosenberg," he barked. "Damn it, this is how you thank me? I woulda expected more from the consigliere for the Genovese family."

I looked at Vinnie. "The Genovese family? Damn it! You said no mobsters."

Rockefeller stood up and pointed at Rosenberg. "This man's a criminal?" he bellowed.

"He's a lawyer," Scarpelli said calmly to both of us.

"For a Mafia family," I retorted, louder than I meant to.

"Shut up," Rosenberg screamed, waving his pistol around.

The goons ripped guns from under their coats and trained them on Rosenberg.

"Put the gun down, Sidney," Vinnie said softly. It was the first time I'd seen him scared. But he was not scared of Rosenberg. I wondered what it was.

Rosenberg looked at the odds, the two apes pointing guns at him, and no one else in the room coming to help him. He set the gun on the table, knocking over what was left of his chips.

Scarpelli walked over and put his arm around him in a fatherly fashion and talked to him softly. I couldn't hear it and frankly didn't care to. Rosenberg was nodding his head, fighting back tears.

I turned to Sanchez, who had been frozen like a statue in the process of counting my chips. "Please, continue."

Rockefeller spoke then. "I apologize, Mr. Spence, Mr. Vaughan. Mr. Rosenberg came to me with the highest recommendation." He looked at Scarpelli angrily.

I wondered at that moment if Vinnie had set me up. Having a mobster kill me would eliminate me from his list of annoyances.

Rosenberg sat down and put his face in his hands. Vinnie picked up his gun and handed it to one of his men, then looked at the group. "Gentlemen, I apologize. If it's any consolation, Mr. Rosenberg is no longer welcome at this establishment."

Rockefeller and Spence started to calm down. I wasn't sure what they were mad about. I was the one that almost got shot.

"I should hope not," Rockefeller commented dryly.

"Mr. Sanchez," Scarpelli said, "please cash in these gentlemen's chips."

"Yes, sir." He continued counting mine.

I sat down at the table and looked at the girl. Her eyes were wide with fear. Despite the adrenaline wearing off, I kept my voice calm and casual. "I could use another mineral water."

She smiled and said, "Yes, sir."

It took some time for Sanchez to count all the chips and hand each man a receipt. I looked at the number and smiled. I could live off of that for a year easily. I guessed I'd been too greedy, but Rosenberg was not a very good poker player. Then Scarpelli's men led Rosenberg out. Just as he left the room he turned and looked at me. "This isn't over. You stole from the wrong guy."

Rockefeller looked embarrassed, as did Spence. I smiled at them and walked toward the exit. "Thank you, Mr. Rockefeller, Mr. Spence. I had an enjoyable time until I was accused of cheating." I smiled to let them know I didn't blame them.

"And I apologize," Scarpelli said. "I'm gonna have a talk with Mr. Rosenberg's boss."

"What will happen to him?" Spence asked, his voice tight with fear. I think he was imagining cement overshoes.

"Oh, nothin', just a stern lecture, I'm sure." The smirk on his face indicated otherwise. And with that Scarpelli left.

I shook the men's hands and said goodnight, smiled at the girl, who smiled back, and left the room. The casino was just as busy, but smokier. Columns of cigarette and cigar smoke rose from every table to mingle with a cloud hanging under the high ceiling. I didn't see my friend from the pool or her date. But I did see Maria Gonzalez. She was wearing a blue dress that did little to hide her svelte form. She was alone at the blackjack table, betting conservatively from what I could tell in my few moments of observing her. I don't think she saw me.

At the cashier's cage, in exchange for my receipt I got my winnings—minus a thousand dollars, I noticed. Scarpelli was watching. I looked at him, letting my anger show. He walked over.

"I didn't know Sidney had such a temper."

"If he can't lose, he shouldn't play," I said, putting the cash in my pockets. It filled most of them. Next stop was the hotel safe. My order to put my winnings there had apparently been forgotten in the excitement.

"I'm more worried about Mr. Rockefeller. A deal like this might keep him from coming back."

"Yes, I would imagine," I said. "Enjoy my winnings." I walked out, keeping my anger in check.

***

It was about eleven by the time I got most of my winnings in the safe, and I had a receipt in my pocket for that amount, along with a couple of hundred dollars I'd kept out. With plentiful funds, I decided to visit a nightclub. The hotel's Casino Parisien usually had big-name entertainment—I think Eartha Kitt currently—but my luck there had been lousy lately. I decided on the Tropicana, since I'd visited the Sans Souci the night before. And yes, maybe I was avoiding the cigarette girl, although I wasn't sure if her mother would let her work there anymore anyway.

I headed out the front of the Nacional to the line of taxis waiting. The doorman, seeing me, waved one over.

"You!" a voice cried out behind me.

I spun around to see Rosenberg swooping out of the hotel like a rotund tropical storm, pointing his finger at me. "I just found out," he was saying angrily, "that you're an adept. I knew you cheated."

I was pretty tired of Mr. Rosenberg. I fingered my talisman and hit him with a fear spell. It was interesting to watch his bravado crumble. I finished it by saying, "What are you going to do about it?"

He almost, but not quite, ran away. He spent a few moments, during which I supposed he screwed up his courage, getting it to maybe half-mast, and spat at me, "This isn't over, Vaughan." Then he almost ran back into the hotel. I watched to make sure he wasn't going to turn suddenly with a gun or something. In the lobby he was speaking animatedly with a man. I recognized him from the casino. It was the fellow my friend from the pool had been with and, in fact, she was still there, hanging onto his arm, looking lovely as ever. She slowly turned her green eyes toward me and gave me a small, unapologetic smile. That'll teach me to keep my mouth shut.

The doorman was holding a taxi door open for me so I thanked him and slipped inside, saying, "Tropicana."

The doorman spoke to the driver, closed my door, and the car pulled away from the hotel.

It was a large, comfortable American sedan and I settled into its wide back seat and looked out the windows at the lights of the city. The locals, and those trying to bring in tourists, like to call Havana the "Paris of the Western

Hemisphere." That was a bit of a stretch, I thought. The historic "Old Havana" was lovely, but not nearly as historic as Paris. Havana had had neither the time nor the resources in its 400-year history to develop the cultural amenities of Paris. There was no equivalent to the Louvre or Notre Dame here. And Havana had the biggest, worst slums I had ever seen. If Mr. Rockefeller's statement was correct that Cuba has the third highest standard of living in Latin America, I'd hate to see the fourth. Maybe Havana's slums weren't as bad as some of the truly poor places of the earth to which I'd never traveled, such as Africa or China. I just didn't know and I didn't want to learn.

But in matters of sex, Havana had supposedly cosmopolitan Paris beat hands down. The city seemed to run on sex—sex to the Latin beat of the Rhumba. Pimps greeted tourists at the airport, albeit discreetly. If you knew the numbers—and they were easy to find—a girl was just a phone call away. There were cafés specializing in B-girls and "Dime a Dance" parlors. And the unescorted women on the street at night were there for one reason alone. I'd never availed myself of any of those women. Cuban women tend to be thicker in the middle than I prefer—last night's waif a rare and delightful exception. And if I was going to have one in my bed—and I have—I wasn't going to pay for it.

I suppose to Middle America even the most innocent of the nightclub shows would be horribly "sinful." Chorus girls in skimpy outfits, Rhumba dances that were like clothed public sex in many ways, and follies-type reviews that left little to the imagination. It was sex for sale, just not as obvious or vulgar as the B-girls. And a lot prettier.

CHAPTER THREE
Havana, November 29, 1958

The taxi stopped at the arched entrance to the Tropicana and I stepped out. Gomez stood by the access in a white tuxedo, greeting each visitor as an old friend, even if he'd never met the person before, while passing judgment on each one's suitability for admission. He looked at me and smiled broadly under his salt-and-pepper mustache.

"Mr. Vaughan!" he cried out, taking my hand and pumping it vigorously. "Welcome back."

"Hello, Gomez," I said. "How do things look tonight?" He knew what I was there for.

He smiled knowingly. "Busy. Do you wish a table Mr. Vaughan?"

"No, I'll just go to the bar," I said, and strolled past looking around.

The Tropicana was an open-air club, with palm trees as part of the décor. Huge arches with open space between them gave the illusion of a roof and, I supposed, helped with the acoustics. For hot nights, there was an air-conditioned "Crystal Arc" room that indeed had a glass-arced ceiling. But this evening wasn't warm enough to necessitate its use.

It was a huge nitery but needed to be—it was often full. There were two stages in two separate areas, with the bar between. One could sit at the bar and watch both shows.

I settled onto a barstool, ordered a vodka martini—no need to stay sharp now—and watched the rooms and the shows. There would be the *de rigueur* Rhumba show at least once a night, a bit toned down from what you'd see in one of Havana's dives. Then there were the dance numbers, with as many as 50 chorines dancing in skimpy costumes. The girls tended to be, like most Cuban women, wider in the hips and waist then the girls one would find in Las Vegas or other American nightclubs. The shows often had a Voodoo theme, which I found amusing and naive. They obviously didn't know the power of what they were playing with. But "playing" was the right word, as they could only go through the motions—or what they thought were the motions—as they had no power to evoke spells. And of course, to draw in the American crowds, name entertainment from the States was available.

The 11:30 shows were in progress and right then on one stage was a line of pretty chorines, and on the other a blonde singer I thought might be Rosemary Clooney. I also looked over the room. I recognized some regulars, including an American industrialist with a dark-haired woman I was sure was too young to be his wife.

A tall, dark man came into view and I smiled and nodded as he walked by with a beautiful brunette girl on his arm.

"Hi, Mike," he said, grinning.

I wasn't even aware his divorce was final, I thought. Probably didn't matter. "Hello, Rock," I replied.

As they walked away, I could see him talking to the girl. She glanced back at me, a look of intrigue in her eye. I gave her a smile and she coolly returned it before giving her attention back to her escort. She might dump him for me, I thought. It had happened before. I mean a movie star is one thing but an adept is...something else, something rarer. And Rock seemed to always end up talking to some of the boys, anyway.

Gomez sat next to me at the bar, interrupting my thoughts, and ordered Scotch.

"Lovely night," he said, as if to make conversation.

"Yes," I agreed automatically. A blonde woman had caught my eye. She was with a couple that was obviously fascinated with each other and she was bored by the chorus line and looking around unhappily.

Gomez, for his part, was watching the industrialist. I wondered if he had blackmail on his mind.

"See that man?" he said, picking up his drink. "The one with the white hair, heavy jowls, sitting with the dark-haired woman that is not his wife?"

"Yes." I smiled at how he managed to work the man's infidelity into his description.

Gomez took a sip of his Scotch. "Do you know who he is?"

"Yes. Runs an American company."

"Not just an American company," Gomez said. "One of their largest defense contractors." I assumed what he was telling me was common knowledge. At the time I suspected Gomez was more than just a maitre d'.

"Interesting," I said with a tone I hoped indicated just the opposite.

"Yes, very," he whispered, apparently oblivious to my opinion. He took another sip, watching his quarry over the glass.

I wondered if the woman was a spy for the Russians and was trying to get defense secrets out of the man using sex. Or if that was just Gomez's theory. Or maybe he was simply interested in extortion. But I'd think that would be bad for business.

Not my problem, so I took my drink and wandered in the direction of the bored blonde lady. A hostess intercepted me and offered to show me to a table and I used a small persuasion spell to get one with a view of the stage and of the blonde, even though it had a "Reserved" sign on it.

Sitting at the miniscule table I glanced at the blonde. Then I turned to look longer. Closer, she was even lovelier. Her features were northern European and her skin was like porcelain.

She noticed my gaze and shyly smiled and looked away, finding the chorine line suddenly interesting. I watched the show, too, but at what seemed to be a tacitly agreed upon time, we both looked at each other, and held our stare. I let a smile slowly curl on my lips. She returned it before again looking at the stage.

This happened a few more times, each gaze getting longer, until our eyes seemed locked and the rest of the room seemed to melt away. I finished my drink and walked over to her table, looking at her the entire trip. The man and woman she was with were still infatuated with each other.

"Hello," I said to the man. "I'm Mike Vaughan."

He looked reluctantly away from his girl and smiled at me. "Hello, I'm Daniel Corbett." He held out his hand and I shook it. "This is my fiancée, Alison Walker, and her friend, Liesl Svensen."

Alison held out her hand and looked at me through her cat-eye glasses, "Nice to meet you, Mr. Vaughan."

Liesl also held out her hand, "Yes, nice to meet you."

"May I join you folks?" I asked after briefly shaking each woman's hand. I noticed how delicate and slim Liesl's hand was.

Liesl looked happy at that prospect, her blue eyes sparkling.

"Of course," Daniel said.

I sat in the remaining chair, next to Liesl. This table, no larger than the one I just left, forced me to sit very close to Liesl, which I did not mind at all. Her arm brushed against mine accidentally and we exchanged a smile as no apology was sought nor needed.

"What brings you to Havana, Mr. Vaughan?" Daniel asked. "Down for the long weekend, as we are? Because of the troubles we got a very nice bargain on our hotel rooms."

"I live here," I replied.

That got his attention. "Really? That must be nice. Do you work for an American company?"

I laughed. "No, I'm a man of leisure."

Daniel looked more impressed. "Lucky you."

I didn't tell him that luck had little to do with it. "Yes, I am very fortunate."

Having made enough polite conversation, Daniel and Alison went back to admiring each other. That was fine with me; it left me virtually alone with Liesl.

"Liesl," I said. "That's a lovely name."

"Thank you," she replied with a shy smile.

We chatted and watched the show. When it ended I asked her to dance. She moved gracefully. She was tall, with long legs showing under her demure petticoats. I held her as close as propriety allowed, looking into her sapphire eyes. At one point I stole a quick kiss and her reaction told me she didn't mind.

Eventually, we excused ourselves from Mr. Corbett and Miss Walker. I escorted her, her arm in the crook of my elbow, to another table. "Shall we stay here," I asked, "or would you like to go somewhere else?"

"Somewhere quiet would be nice," she said with a coy smile.

The Tropicana was located on a large former estate and had acres of meticulously maintained gardens with palm trees forming a canopy giving the illusion of privacy. I led her along a path to a bench. We sat, holding hands. It was dark enough that we had to sit very close to see each other.

"Mike," she whispered, having long dropped the more formal "Mr. Vaughan."

"Yes?" I asked.

She kissed me slowly, yet almost shyly. I resisted the urge to pull her close and kiss her hard. I didn't want to scare her away.

"It must be nice to live in paradise," she whispered a few moments later.

I didn't laugh. Yes, Havana was wonderful. But with the prostitution, mobbed-up gambling, narcotics, poverty, Castro's revolution, and Batista's SIM, I would hardly call it paradise. But rather than disabuse her, I simply said, "Yes—nicer now, though."

She smiled at the compliment.

I kissed her again, more intently. She didn't resist, but instead melted into my arms.

"Mike?" she said later.

"Yes?"

"Can we go somewhere?"

I looked into her eyes to see if she was serious. I saw no deception or uncertainty. She did not seem the type and I was slightly disappointed, to my surprise. "Where?"

"We're staying at the Hilton. I share a room with Alison, but they won't be back for hours."

Again I gazed into her eyes. She meant it.

"I have my own room at the Nacional."

She shook her head slightly. "No. I can't. Alison would know."

I understood. She needed to be in the room, alone, when Alison returned. The logistics of getting from the Nacional to the new Hilton were too demanding. And I could get a room at the Hilton.

"I'll get us a taxi."

"Thank you," she breathed.

***

When Liesl and I walked out of the Tropicana—I worried briefly that walking past her friends would change her mind but they didn't seem to notice her, being nose to nose in their own little world—the doorman waved over a taxi. That wasn't the usual procedure. Normally, the next one in line got the fare. I didn't think about that at the time, having other, happier things on my mind. I did notice the driver was Negro, but that wasn't unusual as Havana had a large Afro-Cuban population, and he had another Negro companion in the front seat. That was also unusual. I looked at the doorman to see if he thought this situation was strange, but he simply opened the door and Liesl slid in. She looked at me from inside, smiling, so I got in with her.

"Habana Hilton," I said.

"Yes, sir," the driver answered. His friend stayed mute.

Liesl held my hand and gazed at me as the taxi moved through the streets, ignoring the driver and his friend. She delighted in the outdoor cafés, still doing business at this time of night, the bright lights, the music, all along Prado Boulevard. I smiled at her enthusiasm.

I was watching Liesl and not paying attention to the route we were traveling. Suddenly I noticed the car was going down a narrow, dark alley.

"Driver?" I asked.

Liesl held my hand tighter and looked at me. All innocence left her face.

"What the hell is this?" I asked.

"Just be calm, Vaughan," the passenger in the front seat said.

"How do you know my name?" I demanded, thinking it might be a stupid question, as Liesl might have said it. But no, she would have called me "Mike."

The car stopped and the passenger turned around and removed his hat.

I gasped. He was older than when I last saw him, with gray frosting the black hair. "Brown?"

"Yes," he said simply.

"What is this?" I demanded, albeit politely. Louis Brown was Frank Kader's lieutenant, and Kader was the head of my guild, the American Meta Association. And I assumed the now mute driver was a well-armed warrior.

I looked at Liesl, who had stopped masking.

"You're good," I said. And I meant it. To kiss a woman and not know she's an adept showed her great ability to mask, and that showed her powers were strong, probably better than mine.

"Thank you," she said, no longer the shy, demure girl from the club. Her blue eyes blazed with her power as she pulled her hand from mine.

"Vaughan," Brown said, "we arranged this meeting for a reason."

"I assumed so," I said, more than a bit disappointed my evening wasn't going to turn out as I had hoped.

"Liesl is a Valkyrie," Brown said.

That explained her power. "And Daniel and Alison?" I asked her.

"Persuasion spell," she said. "Never knew them before tonight. But unescorted ladies aren't welcome at the Tropicana."

"And how'd you know I'd be at the Tropicana?"

"We knew it was one of your regular haunts and that you would show up eventually."

"Why didn't you just ring up my room at the Nacional? Why all the cloak and dagger?"

"Just a precaution," Brown said.

"Against what?"

Brown looked impatient. "Listen, Vaughan, there's a situation."

"What situation?"

"Well, you wouldn't know about it, since you spend your days as a playboy, not concerned about anyone or anything else."

I had to agree; I pretty much didn't care about anything other than my own pleasures. So his intended jibe didn't take. I'd accepted that about myself.

"Kader is being challenged," Brown said.

I looked at him, then at Liesl, then back at him. I detected no deceit or jocularity. "You're kidding?" Kader was the most powerful adept on the planet, except maybe the head of Liesl's guild, and they were allies (and some said lovers). He had at least two very powerful talismans, one of which he'd won in a battle fought over San Francisco that people — lessers and adepts — still talk about.

Brown must have realized what I was thinking. "He's older — his powers have diminished."

"He's not that old," I said. I thought maybe early sixties. He'd been head of the guild for only fifteen years now. That was not a long time for a powerful and careful adept.

"Yes," Louis agreed, looking sad. "He is aging quickly and his health is failing. Healing spells aren't keeping up."

I frowned at that. "Poison? A rune?" Poison would be easier. For a rune one would need Kader's real name. And Kader didn't get to be head of the guild by being careless with his name, I was sure.

"We've checked for those things. It might just be bad luck. Some people age faster than others."

"Who's challenging him?"

"A group out of the East Coast. Used to be part of the guild there before Kader brought them into the AMA."

"Can they do it?"

Brown looked at me with his black eyes. "Yes, unless."

"Unless what?"

"Unless we support Kader."

Liesl spoke up: "My guild will help as much as possible, but we have our own problems."

I looked at her. "How's that? You have the Hammer of Thor, the most powerful talisman in existence."

She took a long, slow breath and looked sad. "At the end of the war there were two surviving Valkyrie and no surviving berserkers."

Yes, I remembered that normally there are only a dozen or so of the blonde female adepts, and a couple hundred male berserker warriors.

"Dagmar and Brunhild recruited as fast as they could, and Dagmar continued after she became Brunhild." The head of the Valkyries is always called "Brunhild."

"Still," Liesl continued, "we are weaker than at any other time in our history. And we have not been able to recruit adequate numbers of berserkers."

"But you have the Hammer," I repeated.

"Yes, and every other guild wants *Mjollnir*. Only the AMA have we been able to trust, and we fear if Kader or one of his lieutenants—" she looked at Louis "—isn't the head of the guild, we'll lose even that ally. Without enough berserkers..." Her voice trailed off. Then she grew strong again. "We don't dare make an enemy of the new head of the AMA."

I choked. Guilds tend to be bloodless in their relationships with other guilds. But to me even that seemed too cynical.

Brown interrupted my thoughts. "So we need to know, Vaughan, can we count on you to help? Will you come to San Francisco to defend Kader and defeat his enemies?"

I looked at Brown. "How do you know I'm not one of his enemies?"

Brown laughed. "You don't have it in you."

I felt insulted, but had to admit he was right. "Well, I'm not your ally either. Who runs the guild doesn't concern me, as long as I get protection."

"So the fact the AMA has protected you all these years, with the threat to take care of any adept, warrior, or guild that harms you, instills no loyalty in you?" Brown asked. Guilds formed for, mostly, mutual protection. If an adept is killed, the guild is duty-bound to avenge the death. I knew that meant at some time I might be called upon to kill someone who'd acted against the guild or a member.

"Sure, I'm loyal to the guild, not to Kader." This was internal, guild politics. I didn't care, I told myself.

Brown looked at me intently, and hissed his words: "Kader is the guild."

"Please, Mike," Liesl said, touching my hand. I looked at her and would have loved to please her. She smiled at me and started to say something when the world seemed to explode. Bright flashes filled the alley, reflecting off old brick walls and the glass and metal of the car. The sound of gunfire hammered at us. The car's windshields shattered. I dropped to the floor, pulling Liesl after me. The shooting stopped for a heartbeat. I was breathing hard, scared to move.

"Hang on!" the driver yelled. The car backed up, tires squealing. The car lurched as it bounced off the walls of the alley. I think the driver was steering without looking, ducking the gunfire that had resumed.

I could hear bullets impacting the front of the car. A loud explosion and the car jerking hard indicated that a tire had been shot out.

The car bounced left and stopped in the street. But this put my side of the car facing the danger. I scrambled away from the door in pure fear. Liesl tried to stop me from crawling over her.

The glass in the windows above us shattered and I felt a thump in my thigh as if someone had hit me there very hard with a closed fist. The car lurched forward and the shooting stopped. I looked up. The warrior was driving the car down a street at breakneck speeds. He had no headlights—presumably they'd been shot out—and I could hear one of the front tires flopping against the fender.

"What the hell?" I screamed.

"Louis is hurt," the warrior said.

"Damn, so am I." I had touched my leg and my hand came away bloody.

"Heal yourself," Liesl ordered me without feeling. She leaned forward. "How is he?"

"Not good. Unconscious."

She said a very bad word in the ancient language.

I put my hand on my leg and ran a healing spell. The pain and bleeding stopped, but I imagined I could feel the bullet inside me.

"Who were they?" she asked.

"I don't know," the driver replied. "I couldn't see them. They had automatic weapons."

"Are you hurt?" Liesl asked him. I noticed the Valkyrie was better in emergencies than I was. I felt shame at that.

"Not really," he replied, jerking the steering wheel. I got the idea the car was hard to control. I could smell hot odors that I thought were coming from the damaged engine.

"You've been shot!" Liesl exclaimed.

"I'm fine!" the warrior insisted.

"We need to get Louis to a hospital," I said, trying to be helpful.

"Where the hell do you think I'm going?" the driver yelled.

"Look out!" Liesl screamed, pointing at a truck coming into our path, barely visible by the neon lights of a nearby bar.

The tires squealed, but I'm sure having one shot out didn't help. The car slid sideways and its front left corner slammed into the side of the truck with a sound of smashing violence as metal must have been ripping apart. We all were flung forward. The warrior went out the opening where the left windshield should have been. I flew over the back of the seat, slammed my head into the hard steering wheel, and passed out—but not before experiencing the worst pain I'd ever felt. Oblivion was a welcome relief.

I woke up with Liesl pulling me away from the wreckage. A crowd was gathering. She laid me down, roughly dropping my shoulders on the concrete sidewalk in the shadow of a dark doorway.

"Brown?" I asked.

"I'm not sure. Dead, I think," she said softly.

"The driver?"

"Dead." The way she said it indicated to me I didn't want to confirm that for myself.

"Should we go back for Brown?"

She nodded her head. "Yes, I will." She started walking away. From my angle, on the ground, I could see her legs were bloody, staining her petticoat crimson, and her dress was torn.

A car zoomed up, scattering the rubberneckers, and squealed to a stop. Three men jumped out, all Cuban but wearing suits and hats like American mobsters. All carried large guns, presumably the "automatic weapons" that were fired in the alley. The crowd evaporated in screams. Liesl pointed at the men and one blew apart like a pile of dry leaves before a hurricane, his gun clattering to the pavement. The other two fired at her, their guns spitting a staccato of death, flashing strobe lights of destruction.

Liesl had her protection spell up early enough and the bullets ricocheted off her harmlessly, hitting and pockmarking the walls of the buildings around us. But she couldn't attack the men while the spell was up. They stopped firing. "Where is he?" one asked. I could see even at this distance his bushy mustache and eyebrows.

I had painfully pulled myself to my feet. My head hurt and my body wasn't cooperating with it; I had too many injuries to know where to start healing.

"Who are you to ask me questions?" she demanded, her powerful voice filling the street. She was not hiding from them what she was or her power.

I reached for my talisman and pointed a fear spell at the men. It seemed to be all I could do.

"Check the car," Bushy said.

The other one, thinner and looking young, moved to the vehicle but didn't take his eyes from Liesl. When he was close enough, he glanced in. "The chardo meta's in there." He must have meant Brown.

Bushy looked at Liesl. "Where's the other one? The other meta?"

"Dead," she said.

He looked at her questioningly. I changed to a persuasion spell, making him believe it.

"How?"

"The crash," she said.

"I need to see the body."

Liesl must have detected what I was doing. "You don't need to see the body."

He still looked at her, his face red in the neon light, giving him a sinister look. The same light made his gun, still pointed at her, look bloodied and dangerous. His expression was uncertain. I increased the power of the spell.

"We don't need to see the body."

"Yes we do," Skinny said. Damn, I'd left him out of the spell.

"The police will be here soon," Liesl said. "This is a country in the middle of a civil war. Gunfire in the capital should bring half the army down on you."

I modulated the spell, even though in my weakened state the effort was about to make me pass out: fear and persuasion mixed.

"Listen," Bushy said, "I know a little bit about meta. Your spell will eventually wear out and then we'll kill you. And I know you can't move and keep that spell on. So we'll just wait. I don't think *we* have to worry about the police."

I wondered what he meant by that, but didn't have time to think about it. The persuasion and fear spells weren't working. I gathered what strength I had left, fingered my talisman, and shot flame at them. It arced across the street reflecting orange off the cobblestones and buildings, and splashed on the pavement in front of them. Damn, I didn't put enough distance into it. The men jumped back from the flames and started looking for the source—that is, me.

Liesl took that opportunity to run.

She sprinted toward me and, passing, grabbed my arm.

"Thank you," she breathed, pulling me along.

I mumbled a reply and decided not to tell her that hadn't been my plan.

"Get them!" I heard Bushy yell behind us.

Liesl pulled me along. I was weak and on the verge of collapsing; that last spell drained all my energy, both physical and meta. I thought I heard our pursuers' footfalls behind us and tried to move faster.

"Wait," I said, stopping. "In here."

Liesl looked at the sign and exclaimed in disbelief, "What? I'm not going in there."

"We can get lost in the crowd," I explained. "And I can't run anymore."

She still looked skeptical. I couldn't imagine she was worried about propriety at a time like this.

It was the best thing I could come up with. I couldn't run any farther and attacking them with meta would result in me dropping to the pavement for a nice long snooze. And

Liesl wasn't attacking either which indicated to me that she was out of ammo too.

"We'll never outrun them," I said.

"Okay," she whispered resignedly, as Bushy's voice echoed down the street.

I pulled her into the Shanghai. If she'd resisted I couldn't have forced her.

The club, if you could call it that, was housed in a run-down theater in Old Havana. I'd been there once before to satisfy my curiosity. There was a box office with an overweight matron inside and a faded sign announcing the admission charges. The highest, for a seat up front, was $1.25. I slapped the first bill I pulled out of my pocket, a 10 spot, onto the sill by the opening in the gilded metal bars and walked in, ignoring the stare of the woman.

Entering, I realized the flaw in my plan: Liesl was the only woman in the audience. An usher, staring at her, led us down to the front row. Liesl, for her part, was staring at the "show." Five girls, too hefty to be chorines, were dancing—if you could call it that—behind cardboard props, in this case, tall garishly painted, green bushes, and taking off their clothes to the catcalls and hoots of the audience and tinny recorded music. I knew how this ended: when naked they would step in front of the props for just a moment before the lights were doused. That alternated with a comic telling dirty jokes in Spanish and the showing of pornographic movies—most boring things I'd ever seen—and even a traditional Rhumba dance, except at the end the girl would be naked—briefly. The Shanghai was probably the most openly obscene part of the city. I sometimes wonder what my Sunday school teacher back in Idaho would think of Havana, and smile at the image of her running across the Caribbean Sea to escape this Babylon of the Antilles.

I glanced toward the curtained entrance to see whether our tail had pursued us in here. I didn't know why, but they didn't immediately follow.

We were shown chairs in the first row and I sat, luxuriating in the ability to rest for a moment.

I kept one eye on the entrance and another on Liesl, who was staring, mouth agape, at the show. I had to smile at that. I took a moment to heal myself a little.

"Are you hurt?" I whispered to her, remembering the blood on her legs.

"Not badly," she replied. "Where are they?"

"They haven't come in," I said, glancing back to make sure. Maybe we'd lost them, I thought hopefully.

Just then the curtain over the entrance flew back and Bushy bounded in, followed by the thin one. Neither was holding his gun. Bushy was looking around the room, his head jerking back and forth. At that moment I cursed Liesl's lovely blond hair. Bushy pointed, seeing her, and they practically ran down the aisle. He reached inside his coat and pulled out a pistol.

The girls on the stage stepped in front of the cardboard bushes, stood for just a moment, smiled somewhat embarrassedly it seemed, and the lights went out.

"Now!" I whispered and grabbed Liesl. I jumped on the stage and pulled her up. I bumped into someone, feeling only skin, but ignored it and headed for the wings.

"Hey," a man called out as we got to the dimly lit backstage.

"Back door!" I barked at him.

"You're not supposed—"

"Back door!" I snarled through clenched teeth.

"There!" Bushy called out behind us. I glanced back at the stage and Bushy was knocking over props and girls running toward us holding out his pistol. The women were screaming and trying to cover themselves with their hands.

"Come on!" I called to Liesl and pulled her toward the nearest door.

Bad choice. It was the dressing room, lined with women in various states of undress in front of mirrors. The women all screamed. I didn't know why, they'd probably been naked on the stage earlier yet they screamed that I was invading their dressing room.

I knew the sound would draw our pursuers.

"Back door!" I called out emphatically.

A couple of them pointed to the back of the room. Liesl ran for it and I followed.

The door led to a corridor, but at the end was a large metal door. I assumed it led outside.

"Can you spell?" Liesl asked, breathing hard.

"Maybe a little." I sprinted for the door. I drove my shoulder into it and it sprang open onto a dark alley.

"Get behind those crates," Liesl said, pointing. "When they come out, hit them with all you've got."

"Right," I huffed. We ran down the alley and I stopped behind some broken wooden crates and turned to watch the door. Liesl stood in the middle.

"What are you doing?" I asked.

"I'll draw them to you. You'd better get them the first time."

Before I could protest, the door banged open and Bushy and the thin guy burst out.

"There!" the thin one cried, pointing at the Valkyrie.

Liesl ran and they gave chase. I had my hand on my talisman and was preparing a spell.

Following her, they didn't notice me. When they were close enough I pointed at them, and this time the fire hit where I wanted it to. The flames slammed into them, knocking them to the cobblestone pavement.

Bushy saw me and fired as he fell. The sound was huge in the narrow alley. I felt the bullet hit and jerk me backwards. The pain was shocking in intensity and my vision turned white with it. Then it started going dark. Before I lost consciousness, I saw both men crumple to the ground in a burning pile.

CHAPTER FOUR
Havana, December 3, 1958

"Did you know," the doctor was saying to me, "that you have a bullet in your leg and the wound is completely healed? War injury?"

"What?" I asked. I blinked. The lights were bright. "Where am I?"

"Almeijeiras Hospital," he replied. His voice was high-pitched. "You were shot."

"Liesl?" I asked.

"Who?"

"Liesl," I repeated slowly. Every word was an effort. "A woman, blonde."

The doctor, who I could now see was a dark haired man with a long nose, shook his head. "There were two dead men, burned, but no woman."

"A traffic accident," I tried. "Two men, Negroes."

"I'm sorry; I don't know anything about that."

I tried to move but found I was too weak.

"You've suffered a concussion somehow. Did you say you were in a traffic accident before you were shot?"

I made a Herculean effort and nodded.

The doctor looked thoughtful for a moment, then said, "Now this will ease the pain."

I felt the needle. Then I didn't feel much for a while.

When I regained consciousness, I was in a hospital bed in a ward. My head hurt a lot and my right arm was in a sling. I couldn't feel my talisman so I knew it wasn't near. I heard two men whispering in Spanish. Being naturally paranoid, I used a spell to increase my hearing. They were discussing a failed plot by the army to overthrow Batista. I ignored them and waited until a nurse came by.

I called to her, "*¡Enfermera!*"

"*¿Si, señor?*" she said, walking over. She was older, wearing the starched white uniform and sensible shoes of her profession.

Oh, great, I thought, more Spanish. "*Tengo que ver al doctor.*" I was in no mood for the extra effort of speaking Spanish or running a translation spell.

"*El doctor está muy ocupado.*"

I didn't have my talisman, but I could still whip up a decent—if weak—persuasion spell. "*Necesito ver al doctor ahora mismo.*"

"*Si, señor,*" she said agreeably and walked away. I didn't like this ward. Looked like where they put destitute patients, and I came in with nearly a hundred dollars in my money clip. Unless I'd been rolled.

And it smelled bad, like once when a cow died on the farm but before we buried it. Mixed with that was the unpleasant smell of antiseptic.

The nurse returned without the doctor. "*Está sumamente ocupado.*"

Damn. I enforced the spell as much as I could. "*Tiene que venir ahora mismo, es urgente, ¡me estoy muriendo!*"

She rushed off, calling "*¡Doctor!*" It didn't take long for him to come this time. He practically ran into the room. It was the same dark-haired, long-nosed one as before.

"What is going on here?" he asked in English. "You're not going to die." He turned to the nurse and questioned her harshly in Spanish.

I smiled at him. "Needed to get your attention—sorry."

He glared at me. "You told her you were going to die?"

"No, I convinced her of it."

He gave the poor nurse a look to wilt healthy plants.

"Don't blame her; I used a spell."

That brought him up. "What? A spell?"

"I'm an adept."

He looked at me. "Why are you telling me this?"

"Because I want out of here. Why am I in the charity ward?"

"Because when you were brought in all you had on you was a small piece of metal."

My talisman. "What did you do with it?" I demanded.

"I have it. I decided if you carried it that it must be important."

I could tell he wasn't carrying it. "Where is it?"

"In my desk, safe."

"Thank you," I said. And I meant it. "But my money?"

"You had no money."

"Damn."

"You were shot in a dangerous part of town. You didn't even have any papers. We are calling you John Doe."

"Good, keep it that way."

"The police want to talk to you."

"Why?"

"You'd been shot and there were two dead men burned to death near you. They were SIM."

Damn, I thought, Batista's secret police. Why the hell where they after Louis Brown and me?

"Also," the doctor continued, "you mentioned a traffic accident. There was one near where you were found. The car, a taxi, which had been stolen, was shot up, and the thief, a Negro, was also shot, although it looks like the accident killed him."

"There was another man," I said.

"I don't know anything about that."

"Damn," I muttered. I assumed Liesl escaped but, if Louis was dead as she said, why wasn't he found in the taxi?

"No cops," I said.

"But—"

I cut him off. "I said no cops. I am an adept—I can make things unpleasant for you."

He looked at me as if trying to decide whether I was serious. I tried to look serious.

"What can I do?" he asked.

"Move me to a private room and tell them I left. Put me under another name."

He looked at me. "I have heard you adepts can heal yourselves."

"That's true," I said. "But I need to rest, first, and I need that piece of metal."

"Ah, your amulet."

"Yes," I said, not bothering to correct him. "And I need you to take this bullet out of my leg."

"Why?" he asked. "You've lived with it this long."

"No, I got it last night."

He looked at me quizzically.

"Or the night I was brought in," I corrected. "How long has it been?"

"Three days."

Damn, I thought.

"But your leg was healed."

"I healed it that night. I didn't realize the bullet was still in me. I want you to take it out. But first, move me to a private room."

It went pretty much like that. I was moved to a private room which smelled and looked much cleaner. When the doctor came to remove the bullet, I insisted that he use an anesthetic that would only numb my leg. I hated the vulnerability of being unconscious and wanted to minimize it. He removed the bullet then handed me my talisman and I healed my leg (again) and head and shoulder. Then I went to sleep again.

I don't know how long I slept, but judging by the darkness out my window it was late at night when I awoke. Perfect. I had a nurse, a young beauty with large doe eyes, bring me my clothes, but seeing how dirty, bloodstained and torn they were, I had her bring me someone else's clothes. They were a pair of gray flannel pants and a white shirt, and were a little large, but they would do. Persuasion spells work so nicely sometimes. I then walked out of the hospital, caught a taxi, and returned to the Nacional. This time of night the lobby was empty. The desk clerk, who recognized me, was glad to see me.

"Mr. Vaughan, we've been so worried."

Yeah, worried I wouldn't pay my bill. "Why?"

"It's been six days since you've been seen."

I tried not to react to that news; I had lost a day or two there somewhere. "Any messages?" I asked.

"No, sir."

Damn, I had hoped Liesl or Louis, if he was alive, would have tried to contact me. "I'm checking out in the morning,"

I said. "Please have my bill in order. And my items in the safe."

"Yes, sir."

I went to my room and packed. I took only what I couldn't live without: some clothes, my razor, and toothbrush were about it. I changed into a suit and went back downstairs. The casino was closed, of course, so I stopped at the front desk. "I need to see Scarpelli."

The desk clerk looked embarrassed and then said, "Just a moment, sir." He picked up the phone and turned his back to me. I heard a few words, including "Scarpelli."

"Someone will be right with you," he said, smiling plastically.

I waited. A short, pudgy man with balding white hair walked out and talked to the clerk, who pointed me out. The man came over. "I'm Mr. Clark. Mr. Scarpelli is no longer employed here."

I looked at him. "Do you know where I could find him?"

"No," he said simply. I was pretty sure he did know, but didn't want to say.

Suddenly the image of cement overshoes popped into my head. What the hell, I thought. "Do you know if Sidney Rosenberg sent three armed SIM to kill me?"

Clark looked shocked, but I didn't know if it was because I'd come right out and said it in public, or I'd guessed the truth.

"I don't know a Mr. Rosenberg."

The truth spell was strong enough. "You don't know Sidney Rosenberg? The consigliere for the Genovese family?"

"No," he said simply. Stronger truth spells tended to make people speak in one-syllable answers.

"Where's Scarpelli?"

"Sent to Chicago."

"Why?"

The desk clerk was looking on, wide-eyed.

"I don't know."

I released the spell and he looked confused: didn't know why he'd told the truth.

"Thank you," I said and returned to my room. I sat on the bed and thought.

The *Servicio Inteligente Militar*, or SIM, was Batista's secret police. They didn't have a reputation for respecting "human rights," which was one of the reasons a lot of Cubans wanted a change in government. SIM officers also weren't above freelancing. They could have been working for Rosenberg or Scarpelli. Or they could have been working for the faction that was challenging Kader. Or they could have been actually working under Batista's government's orders. But that didn't make much sense. I gave up and decided to go to bed.

I slept pretty well with strong alarm spells on the door and windows.

***

The next morning, with my money from the safe—a problem with having lost the receipt was quickly solved with judicious use of a persuasion spell—and my few belongings, went to Rancho Boyeros International Airport and caught a flight to Miami. There I transferred to one of those new Boeing 707 jets to San Francisco. The flight was nonstop and fast: about five hours. It was roomy and comfortable and the noise of the jet was not as jarring as the noise of a propeller plane. I was going to like the "jet age," I decided.

I didn't know why I was going to Frisco. To tell Kader what I knew about Brown? To try and find Louis? Or because at that moment I didn't feel safe in Cuba and had nowhere else to go? I didn't know. I wasn't thinking, I was reacting.

At the SF airport I secured my small case in a coin-operated locker and pocketed the key after putting a strong secure spell on the locker. For such a small space, it should have lasted a few days. Then I got a taxi to the Huntington Hotel on California Street at the top of Nob Hill. The driver was wearing what was obviously an old and too small navy uniform. When I inquired as to why, he glared at me. "It's December sixth, Mac."

"Pearl Harbor," I stated flatly. I hadn't realized the date.

"Seventeen years ago today I was on the USS *Utah*."

I made affirmative noises and he spent the rest of the trip telling me about escaping from the capsizing ship. I didn't listen but instead looked out the car's window.

Everyone talks about how beautiful San Francisco is, but the sky was gray and drizzling when I arrived. Already I missed the sunshine in Havana.

And Havana didn't have hills like what the taxi was trying to negotiate to get to California Street.

The taxi stopped with squeaking brakes in front of the arched entrance to the Huntington Hotel as a cable car clanged by. I stepped out and shivered. I didn't have the right clothes for this kind of weather. I walked up the few low white marble steps to the entrance and the doorman opened the heavy oak door to the lobby. I stepped inside, feeling as if in my short exposure to the elements, the drizzle had gotten to my bones.

In the small lobby was an adept keeping a wary eye on the entrance. With him was a large man I presumed to be a warrior. He had a large bulge under his coat. I nodded to the adept and headed for the elevators. I noticed out of the corner of my eye that the adept spoke to the warrior who picked up a white phone and dialed a number.

I walked to the small alcove where the elevators were and pressed the call button.

The elevator arrived in a few moments and stepping in, I pressed the black button for the twelfth floor, feeling it click in and, while holding it, pressed the button for the first floor. When I let them go they were both indented. I had no idea how this worked; it was technology, not meta. But the elevator started to move and I knew it was going to the thirteenth floor. Hell, I had no idea how an elevator worked. I had some vague notion of a motor pulling a cable. But how it knew what floor to go to was a mystery to me.

The indicator above the door pointed to twelve and then stopped, but the car kept moving. When it did stop, and buttons popped out with duel clicks, the doors slid open and I faced three men. Two were warriors and they both held weapons that looked like little more than a barrel, a handle, and a long box underneath to hold the bullets. My father had been an avid hunter so I knew a little about guns. Both weapons were pointed right at me. I didn't move.

The third man was an adept. He spoke a phrase in the ancient language that translated roughly (very roughly) to "The moon above Atlantis sparkles on the water of the River Non."

I replied, in the same language, "Only in the spring, when the rukhkh eggs are hatching." Yes, it was nonsensical and therefore less likely to be guessed.

"Welcome, friend," the adept said. I didn't recognize him. He was young and his power was not strong, unless he was masking.

The warriors stepped back, allowing me access to the hall. As I stepped off the elevator, one reached in and apparently pressed a button or something, because the doors closed, nearly on his arm, and, I assumed, the car went away. I walked down the hall to suite 1313. They'd remodeled since I was last here. The floor had a red carpet and the walls were covered in flowered wallpaper. I didn't like the look.

The door was open so I walked in. I was shocked by what I saw. Kader was probably in his early sixties, but looked much older. He was slumped in a wingback leather chair. Beside him was a handsome woman about his age, kneeling on the same carpet as in the hall, holding his hand and looking at him. She looked at me with sharp blue eyes as I entered and I immediately recognized her as Brunhild, the leader of the Valkyrie and Kader's rumored lover. Her hair was still blonde but faded and her skin no longer had the look of fine porcelain.

Two warriors were standing behind the chair. One was a large man garbed in a breastplate, helm, gauntlets, and chain mail. He held a double-headed broadax, but also had a pistol in a holster at his hip. I decided he was Brunhild's berserker. His bright eyes sized me up quickly as not being a threat. The other warrior was a Negro in a business suit, holding the same weapons the warriors in the hall had. His dark eyes swept over me as if I were transparent.

Also in the room were other adepts. I did a quick count and came up with 15. They were milling around, talking quietly in groups, seeming subdued and nervous as a group. There were also about 10 warriors, all holding that same kind of weapon. I looked for someone I knew. Conspicuously missing was Louis.

A small Asian man walked up to me. "Who are you?" he asked in nearly a whisper, as if to not disturb the pall of quiet that covered the room.

"Mike Vaughan," I told him, keeping my voice low.

"Kirozow Takada," he said. "You can call me 'Sam.'"

"Thanks. What's going on?"

He walked into the body of the room, forcing me to follow. "We're waiting."

"For what?"

"The Eastern Faction to attack."

I looked at him, sure my eyes were wide with surprise. "Waiting for their attack? Shouldn't we have more adepts here?"

"This is all that are loyal to Kader."

I felt my jaw drop. "This is it?" Suddenly I realized they'd come to see me in Havana not because of my power, but because they were desperate.

"Yes." Takada look angry. "Many are staying neutral. There's still resentment about how Kader consolidated the guilds. He thought decentralizing power would help, but it only made for factions, and now one is challenging him."

I decided at that point I was going to be neutral. I didn't know what force the "Eastern Faction" had but I was sure it was more than 15 adepts and a handful of warriors. But there was one question I wanted answered. "What about Louis?"

"Missing, since he went to Havana to talk to an adept there, along with the Valkyrie that went with him." He looked at me funny just then. I decided it was time to depart. The question was how to leave gracefully.

Just then a rukhkh burst through one of the suite's windows in a spray of broken glass and shattered wood. It screamed, shattering the remaining windows and probably doing much the same to the courage of anyone in the room.

Two adepts attacked it, shooting flames at it. It dove for the nearest, knocked him flat, and ripped into his chest with its obsidian talons. A warrior fired at him, the gun spitting out bullets in rapid succession. Where they hit the huge bird, black feathers erupted and the bird screamed with such pain it seemed to tear at my soul. Its huge wings beat in the air, making a blast of wind that literally knocked men down.

I started backing out, thinking it was definitely time to go while the others were distracted. I stepped into the hall and heard the elevator doors open. Gunfire spat out of it, killing the two warriors and the adept there who crumpled in a mass on the red carpet. The color of the fibers did not hide the blood seeping from under the corpses. Three men stormed out of the car and glared at me. They all had boxy weapons held at their hips. Before they could shoot me, I ducked back into the room.

"They're coming!" someone yelled needlessly.

The battle with the rukhkh was finished, the great bird lying in a puddle of its black blood.

I headed for the back wall near the windows. I knew I was going to have to fight, but I wanted maximum distance between me and the attackers. I pulled out my talisman and started working on a protection spell and attack spells. I considered teleporting to the floor below us, but decided that, for now, that was far too dangerous.

Brunhild's berserker had picked her up and carried her to a corner, set her down, and stood in front of her, challenging anyone to get past him.

I understood her actions even if I didn't agree. This wasn't her guild's fight. If she got involved it could make enemies of the new AMA leadership and her guild. Despite her feelings for Kader, she had to put her guild first and remain neutral.

Kader had also moved, but to stand in front of his allies. His warrior, looking worried, stood beside him. "We will fight them to the death!" Kader called out and for a moment, I was ready to die beside him. But just for a moment.

Two enemy warriors came into the room. They were attacked by Kader and other adepts, and their bodies disintegrated faster than their screams faded. That stopped the warrior attack, and for the moment we seemed safe.

Then, through the broken windows, adepts flew in on the backs of rukhkhs or on carpets. This put me right on the front lines of the action. Flames, lightning, and airbolts diced the air as adepts attacked, defended, and died. The sounds of gunfire, screaming rukhkhs, and yelling men were a cacophony of battle that assaulted the ears.

A young man on a flying carpet pointed at me. I ducked and shot lightning at him. It hit him and he was spun around, fell off his carpet, and dropped to the bloody floor. I looked at that carpet, which settled softly on the floor, and saw my escape. I made my way toward it, but didn't see the rukhkh coming at me. It slammed me into the wall so hard I thought I heard the plaster crack. My breath was knocked out of me and I was momentarily stunned. Its yellow, hooked beak was lowering toward my face when it screamed, lifted its head, and fell with a loud crash to the floor. Its feathers were smoldering where Takada had hit it with lightning. I smiled at him in thanks. He nodded and attacked another adept.

I ran and jumped on the carpet, which bounced a foot or two in the air as I approached. I turned it toward the window, seeing a patch of blue through the gray clouds, seeming to beckon me to escape. But I was knocked off the carpet by what felt like a giant fist. I must have been hit by an airbolt. I lay on the floor, gasping for air, the pain in my ribs making every breath torture.

I still had my talisman in my hand. I touched my side and healed as best I could. The pain was almost gone. I crawled to the carpet.

"They're running!" Kader yelled. I looked up and indeed it was true. The enemy adepts were flying out the windows, or scrambling out of the room into the hall with their warriors. A few were killed while retreating. I was amazed and happy. A cheer broke through the room, and even the berserker smiled.

Kader was bleeding and his warrior was dead. Adepts moved to help him to a chair.

There were dead adepts and rukhkh blanketing the room. Blood and viscera stained the walls and carpet and brought up a smell I wanted to forget, but knew I never would.

Takada looked at me. "That was a good idea."

"What?" I was sure he didn't mean escape.

"Get on a carpet—get in the air to attack them from above."

"Oh, yeah." I was breathing hard, experiencing that drained feeling one has when adrenaline wears off. I was happy to let him think I was a hero.

I was smiling at Takada when a large section of the roof of the building tore away in a shower of broken plaster and torn wood.

"They have a pterodactyl!" somebody screamed.

I ducked falling debris as the roof was peeled back by the pterodactyl's claws. A large piece of ceiling landed on Takada and knocked him down. I moved to pull it off, but a blast of cold wet air hit me from above, slamming me down. It was the downdraft of the pterodactyl's leathery wings beating as it hovered over the opening it had torn in the building. I looked up. It was right above me, its mottled, light gray skin almost camouflaging it against the dismal sky. It screeched a sound that seemed to vibrate me to my core. I knew I was dead if I stayed there, so I scrambled away on my hands and knees. It swooped through the hole in the roof and landed on the carpet next to Takada. It knocked the debris off him with its snout and then scooped his limp body up in its mouth and swallowed him nearly whole. This was a big pterodactyl.

I realized somebody was screaming in uncontrollable fright and it was me.

Adepts and warriors attacked the monster. But bullets bounced off and meta attacks were deflected. There was a reason the pterodactyls survived while other dinosaurs didn't. They were magic creatures—like the Loch Ness monster, the abominable snowman, and its American cousin the Sasquatch—that were semi-intelligent animals that learned to use meta to survive. There weren't many pterodactyls and they live in isolation, mainly in the Amazonian jungle, most thought, as far away from humans as they could get. As far as I knew, there was little that could kill them. How the Eastern Faction got one under their control was a mystery I didn't have time to ponder just then. There were supposed to be ways, but some said those black arts were long forgotten. Apparently not.

I stood and ran from the room, not caring if I looked the coward. I felt only the need to escape and save myself. Kader was dead, or soon would be. It was time to think about how to make friends with the new regime. Warriors were coming out of the elevator again, holding those boxy weapons. The Huntington didn't have stairs, just a fire escapes on the sides. I realize the elevator was a bottleneck. I wasn't going to get out of there that way. The warriors pointed their guns at me and I raised my hands. Behind them was an adept I recognized named Houser. We'd met a few years back at a guild conclave. I didn't like him then, thinking he was an arrogant bastard. I apparently underestimated him. He looked at me. "Vaughan," he called out, "stop!"

I was stopped but perhaps he felt the need to give an order in front of his men. Houser looked at me angrily and pointed. "You backed the wrong side, Vaughan."

"I didn't back any side," I said. "I just happened to be here when you attacked." We were yelling over the din of the slaughter in the suite.

"If you aren't on Kader's side, why are you here?"

"To find out what was going on. I was in Havana and I only heard rumors." I decided that I probably shouldn't mention the part about Louis Brown and Liesl.

"You should have come to me, then," he said.

"I didn't know you were involved." I was talking lightly, ignoring the guns pointed at me and the sounds coming from the room I had just fled.

"Sorry, Vaughan," Houser said. "I don't believe you."

The warriors took that as their cue, and guns that had been held relaxed were suddenly pointed at me. I got the protection spell up in time and the bullets bounced off me. The warriors stopped firing.

"You can't last forever, Vaughan," Houser yelled at me.

He was right. And with a protection spell, I couldn't move, either. At that point defense was not my best option, but it was the first thing I had thought of. I had a feeling of helplessness, knowing that when my spell wore off, or I passed out from fatigue from maintaining it, I'd die, unless I could convince Houser I wasn't worth killing.

Houser turned to one warrior and said, "Watch him. When his spell dissipates, kill him. If he moves, the spell is gone, so kill him."

"Yes, sir," the warrior said.

"Come on," Houser barked to the other warriors and started for the door to the suite, brushing past me. There was only the one warrior between me and the elevator.

The wall crashed in in a cloud of broken plaster, knocking down Houser and his troupe. A wing of the pterodactyl was protruding. The warrior watching me forgot his orders and ran to help Houser. I ran, negating the protection spell but escaping. I sprinted for the elevator and it was still there, waiting. Just before I got inside it I looked back and saw Houser speaking, holding a large talisman in both hands. I assumed it was a spell to control the beast and the talisman was somehow attuned to its being. His warriors were trying to protect him from a flopping leather wing.

I got into the elevator, but it didn't move. I remembered how the guard had reached in to do something that sent it on its way. But the guard was dead; I'd stepped over his body to get into the car. I looked at all the buttons. I pressed a floor button. Nothing happened. From the sounds I could tell the pterodactyl had retreated back into the suite, no doubt mopping up Kader's forces. That meant Houser and his men could be on me in moments. I pressed the "CLOSE DOOR" button and the elevator remained motionless. "Damn," I swore under my breath. I punched the "HOLD" button and it depressed and stayed in. And mercifully, the doors started sliding shut. Just before they closed a gun was jammed between them. Automatically, the doors started opening again. I shot flame out the opening and heard a scream. The gun dropped with a rattling sound and I kicked it off the threshold and jabbed my finger hard on the HOLD button again. Nothing happened. So I tried CLOSE DOOR. Nothing happened. I hit the button for the first floor. This time the doors closed, but not before I saw the burning warrior bouncing off the walls and lighting wallpaper and carpet on fire as he flailed about trying to end the agony. The smell was horrific.

But the flames kept the other warrior and Houser away. Bullets impacted the wall and I realized the other warrior was shooting at me. I scurried to the back of the elevator and crouched on the floor. When the door finally closed completely I heard the bullets hitting the metal. I leaned against the back wall, breathing hard, feeling lucky to be alive.

The car descended far too slowly for my desires. I'd punched the button for the lobby, not knowing what I'd find. If Houser's group was there, I was probably dead. That flying carpet was looking awfully good right then.

As the car dropped, I felt the whole building shudder and wondered what havoc the pterodactyl was wreaking above me.

I decided getting off at the lobby wasn't a good idea. It was probably full of Houser's men and it was small with little chance to escape. Even an invisibility spell would be near useless as the opening of the elevator would give away my presence. I hit the button for the second floor just in time. The elevator stopped and I stepped out. A lot of the doors to the hotel rooms were open. Looking inside some of them it appeared from the disheveled interiors that the denizens had departed in a hurry. I was sure of that; all the lessers probably ran for their lives when the battle started. I explored the floor which was strangely quiet, although the rumblings and gunshots from above could be dimly heard.

Down the hall, on the left of the elevator, I found a window overlooking a very steep street more than two floors below. The Huntington is on the edge of Nob Hill. But here was the fire escape.

I hesitated. On the fire escape, I'd be easy prey for that flying nightmare. But it was busy eleven floors above me.

I opened the window and it screeched as I did—a sound that seemed loud enough to summon a demon, or a pterodactyl.

Once it was open enough, I put a leg out, stepped on the painted metal of the fire escape, and then pulled the rest of my body through the window. I was shocked at how cold it was and how far down it was to the steeply sloping street. And I could see the lowest fire escape was far above the cement—farther than I wanted to jump.

Not knowing what else to do, I scurried down the steep stairs which vibrated under my feet until I reached the bottom platform. Here I could see there was a ladder that reached lower than the platform so the jump wouldn't be so bad. I approached it and noticed it was in two pieces and it looked as if one piece would descend if I put my weight on it. I was studying this, trying to determine how to work it when a rush of wind interrupted my thoughts. I turned but too late: pterodactyl claws grabbed my torso, wrapped around my body like a fleshy vise, and pulled me skyward, the beating of the wings blowing down on me as the claws held me so tight I couldn't breathe. I didn't know why it just didn't eat me. I was sure it would hurt less than what its claws were doing to me and the way my head was hanging down with the blood rushing to it. I tried beating its claws with my hands but it felt as if I might as well beat on hardened steel.

The beast swooped upward and I noticed people on the street looking up in horror. It was amazing how well I could see their faces despite our gaining altitude.

The pterodactyl swung in a tight arch in the narrow space between buildings, and headed for the Huntington's roof. It skimmed over the edge so close I thought it was going to smash me into the tiles of the sloped part of the roof that was around the flat top of the building.

Without warning the animal stopped in midair with a horrible sound of twisting metal and its painful screams. It dropped me, luckily only a few feet to the roof, but I landed on my hip and the pain shot through me. I looked up to see the pterodactyl entangled in the Huntington's neon sign and the metal supports holding it. As I watched, the sign—broken glass tubes raining down—started tilting back on the beast.

I ran, ignoring pain in my chest and legs. The animal and the metal crashed into the roof mere inches behind me it seemed and the pterodactyl screamed, answered by shattering glass in buildings near the hotel. Bells rang in the towers of the cathedral across the street in resonance with the unearthly sound.

I found stairs leading down through the tiled sloping roof to the edge of the building, then a precarious ladder leading down to the fire escape on the thirteenth floor. This time I did not hesitate, but scrambled down the stairs as fast as I dared while hanging onto the damp, dirty and slippery rail tightly, got on the ladder, hoping I didn't slip on the wet rungs and fall to the street, and climbed down to the fire escape platform. I sprinted down the stairs using a spell to keep me moving despite the pain. At the last platform I jumped on the ladder and descended. As I reached the bottom of the first ladder, the second ladder slid down with a rusty squeal as I stepped on the last rung, leaving me less than a foot above the sidewalk. I dropped to it.

And I ran again. Once I stopped to look up toward the top of the hotel. The top of the Huntington looked as if someone had taken a can opener to it, with the roof peeled away at one corner. The neon sign was gone but I could see metal protruding into the sky. I could still hear sporadic gunfire and the angry and painful screeching of the pterodactyl. I didn't know if it was going to die.

I was met by police cars and fire engines roaring up the hill with their lights flashing and sirens screaming. I was sure they were there to protect any lessers. They couldn't do anything for the adepts and, frankly, wouldn't try.

Far enough away to feel reasonably safe, I found a dark alley and rested, needing to after all the spells I had invoked and the physical effort I had expended.

After resting long enough that my heart was not pounding as if someone were beating on my chest with their fist, I walked down the hill again. I didn't know where I was going; I needed to think.

I was getting strange looks from passers-by. I wondered why until I slipped into a Chinese restaurant and found the bathroom. In the mirror I saw that I was covered in plaster dust and blood. The blood was mine. I had a cut on my head that I hadn't even noticed. But once I'd seen it, it started hurting like hell. I healed it and cleaned up as best I could. While doing that I decided I had to get out of San Francisco as fast as possible.

I walked out of the restaurant and waved down a taxi to take me to the airport.

S. EVAN TOWNSEND

CHAPTER FIVE
San Francisco, December 6, 1958

I got my belongings, including my cash, from the airport locker, and bought a ticket on the first flight to a city outside of California. It ended up being to Dallas. Then I bought a ticket on the first trip out of Texas. Each trip I used a different name. I used spells to hear what people were saying while I stood across the room. Any name they mentioned I used, first or last, unless of course it was a female first name, was too similar to a name I'd just used, or was too foreign sounding. From Dallas I flew to Cincinnati, then Seattle. I spent the night in a motel near the airport — secure and alarm spells in place — and in the morning took a flight to Chicago. Very few airports could handle jets which apparently needed longer runways (the stewardess explained when I asked why we couldn't take a jet to Seattle). So I ended up flying a lot of prop jobs, including the one into Chicago.

Why Chicago? I didn't know. Maybe I wanted to find Scarpelli. I did know I wanted to get lost in a big city. I couldn't go to Havana — they knew I went there. Chicago seemed a logical choice, even in December.

***

I stepped out of the Chicago airport into a snowstorm and started wondering how logical my choice was, after all. I hailed a cab and sat in back.

"Where to?" the driver asked.

"Downtown," I said, "a nice hotel."

"Okay," he said and ground the gears on the car before pulling slowly away.

I watched the storm out the car window. The flakes were large and falling softly, but the motion of the taxi destroyed what could be the peacefulness of the snowfall.

I hadn't seen snow like this since I'd left Salt Lake City in 1949.

Growing up in the high valleys of Idaho, snow was just another part of life from October to April. Salt Lake City, pressed up against the Wasatch Mountains, was painted white every winter by inches of snow.

I'd gone to Salt Lake in '44 from my home in Idaho. I was about to turn 18 and, seeing a prolonged invasion of Japan—no one knew two atomic weapons would end the war far sooner than anyone thought possible—and my impending draft coming up, I decided to pursue my ambition to become an adept. Adepts don't have to worry about the draft, or much else the government requires.

Cowardliness wasn't my only motivation. Being an adept seemed to be about the only option available to me to escape becoming another sod-buster like my father (and his father and his father and as far back as family history was known) and spending the rest of my life in dirt. A subsistence existence that was so poor that during the Depression we had to drive back roads because we couldn't afford license plates for the Model T.

I drove my father's Ford pickup truck—the last time I drove in my life—to a nearby Indian reservation. The truck was at least 10 years old and most of its red paint rusted to a brownish patina, one head-light drooping giving it a slightly inebriated look, and the springs in the seats were either poking out of the fabric or collapsed to the point of being harder than the wooden support beneath them. As it barely wheezed its way down the dirt roads of the reservation I stiffened in my resolve to flee as far as I could from the poverty I'd known all my childhood.

A bribe of whiskey to a tribe elder got me the location of an old medicine man. He was living in a shack made of scavenged boards, canvas, and tarpaper. It was scant protection from local winters that left my family's house frigid with ice coating the panes in the windows. There was no furniture—just blankets to sit on.

The Indian was weathered like an old post out on the prairie, as my father would say.

"Who are you, *andabichi*?" he asked.

I didn't know that last word so I told him my name and added, "I want to become an apprentice."

He chuckled at me derisively. "I do not take white men as apprentices."

I had anticipated that. "Is there a meta—an adept nearby?"

He shook his head, making the grey and black ponytails hanging from his head waggle back and forth.

"No, none close."

I sighed, defeated; I didn't know where to go. I did know I had to go home and my father would beat me badly for taking the truck.

"Nearest I know in city by the lake," the old Indian said unbidden. "I traveled there once for a visit. Large city, very strange for me. Powerful adept but polite in the ways of the white man."

Some polite questions and a willingness to sit through his stories got me the name and address. "City by the lake" had to be Salt Lake City.

When I got home my father was furious. Gas rationing wasn't a problem; we were provided all we needed for the tractor and if it got diverted to cars, well, the War Resources Board was none the wiser. But I had wasted, in his opinion, my father's money and had had the pickup when he claimed he needed it. He used a switch on me for the last time that night. He was red with rage as the willow branch snapped against my backside. And he hadn't even discovered that the stash of whiskey he kept hidden from my mother, the bishop, and — he thought — from me, was missing.

After he went to sleep, I snuck out of my room and went to a corner of the barn and dug up a tobacco can. In it was all the money I had been able to save all my life. I returned to my room, tied up some clothes into a bundle, and left, walking for the nearest town. Then I decided that was foolish because that was the first place they'd look. I found the main road, U.S. 91, and hitchhiked toward Idaho Falls which, up until then, was the largest town I'd ever been in, having accompanied my father into town for supplies. At one point I thought I saw a red pickup coming down the road so I hid in the borrow pit. The altitude of the Snake River Plain brings winters early and arctic so it was wet and cold in there, the ground covered in snow and under the snow was mud. The combination seemed to suck the warmth through your clothes and out of your body.

I had to walk to the bus station from where a farmer dropped me at the edge of town. The station was a white concrete building with a hardwood floor and wooden benches. A pinball machine sat unused in one corner. At least it was warm.

I stood in line to purchase a ticket from the old man at the ticket window and barely had enough money for the fare to Salt Lake City.

The bus trip took eight hours, stopping at every town, large and small, along the way: Shelly, Blackfoot, Pocatello, Malad City, and so forth. Everyone on the bus was smoking, it seemed. No one in my family smoked and the haze seemed to sicken me. I lay against the cold window hoping that would help me feel better

We stopped at a place in Utah called "Crossroads" for lunch, but I didn't have much money and was afraid to spend it on food. Embarrassed that I wasn't buying anything to eat, I wandered around outside the restaurant aimlessly, keeping one eye on the bus for it to start loading. The cold was better than the eyes of the other passengers.

The road ran between the Great Salt Lake to the west and the mountains to the east. The mountains were like a thousand-foot high wall, rising suddenly from the flat valley floor. The towns were built right up against the steep slopes.

Salt Lake City was huge compared to Idaho Falls. Cars and city buses—the latter I'd never seen before—were everywhere. I thought with gas rationing there'd be less traffic, but there sure seemed to be a lot (I hadn't seen what it looked like without gas rationing, but I would a few months later and was more surprised then). And there were more people than I knew existed in the world at the time.

I walked the streets, trying to find the address the medicine man had given me. I was cold and hungry and close to spending my precious last few dimes on a meal.

I found the adept's home after figuring out Salt Lake's grid address system, and waited outside in a snowstorm. It wasn't a gentle one like the one I watched outside the taxi window. The snow was small and hard and the wind smacked it into your face with a thousand cold bites. I nearly froze before a man came out. He was dressed warmly in a long coat of wool or some other fabric. He had gloves and a muffler and had his hat pulled down low against the wind. I immediately associated his attire and bearing with money having only seen such fine clothes in the movies.

I followed him, apparently clumsily, for he turned a corner and when I followed he was there, waiting for me. He grabbed me and pushed me against the wall of a building.

"Why are you following me?" he demanded.

"Please, sir," I pleaded. "I was told you're an adept."

"What of it? Do you wish to be turned into a frog?"

I was too scared to realize he was teasing me. "N-n-no, sir, I want to be an adept."

He laughed. "Many boys think they want to be an adept."

"I do, sir."

He looked at me, his blue eyes seeming to bore into my brain. He released me with his hands but still held me with his eyes. "What kind of grades do you get in school, boy?"

I looked embarrassed. "I don't much like school, sir."

"Why?" he demanded. "Too hard?"

"No, sir. It's…boring. And too regular, if you get my meaning."

At that I saw his visage soften for a moment. Then he asked, "Do you like to read?"

"Yes, sir!" My father said I liked to read too much.

"Who are your favorite authors?"

"Mark Twain and Jules Verne, sir."

At that he actually smiled. "Yes, I don't suppose a boy from a small town gets much opportunity to read anything more modern."

I was disappointed that he knew I was from a small town, as if I could act cosmopolitan after a few hours in Salt Lake City.

"What's your name?" he demanded. "Where are you from?"

"Uh, sir, I don't think I should tell you that." Rumor — whispered between schoolboys — was that if an adept knows your name or history they can control you.

He smiled. "Very good. You come around tomorrow morning and see me at my house. I assume you know where that is?"

I nodded, disappointed that he wasn't going to take me in right then. I needed the warmth and food.

"Yes, sir."

He smiled at me and patted my arm, then walked away.

He later told me that he'd spotted me from the house and came out to see if I'd follow. He also said that if I could survive a night alone on the city streets, and didn't give up and go home, I might have what it took to be an adept. I didn't tell him that I didn't have enough money to go home.

That night was terrifying for me. I slept, a little, under a bush beside a house. It was too cold to really sleep and the bush did little to protect me from the wind and snow. In the morning the owner chased me away with a shotgun.

I returned to the adept's house and knocked on the door. He didn't answer, but a man I later learned was his warrior did. I was led inside, and was warm for the first time since getting off the bus. The adept met me in a lavishly appointed room. Again, it was like something you'd only see at a movie house. There were leather chairs and a fire in the fireplace and breakfast was laid out. The adept was there, sitting at the table.

I looked at the food hungrily and he bade me eat. I decided I should mind my manners despite my hunger.

"Full?" he asked when I'd cleaned the plate.

"Yes, sir," I said, lying.

"Good. And the first thing you need to learn is it's 'teacher,' not 'sir.' Do you understand?"

"Yes, si—Teacher."

"Good. And I shall call you 'Student.' But you need to choose an alias, also—something totally unrelated to your real name. And never tell me or anyone else your real name or where you came from."

"Yes, Teacher."

"Most likely you lived there all your life?"

I was about to answer when he held up his hand. "Don't answer. Never give anyone any information about your past. For if I knew the town where you grew up, do you think I could learn your name?"

"Yes, Teacher." I knew adepts kept aliases. I wasn't sure why.

"And if I knew your name, I would have power over you. Did you know that?"

"No, s—Teacher."

"Lars!" he called out, making me jump.

The warrior walked over.

"Get this boy cleaned up and into some decent clothes. He may rest today but tomorrow we see if he has what it takes to be an adept."

"Yes, sir," the warrior said. He looked at me derisively. "Come on, you."

For five years I apprenticed under that adept, a hard job of mostly non-meta duties such as cleaning house and preparing meals. He was part of a small guild of adepts in Utah, Idaho, Wyoming, and Nevada. But he trained me well, and by the time I was ready for my trials and to be fully accepted into a guild, my teacher's guild had been absorbed into Kader's AMA. My teacher really was a kind and wise man and I mourned his death of natural causes.

"How's this?" the driver said, breaking me out of my reverie. "The best place in town."

I realized the car was stuffy with its heater going full blast; the warmth had almost put me to sleep.

I looked out the window at the hotel. I hit the driver with a truth spell. "Do you get a kickback from this place?"

"Yes."

"Is it the dive it looks?"

"Yes."

"I want a nice, quiet place. Where would you recommend for your well-off bachelor uncle?"

"The Allerton, on Michigan."

I released the truth spell. "Take me there."

"Uhm, yes, sir." He was, as most lessers are when hit with a truth spell, confused about why he'd told the truth. But he ignored it and put the car in gear.

The Allerton was a tall red brick building. The clouds were so low I couldn't see the top. I entered the marble-tiled lobby and was greeted by a uniformed bell captain—I later learned his name was Joe—who took my bag and directed me to the dark mahogany desk. There I found out that the Allerton was a club hotel, one of a series across the country set up for single businessmen and women. There were separate floors for men and women, serviced by their own elevators. However, I wasn't in the club. But that didn't take long to solve with the right spells and enough money, and soon I was in a luxurious room looking out on gray clouds.

The bellhop said I had a view of the lake, but I couldn't see it.

I sat on the bed and rested. I had no idea what to do next. I realized I was an adept without a guild. Houser and his bunch had most likely killed Kader and taken the leadership of the guild. But Houser thought I was loyal to Kader and would, therefore, prefer to kill me rather than let me live. There was little doubt in my mind that he'd sent the pterodactyl to finish me on the fire escape.

I needed to think through my options, what few there were. No guild would take me and risk the wrath of the AMA. Even changing my name wouldn't help, at least not for long. As the AMA looked for me, they'd pass my description around and soon I'd be found out. There were two major guilds in North America: The AMA, from which I'd just been forcibly ejected, and the North American Guild, called the NAG, which was mostly the southern U.S. and Latin America. The AMA was the most powerful; Kader had seen to that. He used that power to keep the members safe. Houser would now use that power to make sure I was safe nowhere.

There were minor guilds, also. The French Canadians, the Eskimos, and most Caribbean islands had their own guilds. Cuba's was the *Gremio Cubano* and I was on friendly terms with them. At least, they left me alone and I left them alone. That's pretty friendly in inter-guild relationships. But they wouldn't take me in for fear of the AMA, either.

Discouraged, I decided to sleep, hoping things would look better in the morning. It wasn't paranoia that made me put alarm spells on the door and windows before sleeping.

***

Things didn't look better in the morning, or for several mornings after that. I had checked in as Steve Wendell of

New York City — a name I'd never used and a place I'd never been. I hoped my trail was sufficiently cold. Perhaps I should have flown to a couple more cities before coming here, I wondered. But, like that trip to Salt Lake City, I was worried about running out of money.

The sky did clear once or twice and I saw Lake Michigan. It was a greenish-gray and cold looking body of water, as unlike the Caribbean as a slug in the nose is to a warm embrace.

I hibernated in my room for nearly two weeks. I had room service for meals and a paper to read — the evening edition of the *Sun-Times* was delivered to my room nightly by a bellhop in exchange for a fifty-cent tip — and I watched the television, wondering what people saw in quiz shows and "I Love Lucy" (although a new show called the "The Rifleman" I found interesting).

To be honest, I had developed a case of agoraphobia. First of all, it was absolutely freezing in Chicago, something probably accentuated by my being acclimatized to Havana's weather. Highs in Chicago were in the zero to minus five range. About a week after I arrived, the paper announced that it was the coldest December in seven years and the Chicago River was freezing. The next day, it was declared the coldest December on record. Secondly, a sense of dread had come over me since the battle in San Francisco, because I was sure Houser was trying to hunt me down. I would leave the Allerton and walk along Michigan Avenue, but after a few blocks I'd return, telling myself it was only the weather driving me back and not the constant fear that felt like a cold hand around my neck. Or I'd have a taxi take me to a restaurant that Joe recommended, only to quickly devour my meal and return. If I were a horse, my father would have called me barn soured.

I didn't want to leave my hotel room, much less the hotel.

However, two needs forced me to face my fears. One was money. I was paying my hotel bill weekly and watching my cache of Sidney's money slowly disappear. The added expenses of all the airplane flights getting here and replacing my wardrobe—with a tailor who would come to my room—put a large dent in my funds. I was going to need to raise money shortly, and that meant finding a reliable place to play poker with rich men who were not connected to organized crime. I was afraid that might be difficult in Chicago, and I knew I'd better start long before my need became desperate.

The other necessity was less prosaic. In Havana I had grown used to being in the company of women on a regular basis. It had been three weeks since that last brown girl at the Hotel Nacional. And it looked like I wasn't going to be going back to Havana soon because Houser's minions would probably be there looking for me. I'd read in the society pages about the opening of Lansky's Hotel Riviera shortly after I'd arrived in Chicago, and rued missing what was probably quite a party even though the revolution was still a problem. According to the paper, rebels had threatened to set up a government in the areas they controlled and ask for recognition from the Organization of American States. They were "taxing" companies in the occupied territories but U.S.-owned United Fruit was refusing to pay. The paper said the rebels were hoping that the U.S. military wouldn't interfere.

I was rather hoping they would. I hoped the stupid revolution would be over so if and when I dared, I could return to Havana.

In Havana, everything was out in the open and easy to find. That was the appeal of the city and what brought in the

Yankee tourists and their money. In Chicago, despite its reputation, it took a little work. I tried the hotel's "Tip Top Tap" room, but it had seen better days. It was populated by middle-aged couples and homosexual men.

I needed to find someplace to meet women.

***

"Hey, Joe," I called out across the lobby, getting the bell captain's attention.

"Yes, Mr. Wendell?" he smiled at me across the lobby. It was early evening and already dark and cold outside.

I walked up close to him—his smile not varying at all as I approached. But I seemed to make him a little uncomfortable. "What can I do for you, Mr. Wendell?"

"Joe," I said softly. "Where can a man get some action in this town?" It was the best opening I could think of.

"Action, sir?" he asked, seeming perplexed.

I didn't want to hit him with a truth spell. I'd kept my powers hidden from the staff, thinking they wouldn't talk of the reclusive adept staying in the hotel. "Yeah, you know. A friendly poker game."

Suddenly he looked both happy he understood and disappointed in, well, me.

"I'm sorry, Mr. Wendell, I wouldn't know anything about that."

I was embarrassed, both for him and me. "I'm sorry, Joe."

"That's okay, Mr. Wendell."

We stood during an awkward silence. Then he said softly. "You could try talking to Knolling, the night bell captain, sir."

I looked at him and smiled. "Thank you."

"You're welcome, sir," he said in his normal voice as if nothing unusual had happened.

Knolling didn't come on duty until nine P.M. But it was surprisingly easy. After informing him of what I wanted, he said, "I might be able to get you in a game."

"High stakes?" I asked.

He nodded as he looked elsewhere, obviously thinking. "Yeah, the highest. I'll contact you in a few days."

I agreed and resumed my hermit ways. After the embarrassment with Joe about a poker game, I wasn't ready to ask Knolling about women.

***

The next Saturday, my morning paper arrived with a story a few pages off the front page which related that Batista's forces had made a "thrust" into rebel-held Oriente Province, killing 120 rebels and capturing a leader. The story reported Batista troops were using tanks and equipment bought from England.

Shortly after nine that evening, there was a knock on the door of my room. I used a far seeing spell to determine that it was Knolling.

"You need to go to the Ambassador Hotel," he said when I opened the door. He gave me a room number and a name, "Frankie."

"Any mobsters?" I asked.

He smiled at me as one does at an errant child. "Probably."

I got the feeling that if I wanted high stakes I was going to have to deal with mobsters.

"When?" I asked.

"Now. Game starts at ten."

"Good," I said and started to close the door. Knolling put his meaty hand against it.

"Mr. Wendell," he said, his voice growing more soft and intense. "Now I vouched for you to some pretty tough guys.

You wouldn't want to make me look bad to these fellows. Do you take my meaning, Mr. Wendell?"

I tried to look at him with a confidence I didn't feel, and hadn't felt since Havana. "Yes, of course."

"Good," he said and released the door. Then he stood looking at me expectantly. It took me an uncomfortably long time to realize he wanted a tip. I gave him a fiver.

I changed into a business suit and, putting on my wool dress coat, went downstairs. The doorman caught a taxi for me and I moved as fast as I could from the lobby to the warm taxi as the weather was still amazingly cold, with the breeze off the lake making even the heaviest coat seem like a piece of gauze.

The hotels, mine and the Ambassador, were only about a mile apart, and in warmer weather I would have been happy to walk the distance. The Ambassador was a nicer hotel than the Allerton. It boasted an ornate lobby with comfortable-looking chairs scattered about, a burgundy oriental rug, dark wood paneling, and a large crystal chandelier hanging over the whole affair. There were two men that did seem out of place sitting in some chairs facing the door. They were large men, like Knolling, but wore expensive suits that while sized correctly, just didn't seem to fit them. They sat quietly eyeing the entrance. They looked everyone over as if inspecting a piece of meat. At the time I wondered about them for a moment, and then hurried to the elevators.

I knocked on the door of the room and a man opened it. I was starting to think Chicago was full of large men as this one filled the doorway. He also looked uncomfortable in his suit.

"Yeah?" he growled. I could tell he was trying to be intimidating and to be honest, he was pretty good at it.

"Frankie?" I asked.

"Who wants to know?"

"Steve Wendell," I said.

"The Allerton?" he asked.

"Yes."

He stepped back from the door and said almost politely, "Come in."

The room was obviously a hotel room but the usual accoutrements were missing. There was no bed or dresser, but instead a round table covered in green felt with plush chairs around it—a set up I'd seen countless times for countless games. A bar was standing in the corner, bottles of liquor resting on it along with a bucket of ice. There was an expensive couch with a stunning blonde woman sitting on it. She was dressed expensively in a suit and had large, almost gaudy jewelry. But her eyes were, not sad, but almost dead. She looked me over and then went back to staring at nothing. There were three more men in the room. No one introduced themselves or did much more than look at me and break eye contact. They were wearing dress shirts and suit pants. One had on a vest that was open.

I took off my coat and the man who had let me in, "Frankie" I suppose, took it and hung it in the room's closet.

"Let's get started," the man in the vest—the oldest and thinnest of the bunch—said. He ran his hand through his thinning gray hair and sat.

The rest of us did also, tacitly choosing our seats, except "Frankie," who stood by the door as if to prevent anyone from entering—or escaping. I glanced at the blonde and she was still staring vacantly at nothing.

"Hey, Barbara," the oldest man said to her, "see what Mr. Wendell wants to drink."

She looked at him and smiled, but her eyes remained the same. "Sure," she said in a loud, Midwest accent such as I'd heard often since coming to Chicago. "What can I get ya, Mr. Wendell?" She looked at me, still smiling.

"Mineral water," I said.

One of the poker players laughed.

"Doctor's orders," I explained.

The game started shortly after Barbara delivered my highball glass with ice and mineral water. The game was played with cash, not chips. I tried to break even and perhaps came out a little behind from where I started. The men talked about women, sports, the news—a fire at a Catholic school that killed 90 children occupied a full hour of talk, as some of the men were related to some of the victims—and the extraordinarily cold weather.

They were talking about the murder of a fourteen-year-old girl by her nineteen-year-old boyfriend when the man in the vest announced it was the last hand. No one protested. They continued to talk about the crime. All the men expressed disgust at it and hoped the killer would get the electric chair.

It was nearly seven in the morning but the low-hanging clouds went from black to gray and that was as light as it was going to get. The days were short as it was nearly the winter solstice.

We gathered our bills and stood and stretched. The older man in the vest came over and introduced himself. "I'm Teo Luttazzi. We have these games every Saturday and you're certainly invited."

Frankie looked me over. "You sure, boss?"

Luttazzi threw Frankie a look and it seemed the big man nearly wilted. "Yeah, I'm sure. He's good people. I can sense these things."

Frankie started handing out coats and I noticed Luttazzi and the blonde left together without coats, meaning they lived in the hotel.

The next night Knolling stopped by to ask me how I liked the game. When I said it was fine, he mentioned I was invited back. He apparently had gotten a good report back.

But Wednesday, Christmas Eve no less, things changed. As I was searching the newspaper for anything about Cuba—I didn't think no news was good news—a loud knock on my room door startled me. I used far seeing again and Knolling and Frankie were there. I thought that strange. It was early afternoon and Knolling was off duty and I had no idea why Frankie was there. Knolling also wasn't in his uniform. I put my hand in my pocket to find my talisman and walked to the door.

"Who is it?" I asked, thinking I should.

"Knolling, sir," came the reply.

I could see Frankie looking impatient, with his hand inside his coat.

"What do you want, Knolling?" I demanded, still not opening the door.

Knolling sounded distressed. "Open the door, please, sir. It's about the game Saturday."

No doubt, I thought.

I prepared a quick spell and opened the door. Just as the latch cleared the frame Frankie put his shoulder to the door and pushed it open, knocking me to the floor. My hand came out of my pocket as I tried to catch myself.

Frankie walked over to me and picked me up bodily and dropped me on the bed.

Knolling had followed and quietly shut the door after checking the corridor.

"What the hell is this?" I demanded, looking up at Frankie. My spell was ready if needed and I slipped my hand back into my pocket.

Frankie pulled a pistol from his coat and pointed it at me. "We have a problem, Mr. Wendell."

That's when I realized my talisman wasn't in my pocket. I didn't dare not look at Frankie, but I needed to find it and fast. I could feel the spell dissipating without the power of my talisman to support it.

I looked at Knolling. "What the hell is this?" I repeated. Out of the corner of my eye I saw my talisman against the wall near the door.

Frankie took my head in his hand and turned me to look at him. "I said, 'We have a problem, Mr. Wendell.'"

I tried to look hurt. "Why are you bothering me?"

"We checked," Frankie said, the gun inches from my nose. "There ain't no Steve Wendell from New York. At least nones that have traveled to Chicago for reasons unknown."

I tried to glare at him. The spell was gone and getting my talisman back at that moment seemed unlikely. "You checked up on me?"

"Boss needs to know who he's playing with. Now Knolling here vouched for you, but if you're a Fed, it ain't gonna go down too well for him, you see?"

I again looked at Knolling, who was looking sick. "He isn't a Fed," he said, "he doesn't act like one."

"You stay shut up," Frankie barked at him.

Knolling stayed shut up.

Frankie again turned my head to look at him.

I was starting to get angry. "Do that again and you'll be eating cannoli with the other hand," I growled. Yes, it was a bluff.

Frankie laughed. "The boss told me to find out who you are."

I just looked up at him, trying from that position to not seem as intimidated and worried as I was. "My name is not Steven Wendell and I'm not from New York."

This news didn't seem to surprise Frankie but it did seem to anger him. "Then whos are you?"

I wasn't about to tell him my real name, or where I was from. "Until three weeks ago I was living in Havana. My name is Michael Vaughan." This was not the tactic I wanted to use, but it was the best I could think of with that pistol in my face. If it was mobsters that hired the SIM to attack me in that alley in Havana, I might be telling them where to find me.

Frankie looked at me, trying to decide whether to believe me. "Why'd you leave Cuber?"

"I had a run in with the SIM. They thought I was running guns to the rebels."

"Was you?"

I smiled. "No. But a friend of mine was and the SIM's motto is guilty until proven dead."

Frankie still looked skeptical but he lowered the gun. "We'll check it out," he said.

For a moment I worried that they might have contacts in the SIM and my story would be proven false. I took a chance. "Do you know a Vinnie Scarpelli?"

I could tell by the look on his face he did know him and didn't think much of him. "Yeah."

"Ask him, he knows me."

Frankie looked at me. "I will." He put the gun away and walked toward the door.

"Game Saturday?" I asked casually.

"We'll let ya know."

He walked out and Knolling looked at me for a second, perhaps hoping I'd just saved his bacon, and then followed, pulling the door closed. I bounded across the room and scooped up my talisman.

Then I realized the mistake I had made. Scarpelli knew I was an adept.

CHAPTER SIX
Havana, November 26, 1963

I awoke with a start. Then the pain hit. My arm was in agony, suspended over my head, held by the handcuffs. The rest of my body ached from sitting on the cold, stone floor. I couldn't believe I'd fallen asleep while thinking about the events of five years ago. Then I remembered the bugs and almost jumped despite my condition as I noticed them on my legs and shirt. I used my free hand to bat them away, shuddering at the horror of them. I hoped none were poisonous and spent a few moments feeling my body for bites.

I finally calmed down, berating myself for my unmanly behavior. In other circumstances the bugs would have been unpleasant but here they just added to the terror of my situation.

I calmed myself by spending a moment wondering what ever happened to that cigarette girl from the Sans Souci. She might have mouthed off to the wrong revolutionary and ended up some place like this—a fate no one deserved. I wondered what happened to Sidney Rosenberg. Or the blonde from the pool who seemed so sweet but ratted me out to Sidney.

Then I shook my head to clear it. A trip down memory lane wasn't going to keep me alive.

I had no idea how long I'd slept. And as I slept, my talisman and the adept who'd stolen it were getting farther and farther away. It was time to do something.

I kicked off the worthless shoes they'd given me and pulled my left foot up as close to my face as possible. The muscles in my stiff and cold legs protested, but I still used my free hand to pull my foot closer so I could see the bottom.

I spent a few minutes sharpening a fingernail on the stone wall, and then dug into the skin of my sole. The skin had grown thick over the years. One of the first things you learn as an apprentice adept is to always, always, always have a back-up. The CIA emphasized this, too. It was amazing to me how much the two vocations meshed.

This was my back-up of last resort. If this failed I was probably dead. I found the wire (if I thought about it I could feel it under my skin) and gingerly pulled it out. That was only slightly agonizing. It was short, about three inches long, and stiff (it was a straightened paper clip, actually). It was difficult to handle until I cleaned the blood off with my pants. I had tried to stay in practice, especially since I started working for the CIA, but the lock on the handcuffs still took a good ten minutes as I was unfamiliar with its design.

Once free, I had some choices. I rubbed my sore wrist while I thought about it. I could teleport to the corridor outside my cell, use a glamour spell to disguise myself as a guard, and walk out. Two problems: *imprimis*, without a talisman I couldn't maintain a glamour for long and, *secundus*, I'd probably need keys at some point, as teleporting where one can't see is dangerous. I had taken a good look at the corridor outside my cell when they brought me here and it was empty. I'd have to risk that maybe someone was walking by. But I wasn't about to teleport somewhere I couldn't see and hadn't seen before. And without a talisman, farseeing was out of the question, as was invisibility. Of course staying in the cell was not an option. It seemed I had all the choices of one of Hobson's customers.

I slipped my shoes back on and walked the one step to the door, trying to avoid stepping on critters as the sound of them crunching under foot was repulsive. At the metal door, I tried to listen for footfalls or other indications of someone being out there. I didn't hear anything, so I popped into the corridor and startled a passing guard so badly he fell backwards. I jumped on top of him, straddling his chest, grabbed his head in my hands like a melon, and bashed it into the stone floor. It made a sound not unlike that of a ripe melon falling to a hard surface. He was unconscious immediately. I looked at him. Blood was seeping out from under his skull, but he was breathing.

He had a large key ring on his belt and one of the keys opened my cell door. I dragged him in, leaving a trail of blood on the floor. I used my shirt to wipe it up as best I could, but still there was a red stain on the dark grey stone. That gave me motivation to move fast but I hoped anyone else would think it belonged to a prisoner. I was sure prisoners bled often in this place.

I went into the cell and looked at the man. As I did, the door swung shut on its own. I cursed myself for not propping it open. The guard was about my size if a bit chubby, so I pulled on the uniform. His shoes were a little small and my left foot was in agony from the impromptu wire-ectomy I had performed, but I got them on as best I could. I left him in his skivvies, with my bloody prison garb lying nearby.

The door couldn't be unlocked from this side, so I had to teleport to the corridor again. Without my talisman, these two quick spells were making me weak. In the hall I stood very still as I tried to feel for my talisman. If it was near I should be able to sense it. I felt nothing except pain in my foot. I remembered the way they'd brought me in, but that seemed the long way. Plus I didn't really want to see "*La paredon*" again. Luckily, I have a good sense of direction and after taking a few corners and nodding politely to the other guards I encountered, I found myself at a double-door exit from the prison. There were two large steel doors and a smaller door cut into the left one. I opened the small one and stepped into the courtyard, blinking at the bright sunlight.

For some reason I was surprised that it was day. Then I remembered that the prison had no windows. The sky was brilliant blue and the sunshine the wonderful light I remembered. I smiled up at the sky and let the sun warm my face. But looking up I also noticed the high stone wall topped with triple loops of concertina wire. Spaced towers held guards holding AK-47s. I recognized the curved magazines and the extended front sights from my CIA training. I knew they were a deadly and dangerous automatic weapon provided to Castro by the Sovs.

There was a small group of guards in the corner of the courtyard, probably enjoying staying out of the sun in the shade of the wall. They ignored me.

A guard shack was beside the gate of double chain-link fence with barbed wire on top. The gate guard looked surprised to see me as I walked up.

"What are you doing here?" he demanded in Spanish. He was a big guy in most dimensions. "Your shift isn't over yet. Who's your supervisor?"

I spread my hands, palms up. "The prisoner that was brought in says he'll talk now to the adept." My Spanish has only gotten better since working for the Company. I looked around the shack while speaking. There were two switches labeled PUERTA EXTERIOR and INTERIOR PUERTA and each had an ABIERTO and CIERRE position.

"The adept is gone. He won't return until later this morning. Now who is your—"

I had no need of more information from him so I touched him, using a sleep spell on him. I grabbed him before he fell and guided him to an uncomfortable-looking metal chair. I left him there, snoring softly. I looked around to see if anyone had noticed our little drama. The guards in the towers weren't paying attention and the small group by the corner was involved in a lively conversation and too busy to notice.

I grabbed the black bakelite ball at the end of the silver metal lever marked INTERIOR PUERTA and slid it over to the ABIERTO position. The first gate slowly clanged and screeched aside. The noise was such that I again looked around. Guards in the towers were looking at me. I tried to act nonchalant, as if I was authorized to do what I was doing.

I tried to put the PUERTA EXTERIOR lever on ABIERTO but there was some sort of interlock that prevented it. I remembered that when we got there, the inner gate didn't open until the outer gate closed behind the car. I waited until the inner gate was about halfway open and pulled the lever back to CIERRE. The gate started to shriek closed. Just before it shut I slipped through the tightening opening into the space between the gates. A guard in one of the towers started yelling at me. I couldn't make out what he was saying, but he pulled his assault rifle off his shoulder and jerked back the bolt. Even at this distance it seemed I heard the safety snick off.

I teleported the short distance to the street just beyond the outer gate. I heard a lot of yelling behind me, so I ran using a spell to make me run farther and faster than most Olympic gold medalists. I zigzagged through the narrow cobblestone streets, hoping to lose any pursuit. It must have been early morning, as the streets were fairly empty. I did see some residents going about their business, almost universally unhappily.

Feeling safe, and exhausted, I stopped, bending over and breathing hard. I saw a stoop and crawled under it into the shade. For some reason the sunlight that had seemed so delightful before was now oppressively hot.

I rested for six hours before I had the strength to continue on to my last hope.

***

A few years before some people at the CIA had decided that in order to protect the American Way of Life the leader of a small African nation needed to be eliminated. It seemed he was getting a little too cozy with the Soviets. They couldn't take direct action lest they expose the CIA's hand in political assassination. So they found some indigenous people who, unhappy with the target for whatever reason, were willing to kill him. The CIA provided weapons, intelligence, and maybe even some training. The proxy assassins burst into a cabinet meeting and in a hail of gunfire killed everyone in the room before security forces managed to stop or kill them. Everyone, that is, except the target. When I was told that story, over beers, by a fellow NOC agent who'd seen a lot—he'd started in the OSS days under William "Bull" Donovan—I began to worry about my career choices.

Wandering the streets of Havana, I was still worrying. Well, if Gomez came through with his promise I could quit the CIA. And if not, I would kill him myself.

But even though my mission was a CIA operation, it wasn't a total screw-up. My first contact had been compromised. I had a back-up. I knew my way around Havana from the old days, but in daylight it was even more depressing than at night. It looked as if nothing had been touched since Castro seized power in early '59. Buildings and streets were starting to show the early stages of disrepair. The people didn't look very happy as they went to work. Everywhere were bigger-than-life posters of Castro, Lenin, and Marx: the unholy trio. Red was predominate anywhere there was new paint. The neighborhood I was in was poor before the revolution. It looked no better now. I remembered Havana's sprawling slums, which seemed to have grown in both size and population. I did notice something I didn't remember seeing before: fear. The fear in the eyes of everyone, including the children. Yes, Batista dealt harshly with opponents, but if you minded your own business he and the SIM would usually leave you alone. A few innocents were swept up in their dragnets and guilt by association happened occasionally. But that didn't seem to dampen the Cuban's obvious and ubiquitous *joie de vivre*.

But now everyone looked afraid. The joy of the Cuban people seemed drained from them. I was eyed with a combination of suspicion, dread and something else. It took me a while to figure it out: they despised me for my uniform.

The address I had I remembered being in the commercial district, not residential. But I found an apartment building housed in what used to be an American sugar company's building. Inside, I climbed narrow stairs to the fourth floor. It looked as if they'd gutted the interior and then built apartments inside in the usual casual craftsmanship of centrally planned markets. Skinny children were playing in the halls until they saw me then they grew quiet. I knocked on a door.

"¿Hola?"

"Soy Ramon. ¿Dónde está Emil?"

"Emil está en Miami."

Sweeter words were never spoken.

The door opened just enough for me to slip through and I did. I was in a room about 15 by 15 feet large with mattresses and sparse furniture strewn about. There was a small alcove with a hotplate and some shelves. The shelves were bare. The paint was already peeling from the walls and ceiling.

My host was a small, muscular man who looked 60 but was probably much younger. He wore baggy, dirty pants and no shirt. He looked over my uniform with trepidation.

"¿Habla inglés?" I asked.

"Of course I speak English, you stupid twit." He spoke softly despite his obvious anger. I presumed the walls were as thin as the children playing in the hall.

"I was captured at my contact's house. I escaped."

"That explains the uniform." He turned to walk into the room. There were long, serpentine scars on his back. "Take it off. I'll get you some clothes you can wear."

"Thanks."

"Don't thank me yet."

"Do you know what happened to my contact?"

The man was digging in a pile of junk in the corner. The prospects of getting decent clothes out of that seemed small. He managed to shrug. "Dead. Or soon will be. Since *Playa Girón* Castro's been one paranoid bastard."

I remembered that *"Playa Girón"* was what Cubans called the Bay of Pigs invasion.

"I wonder how my contact was compromised." It was a rhetorical question, but he answered it anyway.

"He was burned." He turned around holding a cardboard suitcase.

"Burned? Who the hell burned him?"

The man opened the suitcase and pulled out some clean, folded clothes. "Try these on."

I raised my voice. "I said, 'Who burned my contact?'"

"Keep your voice down, damn it! Just speaking English can put you under suspicion. My neighbor—" and he jerked his head in the direction of the next apartment "—is chairman of the Neighborhood Revolutionary Defense Committee."

I whispered, "Who burned my contact?"

"Johnson."

I was trying to think of somebody in the Company named Johnson. I could think of at least ten, but no one who'd have any motivation to burn my operation even if they knew about it. "Who?"

"Lyndon Baines Johnson. The new President of the Estados Unidos."

"What the hell do you mean?" I barked at him.

"I said, 'Keep your voice down.'"

I looked at him and nodded acquiescence.

He continued in a low voice. "Apparently when he was briefed on your mission he decided to end it in order to improve relations with Russia or something. I was instructed to tell you to abort if you made contact with me. They were desperate; they couldn't find your primary contact and you'd already left Miami. They asked me but I couldn't locate him either. So they must have burned him. And you. You and he were sacrificed on the altar of Realpolitick. It's not the first time; it won't be the last."

"How?" I was unhappy to learn my instincts about Johnson were correct. Hell, he might have stopped the operation just to show he could and to establish control over the CIA and its director.

"I don't know. Let it slip to the Russian ambassador at the Ugandan embassy's independence anniversary party, or some other Washington social function, that there might be an attempt on Castro's life and a certain Jose Perez of 213 Karl Marx *Bulevar* in Havana, or whoever the poor bastard was, may be involved."

"Damn," I whispered. Then I changed the subject. "Do you have any disinfectant?"

"Why?"

"I hurt my foot."

"How?"

"Escaping."

That seemed to satisfy him. He set the clothes aside, dug in his junk pile, and came out with a CIA-issue first aid kit. It even had a plastic card in English and Russian explaining how to treat minor injuries (at least I assume it said the same thing in Russian; it might have instructed to drink sulfa and put the penicillin on the wound). I kicked off the too-small shoes, sighing at the relief from pain I realized I'd become accustomed to, then tended to my injured foot, applying sulfa — ouch! — and a bandage. I was as likely to heal myself without a talisman, even for something that small, as I was to flap my arms and fly to the Moon. It takes strong meta to heal.

"So I guess you can lay your finger aside your nose and return to wherever you came from," my host said, handing me the clothes.

"It's not that easy," I answered, starting to undress.

"I don't care how you do it, just leave. I'll have to burn that uniform; can't risk getting caught with it."

"No, I mean I can't leave."

The man looked at me as if trying to decide whether I was telling the truth. "Why not?" he demanded.

I wasn't about to admit to him that I had lost my talisman. For one thing, one didn't discuss such things with lessers. "I am unable to leave the way I came. I need an exfiltration."

I could tell the man was debating internally about asking for more information. "Fine," he said, waving his hand. "It'll take a few days to arrange. Come back in three days. Don't come back here for any reason before then. Understand? I'll burn you myself if you do and that will only make me safer."

There was a time I would have killed a lesser for threatening me like that. But now I didn't want to expend the energy and, I hated to admit it, I needed his help. I finished dressing. "What am I supposed to do for three days?"

"Stay the hell out of sight."

He turned his back to me and I saw the scars again. I thought I'd try to be friendly with him. "You must hate Castro for what he did to you."

The man turned and glared at me. "Castro didn't do it. Batista did. I was captured with Castro at the battle of the Moncoda army barracks and spent two stinking years in one of Batista's prisons. That's where I got these stripes. When the general amnesty came, I found I had no job, no future, no family other than the revolution. So I fought with Castro, until the bastard turned out to be a Red.

"I'm a hero of the Revolution. Perfect cover, don't you think, as long as I parrot their communist propaganda? Now don't screw it up, and get out of here."

I could tell the conversation was over. I was dressed so I left. As I passed the neighboring apartment's door it opened a crack and a man peered out with narrow, beady eyes. I assumed that was the Revolutionary Block Captain. I gave him a little spell of reassurance. It'd be days before he'd be suspicious of anything again. He smiled at me, showing a few sparse teeth, and closed the door.

***

An adept without a talisman is a pretty poor adept. But I was hoping that with the information Gomez promised me I could survive in the North American Guild until I could acquire a new talisman. Maybe even have one provided to me if some of the information was damaging enough to some powerful adept. So I had to leave Cuba by submarine; I'd lived with worse humiliations, some very recently. But if I were to get in the NAG (funny acronym, I know) and get that information Gomez had on the NAG leadership, I had to get his "precious item." I was going to be really unhappy if it was something silly like money.

I had plenty of time, so I found the address Gomez had given me and staked it out for a day. Before Castro this was a middle-class (albeit small) neighborhood for middle managers at the sugar companies or the clubs and hotels. Now it was just like the rest of Havana: run-down and poor looking. The houses were small and close together with small grassless yards. They seemed to all be slight variations on the same plan. Almost all needed a coat of paint or some repair of some sort. There were cars in front of most of the houses, but few of them seemed to be able to move. Some were even up on blocks, their tires and wheels missing.

It would have been easier invisible, but my CIA training helped. I found a place where I could watch the house, stay in shadow, and not be conspicuous. When I got hungry, I foraged for food in the houses that were empty during the day. I didn't find much so I thought it was good that I wasn't used to eating a lot.

From my hiding spot, I saw people coming and going from the house. It looked as if a family lived there. One resident was a beautiful girl about nineteen or twenty. Even in her faded sundress she was gorgeous. I fantasized about taking her to the Tropicana or Sans Souci, pre-revolution, me in a white tux and her in some strapless black dress and high heels. Poor girl had been born a few years too late.

Finally, about nine at night, I approached the house. I knocked softly on the door. An old lady I'd seen working around the outside hanging laundry opened the door just a crack. She looked me up and down but didn't open the door.

"¿Qué usted desea?" What do you want?

"Soy un amigo de Gomez." I whispered the name.

Her eyes grew big and she backed away from the door. I entered. While the outside of the house was as dilapidated as its neighbors, the inside was immaculate though everything looked old and nearly worn out. A crucifix hung prominently on one wall, and an icon of Mary (I think) holding a heart on another.

"¿Usted habla inglés?" I asked.

"No, pero mi hijo habla ingles. Está en la cocina." And she disappeared into the back of the house.

A young man, about 30, came out. He was dressed in work pants and a t-shirt with suspender straps hanging around his hips. He looked intelligent. The old woman followed, looking worried.

"Who are you and what do you want?" he demanded.

I decided to make this quick: "I'm a friend of Gomez's. From the States. He asked me to pick up something for him here and take it back."

"Can you get it back to the States?" he asked.

I nodded. "Yes."

He turned to the old woman. "*Madre, trae a Bonita para aquí.*"

"Excuse me," I said as the old lady left again. "Did you say, 'Bonita'?"

"Si."

"What is 'Bonita'?" Other than a woman's name meaning "beautiful," I meant.

Before he could answer, the woman returned with the 19-year-old girl. She was still in her yellow sundress.

"*Éste es Bonita,*" the old lady said.

"I don't understand," I said. "Where's the item?"

"*El espía americano no entiende,*" the young man said and laughed bitterly. The old woman cackled at me while the girl, Bonita apparently, looked unhappy.

The young man turned to me. "This is Gomez's daughter. He had to leave without her when Castro took over. Her mother died years ago, so we have been taking care of her because Gomez was a friend of ours. But now you will take her to America."

The old lady and the man grinned at me happily, as if I was Santa Claus or the U.S. Marines, or something. The girl looked embarrassed, refusing to make eye contact with me.

I said a very bad word in the ancient language.

***

"I told you not to come back!" He closed the door behind me. "Do you want me to end up on *la paredon*?" He was hissing his words, trying to whisper angrily.

"The situation has changed. There will now be two packages."

He shook his head. "Impossible."

"I have to take someone else off the island," I emphasized.

"Your exfiltration is arranged for the day after tomorrow. I can't change it."

"How?"

"Sub. You'll have to swim for it."

"A sub can take one more person."

"Can they swim to the sub?"

Actually, I had no idea. "Yes."

"Didn't they teach you any tradecraft? If the sub sees two people it'll submerge. It may even open fire. And I can't contact the sub before then. It's impossible."

Again, it looked as if I had no choice. "What if I don't show up?"

"They'll leave almost immediately if you're not there."

"Then I need to get in touch with the local guilds."

"The guilds went underground when Castro outlawed them in '60." Not that even a Communist government could control adepts, but it was probably easier to stay out of sight than constantly deal with Castro's police forces.

"I know. How can I contact them?"

"I don't know."

I could tell he wasn't telling the whole truth. "If you don't tell me there's a greater chance I'll get caught; and if I do, I'll tell them about you."

He let out a long breath. "Okay, maybe old *señora* Salinas downstairs can help. She's in the apartment directly below this one."

"Thank you," I said, and went out the door.

"¡No vuelva," he called after me, "y sola vaya!"

I didn't intend to.

***

Señora Salinas was very helpful. She told me where to find the leaders of the *Gremio Cubano*. Most were hiding in menial jobs; some were in the government. She had heard about Castro's adept. She was afraid of him and suggested I go nowhere near him.

I found the head of the *Gremio Cubano* working as a taxi driver. I got in his cab in front of the Hotel Nacional, which was now full of Russians, judging from the pasty white, overweight people walking in and out of it (the CIA estimated there were 16,000 Russian "advisors" in Cuba).

The driver didn't bother looking at me when I got in. "*Kuda vas otvezti, tovarishch?*" he said as if he'd learned the Russian phrase by rote.

"I need your help," I said in the ancient language.

He looked in the cracked rear view mirror. "*¿Quién diablos es usted?*"

"An adept. I have no guild." I stuck to the language of the guilds.

"Then I pity you," he said in the same language.

"I also have no talisman."

He laughed hard at my expense. "You do not have much, adept."

"Teacher, my talisman was stolen by an adept working for Castro."

He watched me through the mirror for a moment. "I know who this is. He was once part of our guild, but he decided to become a *comunista*." The last word he said in Spanish. There is no equal in the ancient language.

"I need my talisman back."

The man drove the car away from the curb. "It was starting to look suspicious with us just sitting there."

"I understand."

We drove along the Malecon, giving me a spectacular view of the sea and making my heart ache for the Havana I had known before the revolution.

"You cannot go against him without a talisman. He is very powerful."

"That's why I need your guild's help. You must have spare talismans. I would give you my name to borrow one."

"Why would I do that?"

"Would you like to be rid of this *comunista* adept?"

"Very much so. He is protected by Castro, as he protects Castro."

"If I try to kill him, there is no risk to you other than losing a talisman."

He drove silently for a while. I looked at the sea, the beauty of which even Castro couldn't diminish.

"I agree," he finally said. "We'll be at our destination shortly."

We drove into Habana Nueva and stopped in front of one of the ubiquitous apartment buildings. The driver led me to an apartment. It was slightly larger and a lot cleaner than my contact's place. The leader of the Cuban Guild took a cigar box down off a shelf. He removed an object. It was a piece of a rifle barrel.

"This is a talisman that has been in Cuba since the Spanish-American war. An adept killed a Spanish soldier and took this as his talisman. It is not the most powerful talisman there is, but it should serve you well."

I took it and felt its power. After so long without a talisman, it was almost like a strong intoxicant.

The driver took out paper and a poorly made pencil. It had Cyrillic writing on it that probably said "Made in USSR."

"I am sorry, I have no envelopes. You'll have to trust me not to unfold the paper."

I wrote my real name on the paper, folded it in quarters, placed a spell on it that would counter a far-seeing spell from being used to read it, and handed it to him. He put it in his pocket. I knew that if he opened that paper and read my name he could kill me with very little effort.

"Can I find you in front of the Nacional?"

"Yes, the Russian Communist Party leaders love their tours of exotic Havana."

"I hope to see you soon."

"Is there any place I can take you?" He suddenly seemed anxious to help me.

"Do you know where I can find this adept?"

"Yes. Castro gave him a villa in the hills outside the city. I can take you near there. Best to wait for night."

"Thank you, Teacher," I said, lowering my head. I was genuinely grateful.

CHAPTER SEVEN
Chicago, December 25, 1958

Christmas afternoon the phone in the room rang. It was Luttazzi. "If you haven't had Christmas dinner yet, Mr. Vaughan, it would please me to have the honor of your company in my hotel suite."

I thought surely he wouldn't invite me to his hotel to kill me. "Sure, I'll just have the doorman get me a cab to the Ambassador," I said, hoping he'd take the hint that someone would know where I went.

"Don't bother; my car will be there shortly. Black Cadillac."

Of course, I thought. "Thank you."

By the time I changed into a suit and got down to the lobby the car was waiting, running at the curb. It was all sheet metal and chrome with fins and what looked like a toothsome grille. The driver, who moved fast for a big man, jumped out to open the back door for me. I climbed in and was alone, which for some reason surprised me.

The short trip was made in silence and the car dropped me in front of the Ambassador, the driver's only spoken words telling me which room number. In a few minutes I was knocking on the door of Luttazzi's suite.

Frankie opened the door. "Come on in," he said, almost politely.

I stepped into the expansive, opulently appointed room dominated by a large oak table. It was covered with food. I'd never seen so much to eat in one place, even when my extended family, including grandparents, aunts, uncles, and a crowd of cousins all came over for Christmas or Thanksgiving dinner. The selection of dishes was interesting. From the door I could see, and smell, lasagna, a roasted turkey, a ham, a couple of kinds of pasta I didn't recognize, yams, mashed potatoes, gravy, cranberries, string beans, and rolls. However, none of it looked homemade but had the too-nice look of restaurant food. The smell was overpowering, making me feel instantly famished.

"Boss will be out in a minute," Frankie said, holding out his hands. I handed him my coat and walked to the table.

Luttazzi came out with Barbara. He was wearing a black smoking jacket, and she was overdressed in some emerald evening gown with sequins at the shoulders. She did look lovely in it if you ignored her store-mannequin eyes. Luttazzi walked over and put his hands on my shoulders. "Thank you for coming, Mr. Vaughan. *Buon Natale!*" I thought for a second he was going to kiss me.

I was a bit perplexed, but I smiled and said, "Thank you, Mr. Luttazzi." I had decided on the ride over I'd better be polite.

"Call me Teo, please," he said, with a laugh. He released me and sat down and held out his hand, indicating the rest of us should sit also.

Frankie and Barbara sat across from each other, and I sat across from Luttazzi.

The dinner bordered on the bizarre. Not only the combination of dishes, which was like nothing I'd ever had before, but Luttazzi did most of the talking. Frankie and Barbara, who both obviously worked for him but in vastly different capacities, ate quietly and only spoke in order to respond to questions put directly to them.

"Do you know why," Luttazzi asked pointing at me with his fork, "they call Chicago the 'Windy City'?"

I'd experienced the gales between the buildings. "Uhm, the weather?"

Luttazzi laughed. "No! The politicians."

I nodded and said something like, "Oh, I see."

"Yeah," Luttazzi continued, "they think our politicians talk too much. But you know who talks too much? That Kennedy. What's his name?"

I shook my head. I had no idea who he was talking about. "I don't know."

"Robert," Luttazzi said. "Chief Counsel Bobby Kennedy and that damn McClellan Committee. Do you know Momo's been subpoenaed?"

"Momo?" I asked, afraid I was displaying my gross ignorance of lesser politics.

"My boss, Sam Giancana."

I blinked and looked at him. "I thought you were the boss."

Luttazzi laughed—a sound that could fill a large room. I couldn't help but smile, despite feeling the butt of some joke. "Naw. I'm just a lieutenant. Momo's the real *Capo* in Chicago."

"Momo?" I asked again.

"Yeah, Momo. That's what we all call Giancana. At least those he lets call him that." He smiled at Frankie and Frankie smiled back. They were smiles not of joy but of mirth, seemingly at someone else's expense.

I kept eating my turkey and lasagna.

"His brother's going to run for president, you know," Luttazzi said.

I looked at him. "Momo's?"

Luttazzi laughed again. "No, Bobby Kennedy's brother. Joseph P. Kennedy, Jr." Luttazzi got silent suddenly. "Might win, too," he finally said as if that were some secret. I watched him for a few minutes to see if he was going to continue but he didn't.

Without warning he looked at Barbara. "Go get the struffoli."

Struffoli turned out to be pastry balls dipped in honey. It was amazingly good and I caught myself eating more than I intended.

After the struffoli, Frankie made a call and a troop of white-jacketed waiters came in from the hall to start clearing up the dinner and the large amount of untouched food. Luttazzi made a point of greeting each of them, most by name, and handing each a bill of undetermined denomination. The meal cleared, Luttazzi led me to another room of the suite.

"Cigar?" he asked, taking two from a wooden box.

"No, thank you; I don't smoke."

"Good for you," he said, patting me on the back. "Don't smoke, don't drink. You'll live forever."

Frankie followed us in and stood by the wall. I almost laughed when I realized that Frankie was acting just like a warrior working for a guild leader.

Luttazzi sat in a large leather chair and lit his cigar. I sat in an identical chair facing his. It was very comfortable and I could imagine it would take some work to stand up.

I glanced around the room. There were only a too-small window and the door Frankie was standing next to if I found I needed to leave.

"You said you were in Havana three weeks ago?" he started.

"Yes," I replied.

"This revolution," he said looking at his cigar, "it's bad for business."

"I can understand that. I know there were fewer tourists." I had actually liked that; my favorite places were less crowded. But I knew the mob was skimming millions of dollars off the casinos. Everyone knew Meyer Lansky was a mobster and had his fingers in just about everything in Havana. And Batista took bribes to look the other way. No one knew what Castro would do if he won the war.

"What do you think of Castro?" he asked, as if reading my thoughts.

"I don't pay much attention to politics," I answered honestly.

"Oh." He smoked his cigar a few moments, letting me watch him, then said offhandedly, "I talked to Scarpelli."

I tried not to react, but put my hand in my pocket to touch my talisman. "Yes?"

"He vouched for ya. But he also had some interesting news."

I figured here it came.

"You see," Luttazzi said, looking at me, "there was some trouble in Havana. Caused some tensions between the families. And it had to do with an adept cheating at poker and Scarpelli knowing about it."

"Where is Scarpelli?" I asked, hoping to change the subject.

He took a drag on his cigar and blew smoke rings toward the ceiling before answering. "He's...lying low. It would be best for him not to be in the country right now. But Havana's no good now either and the old country is, well, Scarpelli's just not an old-country kind of guy, if you know what I mean."

I wasn't sure, but I didn't protest.

"But the matter at hand," Luttazzi said, jutting the red end of the cigar at me. "Scarpelli didn't have much of a choice, he said."

"Why's that?" I asked, glancing at Frankie, who was standing still like a piece of furniture.

"Said the adept used a spell on him."

I let out a small laugh.

Luttazzi eyed me. "Is that not true?"

"Unless you call bribes a spell."

Luttazzi looked angrily at me. "What do you mean?"

"Oh, I suppose he was worried I'd put a spell on him. But he took his twenty percent willingly."

"Excuse me?" the mobster asked, still seething.

I explained my arrangement with Scarpelli. "He'd lend me the cash to get into games. I'd pay him back plus twenty percent."

Luttazzi recovered and looked relaxed. I had a feeling he was used to controlling his emotions — or at least covering them. "I see." He smoked his cigar, looking thoughtful.

"This trouble with the families?" I asked. "Sidney Rosenberg involved in that?"

The mobster nodded. "Yes." He didn't seem inclined to answer any more questions.

"Someone tried to kill me that night," I said. I didn't know if this was the right approach and the wrong approach might get me killed. "The SIM."

Luttazzi took a long drag on his cigar and then tapped some of the ash on the tip into a golden ashtray. "Wasn't Sidney. He doesn't have the—" he looked at me "—the power."

"Do you know who?" I asked, hoping my voice was polite and respectful.

He shook his head. "No. It wasn't any of the families, I can tell you that."

I thought about that. Who else could hire the SIM to attack me and Louis, who were obviously their targets?

Luttazzi interrupted my thoughts. "I didn't lose much money Saturday."

I realized what he meant. "I didn't cheat much; I was feeling out the situation."

"A wise move," he said with a chuckle. "I won't play poker with you again. But I could use someone like you. I've learned some other things about you. Your guild is looking for you in order to kill you. You're a rogue adept. You're in hiding and have nowhere to go and no friends in the world."

I just looked at him. I had no idea how he knew all that but the underworlds of crime and of the guilds often intersected.

Finally I whispered, "I need money."

"A thousand a week do ya?" he asked.

Without thinking about it, I nodded.

"Good." He stood and walked to a table, opened a drawer in it, and pulled out a stack of bills with a rubber band around them. "First week's pay." He threw it at me.

I caught it and realized it was that easy. I was working for the mob, organized crime, La Cosa Nostra.

Luttazzi's tone changed. Suddenly he was talking to me the way he talked to Frankie or Barbara. "Go to your hotel and wait. We'll contact you. You'll meet Momo soon."

I nodded and followed his orders.

***

No, I wasn't proud of or happy with this turn of events. I was amazed at how easily and cheaply I'd been bought.

The next night Knolling knocked on my door shortly after nine. "Luttazzi says I'm supposed to take care of you. So anything you need, you just ask, okay?"

I mumbled my thanks and closed the door. The twenty 50-dollar bills Luttazzi had given me were sitting on top of the room's TV, where I'd placed them when I returned Christmas night. I guess adding them to my cache would make it feel permanent. I was still wondering if there was a way out of this deal.

The next day was Saturday and I spent the day staring at that stack of bills. I started thinking this wasn't too bad of a deal. It would keep me flush and could protect me from Houser. It was like joining a guild. They weren't so different from the Mafia, after all. I knew guilds sometimes did things that were best not dwelt on. Guilds and the Mafia were immune from the law, guilds more so, in fact. Kader had never been subpoenaed to appear before a congressional investigation.

I picked up the money and put half of it in my money clip and half in my stash. I might as well make the best of the situation, I decided.

Knolling came that night to check on me shortly after nine. This time I looked at him and asked, "Where can I meet women?"

He grinned. "What kind of woman?"

***

Yes, those relationships were shallow and meaningless. But they were about the best one in my position could hope for.

I remembered shortly after I began my apprenticeship, while scrubbing tile in my master's bathroom, he walked in, leaned against the wall, pulled out a cigarette and lighted it, and looked me over with what I learned were his very perceptive eyes.

"Do you realize what it means to be an adept?" he asked.

I swallowed hard. "I think so, Teacher." At that time it seemed to be a lot of unglamorous hard work, not unlike my life on the farm, except not as dirty or smelly.

He continued to look at me. "Did you have a sweetheart back home?"

I kept working, heeding his advice about not talking about one's past. At this point it was easier for me not to say anything. Lying was not second nature to me yet as it was something harshly punished back home. Instead I coughed as the cigarette smoke reached me. I wasn't used to being in such close quarters with a smoker.

But I thought about my old sweetheart back home, the girl with the curly brunette locks and hazel eyes, in her pinafore dress. She'd wanted to be married in the about-to-be-completed Idaho Falls temple (after my stint in the Army and my two-year mission, of course), find a piece of land to farm, and have our full share of children.

"Oh, Johnny," she would gush, sitting on my parents' front porch, my aunt just a few feet out of earshot, "it'll be so romantic! You'll come home in your uniform and I'll be waiting for you—I will! And then you'll have to leave for your mission, but I'll wait for you—I will."

She gushed out her plans for my life.

"Then we'll be married in the temple. My father has some land and we can start farming there. And we'll have cute blond children and I'll bake cookies for them while you work the fields and come to the house and we'll read the Bible and the Book of Mormon."

I almost shuddered there in my master's bathroom at the thought of what she had planned for me.

"Any brothers or sisters?" he asked, ignoring my silence.

Of course, I didn't say. I was the third boy, fifth child. And had three younger siblings, two girls and the youngest, Josh, aged seven. I'd heard some older women at the ward call him a "change of life baby." At the time I had no idea what they meant.

My master smoked his cigarette silently for a few moments, watching me work, watching me think.

"You realize," he finally said, "you can never see them again. Never contact them again. Never even tell anyone about them. The sweetheart, the friends, the brothers and sisters, the parents, grandparents, none of them."

I didn't say anything, but my breathing must have given my thoughts away. My "sweetheart" I was glad to be away from. My father I wouldn't miss, I told myself, knowing it wasn't totally true. My mother, yes, I missed some. But my brothers and sisters, that was hard. Especially tough were my two little sisters, whom I had protected from schoolyard bullies and our older siblings.

"Do you know why?" he demanded in a soft voice.

"Could lead someone to my name," I said, holding back tears.

"Yes," he answered simply. "Adepts cannot have families. No wives, no children, no contact with relatives. And, unfortunately, few friends. The power struggles and jealousies are too great with adepts, and lessers are either afraid or fawning."

He stopped to take a drag on his cigarette. "Think about that, before you go too far with this apprenticeship."

"Yes, Teacher," I replied, and brushed a tear from my eye with my wrist, my hands dirty from the work.

"You can, at this point, still go home," he stated simply.

He walked out without another word and I continued scrubbing.

I never did go home. After a few years the desire to do so left completely.

***

The next morning, after paying cab fare home for the lovely yet vacuous blonde I'd met in the club Knolling recommended, I threw back the curtains of my room and looked out on a blue sky with a few white clouds. I didn't feel the cold radiating from the glass as I had on previous days. I smiled, feeling almost as happy as I had in Havana. I got dressed and went for a walk, going to the Navy Pier. Temperatures were in the fifties and I soon removed my coat and carried it, the exercise of walking enough to keep me warm. The pier was being used by the University of Illinois as a campus, which I found amusing. It was Sunday, so there were no classes and I had the place pretty much to myself. I looked over Lake Michigan, which that day looked almost blue. Things seemed to be looking up for me for the first time since that poker game with Sidney Rosenberg in Havana. Walking back to the hotel, I found myself whistling a tune and smiling at strangers.

Even the news out of Cuba seemed good in the newspaper that evening. Rebel troops were retreating in front of Batista's army, although rebel radio claimed to have captured a seaport, 120 soldiers, and a "Catalina flying boat." I thought what a strange war when capture of a "flying boat" was news-worthy.

***

I was awakened the next morning by the phone in my room ringing. It was Frankie. "Boss wants to see you."

"When?" I asked, still not fully awake and probably sounding like it.

"Now. His car's on the way."

"Damn," I breathed. "Okay." I picked up my watch. It was just after eight.

I showered quickly and dressed in a suit and went down to the lobby. The same black Cadillac was waiting for me. The large driver was looking impatient.

"Not good to keep the boss waiting," he said as he opened the door for me.

The drive to the Ambassador was quick. I got the feeling the driver didn't want to be blamed for my tardiness.

Luttazzi met me in his hotel suite. I noticed Barbara wasn't there or, if she was, she was staying in one of the other rooms.

Luttazzi looked annoyed, but didn't complain about my being late. "You're going to meet Momo," he said without introduction. He walked over and straightened my tie, looking me over as a father would a son. "You call him 'Mr. Giancana' unless he gives you permission otherwise. Understand?"

"Yes," I said.

"He has a temper, so watch your mouth." He was straightening my lapels and picking imaginary lint from my jacket

"Okay." I felt like when my mother took me to meet the bishop. I wondered if he was going to use spit to fix my hair.

Luttazzi stepped back and looked me over. "Don't mess this up for me," he said and I realized then that he, too, was afraid of Giancana.

AGENT OF ARTIFICE

We rode the elevator to the floor above. Getting out we came face-to-face with two large men standing in the hall. I almost thought I should give them the password. But instead they greeted Luttazzi politely and we walked by. It was a short walk to the door of another suite. The hall had dark wainscoting and patterned wallpaper with small chandeliers spaced evenly matching the spacing of the pattern in the dark carpet.

I walked in to the suite and was surprised by the simplicity of the room, especially after the luxury of the hall. The room looked more like a business office, albeit an expensive one. There was dark wood paneling on the walls and a thick red carpet. Comfortable looking chairs were spaced around the room, but they were all empty. There were four men standing looking bored. Three of them were smoking. I imagined they were Giancana's "warriors," although I was sure they were called something else.

Behind a wooden desk sat a thin man. His white hair was balding and he had a grizzled mustache. He looked at me and his dark eyes seemed empty, yet blazing with rage.

The desk amused me because I didn't imagine running a mob was a paperwork-intensive job. I must have smiled because the man behind the desk scowled at me.

There were no chairs before the desk, and Luttazzi and I stood there. "Momo," Luttazzi said using a respectful tone I'd never heard from him before, "this is the meta I told you about." Luttazzi stepped back leaving me alone in front of the desk. I wasn't happy to be called a "meta"—adepts consider it insulting—but I didn't feel as if I was in a position to protest.

Giancana looked at me as if trying to pierce my soul. "What's your name?"

"Michael Vaughan," I said, amazed that my voice seemed tense with fear. I hadn't realized that the mobster scared me until that moment. He seemed to be constantly on the verge of explosive anger.

His eyes did not move from probing me. "You don't look Welsh—more like a Swede. What can you do?"

I wasn't sure what he meant. "I don't do parlor tricks, if that's what you mean." That sentence took amazing courage to say.

He glared at me and for a moment I worried he was going to order his men to kill me.

"What good are you to me? How can I believe you're a meta?"

I again ignored the use of the insult "meta" and slipped my hand in my pocket. The men, who had been looking bored, suddenly reacted, and I had four pistols pointed at me. I pulled my hand from my pocket. "I need my talisman; it's in my pocket."

"Slowly," the biggest man said, his silver revolver pointed at my head.

I nodded and put my hand in my pocket again and pulled out the talisman. I did something I had never done before. I held it between my thumb and forefinger, showing it to them to prove it was nothing dangerous, at least in the sense they were thinking.

"Okay," the big man said and slipped his gun inside his jacket with practiced ease. The other three followed his lead.

There was a pitcher of water on Giancana's desk, and a small table with a lamp on it in the corner of the room behind him. I turned to the goon closest to the table. "Please take the lamp off that table."

The room watched as he did, setting the lamp on the red carpet.

I went invisible.

"Damn!" Luttazzi yelled. The apes against the walls again pulled their guns, but I wondered what they were planning to shoot.

I moved to the desk and picked up the pitcher of water. The men gasped as the pitcher must have seemed to move on its own. I set it on the table and walked away. Almost everyone was looking at the pitcher. I stopped maintaining the invisibility spell and pointed at the pitcher. The water flashed to steam and shot out of the top of the container with a roar. Everyone in the room ducked and someone shot the pitcher, shattering it.

"Holy Mother of God!" Giancana almost screamed. He gave the gunman who shot a look, and the man seemed to cower and try to make himself look small.

It took them all a few moments to realize I was visible again, standing in front of the desk in the same position. They might not even have realized I'd moved.

Giancana looked at me as if he was trying to decide whether to kill me or be amused. Finally he said, "Don't ever disappear like that around me again. You understand that?"

"Yes," I said. I was actually rather amused myself and my fear was gone, since I knew my meta skills would protect me.

"Can you do that," Giancana pointed at the pitcher, "to a person?"

"Yes."

"They'll explode?"

I shook my head. "No. But it hurts a lot and can be fatal if done long enough." I left out that they'd better not be an adept.

Giancana leaned over his desk. "Can you read minds?"

"No. But I can make people tell the truth."

Giancana smiled in a malevolent manner. "So can I."

I ignored the fear that twisted my stomach that statement caused. "My way's probably faster and…less messy."

As if to change the subject, I quickly added, "See and hear through walls, closed doors, unless an adept's placed the proper spells on them. Same for envelopes, face of playing cards—"

Giancana cut me off. "That's how you cheat at poker?"

"Yes."

Giancana laughed. "Scarpelli told me about that yesterday. It took some convincing. Too bad you weren't there."

"Is Scarpelli dead?" I asked.

"No," he said simply. I decided that line of conversation was over.

"Can you kill someone?" Giancana asked, as if that was his real interest.

"Yes," I said softly. "But I need their name, given and family. And it's difficult." I lied, hoping he wouldn't turn me into a hit man.

"You lived in Cuba," Giancana said, apparently satisfied with my answer. "What do you think is going to happen there?"

I shrugged my shoulders. "I have no idea. All I paid attention to was the gambling and the women." I smiled, hoping he'd think this amusing.

Apparently he did, because he laughed. "Money and broads!" he exclaimed. "Yeah, I know your type." He paused a few minutes, chuckling. "I want you to move into this hotel," he finally said. "When I need you I want you close. Luttazzi, get him set up in a nice room."

"Sure, Momo."

"Thank you, Mr. Giancana," I said, not knowing what else to say.

"Call me 'Momo.'"

***

I didn't see "Momo" again until New Year's Eve. By then I'd moved into the Ambassador, down the hall from Luttazzi's suite.

Luttazzi warned me that Giancana wasn't in a good mood. He'd made a lot of money from Havana, but the revolution had reduced the tourist trade and thus the gambling and prostitution, and it looked as if even that was about to dry up completely. The day I met Giancana, the headline on the front page of the Sun-Times was "Cuban Revolt Nears Climax" but it looked as if either side, Castro or Batista, could win, with each claiming victories. On the thirtieth, there were reports that that one of Castro's top lieutenants, an Ernesto Guevara, had been killed in the fighting southeast of Havana and that the Dominican Republic might be sending troops and equipment to support Batista. But the story was mostly about rebel victories. Castro's troops were openly fighting Batista's army.

On New Year's Eve it was reported that Batista had flown his sons to New York, seemingly an admission he knew the end was near. Castro was declaring over rebel radio that the end of Batista's government was "imminent."

There was a New Year's Eve party in Giancana's suite, which was adjacent to the "office." The room was more luxurious than Luttazzi's with gold curtains and marble flooring. It had been decorated with streamers and balloons and a large banner reading "HAPPY NEW YEAR 1959." Momo, appearing out of place in a tux, tried to look festive, but when I overheard him talking, "Castro" and "Batista" and occasionally "Meyer" were peppered throughout the conversation.

The party was full of beautiful women, but they all had the same empty-eyed look I first noticed in Barbara. Their smiles, their laughs, their entire manner seemed to be an affectation. They didn't appeal to me. I noticed they would disappear with Momo's men only to return later, and that only increased my feelings of repulsion for them.

About ten, I made an excuse to Momo, who was too preoccupied to care, and left. I went to the club Knolling had sent me to. I met a tall, raven-haired girl with lovely blue eyes and skin so white it seemed almost translucent. She kissed me at midnight and we returned to my room at the Ambassador about three, after both of us had drunk too much champagne.

On New Year's Day, Luttazzi invited me to his suite to watch football games. The Iowa "Hawkeyes" beat the California "Golden Bears" in a game I completely did not understand. Luttazzi seemed puzzled that I didn't understand football or care about the outcome of the game (he was rooting for Iowa).

A crisis in Berlin pushed Cuba off the front page that night, but the news was good. Batista was reported to be in his presidential palace "amid reports he hoped to announce a sweeping victory over Castro's insurgents by the dawn of the new year." Rebels, outnumbered ten to one, were in retreat. I went to bed thinking maybe Giancana could protect me enough that I could return to Havana after the stupid revolution was over.

The next morning the phone in my room rang, waking me up. I looked at my watch; it was just after six.

"Hello?" I mumbled into the phone.

"Momo's livid. He wants to see you." It was Luttazzi. "Now."

"I'll get dressed."

"Don't bother." The line went dead.

I pulled on the hotel-provided robe over my pajamas and took the elevator to the floor above. The guards at the elevator looked agitated and I could hear yelling. It sounded like Giancana was yelling at the top of his lungs.

I entered the room where I'd had my "interview" a few days before. Momo was standing, yelling at Luttazzi, pounding on the desk near a newspaper. "You get that Jewish bastard on the phone. I want to know what the hell is going on down there!"

He noticed me. "You!" he said, pointing at me.

I stood passively, not knowing what was going on.

"You!" he repeated. "Can you kill Castro?"

I blinked. "Yes." Then I realized what he'd asked. "Why?"

Momo picked up a newspaper that was on his desk and tossed it to me. I caught and opened it. In large type the headlined proclaimed: "Cuba Rebel Chief Castro Proclaims New Regime; Batista Flees Country." Out of curiosity I started reading the article.

Momo grabbed the paper from my hands and put it on his desk pointing to a paragraph in the second column. "Look!"

I bent over to read it. There were riots and looting in Havana. American-operated casinos were "wrecked."

"If they wrecked the Riviera!" Giancana screamed. "Do you know how many millions of dollars I put into that joint?" He turned on Luttazzi, who was on the phone. "Get me Lansky!"

"The operator says the lines to Cuba aren't working, Momo."

Giancana screamed every profanity I'd ever heard, and a few I hadn't.

I ignored it and scanned the story. Batista had flown to the Dominican Republic early in the morning of New Year's Day. His family had flown to the U.S.

The story in yesterday's paper, which we were reading after Batista had fled and Castro declared victory, was a lie. I had gone to bed thinking Batista might win a war he'd already given up.

Giancana looked at me when he calmed down. "Can you kill Castro?"

"Yes," I said. "I need to know his name."

"Fidel Castro!" Giancana screamed at me.

"Is that his full name?"

Giancana blinked and looked at me. "I don't know," he yelled.

"Then I can't kill him."

"You can God-damn well try," Giancana screamed.

I looked at Luttazzi, who gave me a pleading look.

"I'll have to be alone."

Giancana glared at me but said, "Go."

I returned to my room and called the front desk, asking them to please bring me all the morning papers. I was hoping some story might have a clue to Castro's full name. None did, but I learned about mobs roaming the streets of Havana rioting and looting. Some looters were shot by police, who were trying in vain to maintain some order in the vacuum left by Batista's escape. There was a general strike on—that was probably why the phones didn't work—and what few tourists that were left in Havana couldn't get food. The U.S. was sending a ship to get them out of there.

I locked the door to the room and closed the shades. I sat in a comfortable chair with my talisman in both my hands and began invoking the rune in the name of Fidel Castro. I was nervous. Most world leaders hire guilds to protect them. It's one of the guilds' main sources of money to pay warriors' salary, rent on buildings, and all the other things money requires. I didn't know if Castro had protection, and if he did, how strong it would be.

But nothing happened. I spent most of the morning at it. The only explanation was that I didn't have his name right.

Around noon I returned to Giancana's office to report failure. He flew into a rage, demanding to know "What the hell good are you?" and at one point threatening to kill me. He pulled a gun from a drawer in his desk and pointed it at me. I stood calmly, but placed a protection spell around myself. When Giancana noticed the shimmer, he looked at me, his eyes wide.

"What the hell is that?"

"Protection," I replied calmly.

He studied me for a moment and finally put the gun down. He almost looked afraid. I think at that point he realized he couldn't control me the way he controlled others. "Get the hell out of here," he finally said.

I walked out, not bothering to explain that I might have been able to do the job if Giancana had been able to get me Castro's full name. I didn't really want to kill Castro anyway.

CHAPTER EIGHT
Chicago, January 2, 1959

I was angry and decided to go for a walk. The weather was still what the papers were calling unseasonably warm. I walked the half-block east to the lake and then south along Lakeshore Drive. The bare trees looked like claws against the blue sky and that matched my mood. I just kept walking.

I thought about what I had done and where I was. A little over a month ago I'd been in Havana, living as I wished with plenty of money and plenty of companionship. I missed it more than I'd realized, and it appeared there was little hope of getting that life back. Sure, maybe Castro would take his bribes and after a short period of chaos, everything would be back to normal. But somehow I doubted it. And I was still without a guild. I was a rogue adept. Life is usually hard and short for a rogue. I could try to join another guild, but which would take me? The American Meta Association was the most powerful guild on the continent, and Houser was now head of it. No other guild would risk his wrath to protect me unless I could bring them some value. The European guilds would have the same attitude. But I'd spent most of my time as an adept using my powers to meet my own hedonistic desires. I was no good to anyone. And apparently I was no good to the mafia, either.

The days were still short, and when the sun went down the breeze off the lake was bitterly cold. I hunched my shoulders over and walked west until I came to Michigan Avenue, and there I caught a taxi back to the Ambassador.

In the back of the hot, stuffy car I thought about working for Giancana. I didn't want to work for him, and there was no guarantee he could protect me from Houser. Or from himself. I did it only for the money, which didn't make it better; in fact, it seemed to make it worse.

The taxi stopped in front of the hotel, and I paid the fare and stepped inside. At least I needed to go to my room and get my money. I'd leave the thousand—what they'd paid me so far.

In the lobby were Giancana's two goons that were always there. Spotting me, one picked up a house phone and made a call. The other came over to me.

"Boss's looking for you. Where ya been?"

"I went for a walk," I answered and stepped past him.

He reached out and grabbed my arm. I looked at him in a manner he couldn't mistake as friendly. "Take your hand off of me," I said, as if I expected him to obey.

He did but he glared at me trying to be threatening.

I looked at the one on the phone. "Tell him I'll be up soon."

He spoke into the phone and looked unhappy, but hung up the phone. "Boss says not to keep him waiting."

I turned toward the elevator and that's when I saw her. She was in a red dress suit and her blond hair was up and under her hat, but I still recognized her. She looked at me with her blue eyes.

"Liesl?" I whispered.

She smiled and nodded.

I resisted the urge to scoop her up in my arms and hold her close.

Instead I walked over and took her hand. She smiled wider and whispered, "We need to go someplace."

I nodded and turned to the goons. "Tell the boss I'll be back later."

Liesl gave me a funny look at that, but didn't ask questions.

The goons gave me exasperated looks that I ignored.

I said, "Let's go," and we went out and the doorman got us a taxi.

"We felt you," she said. We were in the back of a taxi, going south on Michigan. She'd given the driver an address I didn't recognize, but that wasn't surprising as I basically knew two places: the Allerton and the Ambassador.

"We?" I asked.

"Louis and I."

I smiled broadly. "Louis Brown is alive?"

"Yes," she whispered, glancing at the driver.

"How?"

She shook her head. "Not here."

In the back seat of the taxi my discipline broke down and I pulled her into my arms and held her. She resisted for a moment and then relaxed into the embrace, chuckling. "Easy there, fella," she laughed, as if talking to an errant animal.

I released her, but continued to hold her hands as we talked.

She demurred to answer any more questions until we arrived at a nearly dilapidated brick house in the south part of the city. I didn't like the looks of the neighborhood, but had no doubt we'd be safe from petty criminals.

As she walked up the brick stoop with cracked mortar and a few missing bricks I felt a secure spell end. She opened the door and walked in. I followed. The inside was not in much better shape than the outside. We were in a short hallway with doors leading in different directions. There was peeling wallpaper of an indeterminate pattern and a threadbare rug that seemed more dirt than fabric. I could see into the kitchen. A man was washing dishes but I didn't recognize him. He wasn't wearing a jacket and he had a leather holster around his shoulders and a large black gun in it under his arm. Things must have been bad if they had their warriors doing housework.

"I'm sorry for the condition of the house," she said, sounding genuinely embarrassed. "We don't have many resources." She spent a few moments reworking the secure spell on the front door.

Brown walked out of one of the doors and looked at me. "We've been looking for you ever since we heard you survived the battle in San Francisco."

"Where were you?" I asked.

"Recovering," Liesl answered. "I went back to the car wreck. The driver was dead, but Louis was alive, barely. I got him to a doctor. It took two weeks for him to regain consciousness and heal himself."

"And you just left me?" I demanded.

She shook her head. "No. By the time I got back you were gone. I didn't know what happened to you. I decided you must have run off."

"You could have checked on me after I killed the men that were trying to kill us."

She looked right at me. "I'm sorry; Louis was a little more important than a cowardly adept."

That hurt.

To cover it I said, "How did you know I was in Chicago?"

"We didn't," Brown explained. "Must be coincidence."

I looked at him, not sure whether to believe him. But there was no reason for Brown to come after me, I didn't think.

"This morning," Liesl continued, "we felt someone attempting a powerful rune. We got in the car and traced it to that hotel."

Damn, I thought. Who else felt that rune?

"But I couldn't go in," Brown said, "without drawing undue attention to myself and I needed to get back here to keep watch. So Liesl went in and waited to see if she could find the adept."

"But I needed nicer clothes, so I found a shop and helped myself to this," Liesl said, indicating her suit. She did a little curtsey as if modeling it. "And by the time I returned you'd apparently left."

"Wait," I said. "'Keep watch' on what?"

"What?" Brown asked.

"You said you had to get back here to 'keep watch.' Keep watch on what, exactly." I wondered if there was some secret they wouldn't want to share with me.

Louis and Liesl looked at each other. Then Brown said, "Come in here."

He walked back into the door he'd come out of. The warrior turned and looked at me while he dried dishes. I ignored him and followed Louis. Liesl came into the room after me.

The room was dimly lit and had a strange and unpleasant odor. Growing up on a farm I was used to powerful unpleasant smells. This one was subtle but no less repulsive.

There was an old iron bed in the room's center. A stand, something like a metal coat rack, was beside it with a glass bottle of clear liquid hanging from it. A tube ran down into the arm of someone in the bed. It took a moment for my eyes to adjust to the dark. "Kader?" I whispered. "How?"

"Brunhild negotiated with Houser after the battle," Liesl explained, walking over and picking up the old man's hand to hold it gently. "He allowed her to take him with her. She couldn't stand . . ." she let her voice drift off.

"Houser knew he was beaten, no longer a threat," Brown continued the story. "He let Brunhild take him away."

"He's alive?" I asked, incredulous.

"Yes," Brown said, "barely."

"A rune?" I asked.

"It must be," another voice said.

I turned toward the source. An ancient man walked slowly into the room. He was stooped over, a posture which clashed with his cowboy boots, jeans, and plaid shirt. "I can identify no disease or poison," he said. "That only leaves a rune."

"You brought in a doctor?" I was amazed.

"Doc Addleman is no ordinary doctor," Brown said.

Addleman ignored this exchange. "I'm keeping him alive with IV's. But I'll be damned if I can figure out what's wrong with him. Like no rune I've ever seen or heard of. He's slipped into a coma."

I decided the old man wasn't an ordinary lesser doctor, speaking of runes as he did.

"So someone knows his name," I said.

"Someone working for Houser," Liesl added.

"Unless," Addleman said, "this is a rune that doesn't need a name to work."

"Against an adept?" Brown laughed bitterly. "Never happen."

Addleman shrugged his thin shoulders. "Pretty soon I'll have to use a feeding tube," he said. "He's not coming out of it."

"He's been unconscious for about a week," Liesl said, her voice tight with worry. "He's just getting worse."

I looked at the surroundings, then at Liesl. "Why are you living like this? The Valkyries have resources."

She shook her head. "Brunhild can't challenge Houser. She's taking a risk allowing me to help."

I knew what was coming next. I didn't feel comfortable in that room. I realized the smell was oppressive. I wondered if it was the smell of decay. I walked back out into the hallway and Louis and Liesl followed.

"I have some money," I said. "A little. I can get more." I didn't really need the thousand a week Giancana was paying me, since he was also paying for my hotel room and room service.

"That would help," Louis said, but I heard in his voice that he wanted to say more.

"But?" I asked.

He looked at me, his black eyes looking tired yet angry. "But nothing. There's nothing else you can do, I guess."

I looked at Liesl, hoping for some understanding there. She looked away. I had forgotten she didn't have a very high opinion of me.

I gave them all the money I had on me except the silver, maybe a hundred dollars, and promised to return the next day with more. "Five hundred a week help?"

Liesl almost looked grateful when I said that.

There was a thick silence in the hallway. "I have to go," I said. I had almost forgotten that Giancana was looking for me.

"I'll call you a cab," Liesl said and walked into another room.

Brown looked at me. "I didn't want to say anything in front of Liesl, but I have to know."

"Know what?"

"How did you survive the battle in San Francisco? Brunhild said Houser killed all that were loyal to Kader."

"I escaped," I replied, hoping he'd ask no more questions. It was the truth but not the whole truth.

He stared at me for a long time as if to ascertain whether I was lying. "I have work to do," he said and walked away.

Liesl came back a moment later. "Taxi's on the way."

"Give me your phone number so I can contact you." It was easier than meta methods.

She did, then also left me.

I sat on a wooden bench in the hall and waited alone for my taxi.

***

Walking into the Ambassador lobby, I expected Giancana's men to accost me. Momo was probably livid at my ignoring his orders.

But the men were strangely quiet, sitting in their chairs facing the lobby. Out of curiosity I walked over. Both had their eyes open, but I realized they weren't blinking. Or breathing. I saw no signs of violence. I touched one and felt it. They'd been killed by meta.

I turned and ran for the revolving door to the street. I pushed against it to escape and the heavy door moved with agonizing sluggishness. Just as the pane of glass behind me closed against the arc of the door's frame and before the pane I was pushing came free on the outside of the arc, a large man stepped in front and pushed against the door. He laughed, looking at me as I struggled to push the door against his massive weight. I turned to go back into the lobby, but another man was there. In one hand he had a pistol. The other he used to reach down and clicked something, and then the door wouldn't move at all in either direction. I was trapped. I turned to look back outside. The man there had stepped back, since he knew I couldn't escape, and pulled a gun from inside his coat and aimed it at me.

I berated myself for not using a strength spell against him. But as the muzzle of the barrel came level with my eyes, I knew if I stayed there a moment longer I'd be dead.

I teleported to the sidewalk behind him as he started shooting. After three shots he realized I wasn't there. He started to turn, looking for me, but it was too late. I grabbed his neck and he fell to the cement. His gun clattered to the sidewalk next to him.

The doorman was lying on the sidewalk. I touched him. He was alive, but unconscious. I waved frantically for a taxi, but none seemed near. I ran south, hoping I'd find one.

The fire must have come from an upper window. I saw the orange reflection on the shiny fender of a car and ducked into the busy street. The flames slapped into the cement and splattered the building and cars parked on the curb. I looked up and saw an adept pointing at me, fire arcing from his finger. He was aiming it toward me, the flame crossing the hood of a parked car, leaving a black trail of scorched paint and dots of orange flame behind.

Cars were honking their horns and I heard brakes squealing. I turned to see a taxi about to run me down. Now there's a taxi, I thought indignantly as I jumped out of the way, twisted to keep looking at the adept, and shot an airbolt at him. It missed and crumpled the bricks beside the window causing some to fall out and smash to the sidewalk. The adept ducked inside, and that ended the flames coming at me.

"Hey!" someone called and I looked back. The man that had locked the revolving door was running down the sidewalk toward me, waving his gun.

I went invisible which was dangerous in the middle of a busy street. I danced around the cars and made it to the sidewalk across the street from the hotel. I watched. The man with the gun, the warrior apparently, was looking for me. The adept poked his head out the window. "Where is he?" he yelled.

"Went invisible," the warrior yelled back.

It was almost eleven at night and I wasn't worried about anyone seeing my shadow. But a good adept could find me.

Then I saw them: Houser and another adept. They walked out of the hotel together. They were talking animatedly. Because of the traffic noise I couldn't hear them, and I didn't want to risk my invisibility to use a spell to listen in.

Houser looked at the warrior I'd touched. Houser put his hand on the man's forehead and the warrior sat up blinking. He looked at Houser and started talking excitedly, waving his hands in desperate motions. I assumed he was explaining how I got away. The second warrior walked over and all four started talking. I was sure I was the subject.

I headed south and when I was out of sight of Houser, the other adept, and the warriors, I let the spell end. I found a phone booth and called the hotel. I asked the hotel operator for Luttazzi's room.

"Yeah?" It was Frankie.

"It's Vaughan," I said.

There was silence; then Luttazzi came on. "Where the hell are you?" he demanded.

"Down the street at a phone booth. I was attacked trying to get into the hotel."

"Who by?"

"An adept named Houser and his...muscle."

There was more silence on the other end. Then he said, "Someone named Houser was looking for you. He somehow convinced Max to bring him up." Max was one of the dead mobsters in the lobby. Houser must have used a persuasion spell on him, I decided. "After he talked to Momo, the boss wanted to see you, find out why, but Max and Ernie said you left with a broad. A real looker, they said. Giancana was pissed."

"Is Giancana okay?" I asked. I wasn't sure why I cared.

"Of course. He told this Houser you weren't here, and he thanks him and leaves."

"He didn't leave. He and his men just attacked me in the lobby. Max and Ernie are dead." Must have killed them to keep them from warning me.

Luttazzi spat out a very bad word in English and one or two in Italian. "Where are you exactly? I'll send a car."

"No," I said. "I have to go. Houser knows where I am and he won't stop until I'm dead."

"Momo's not going to like that." His voice indicated he was worried about himself as well as for me. "I tell Momo this Houser attacked you, and Momo will have him killed."

"He couldn't kill him any more than he could kill me," I said. "But I have a problem."

"What?"

"I need my money, in my room. I have to get back into the hotel."

Luttazzi sighed. "I could have Frankie bring it to you." I guess he'd decided I was actually leaving.

"No, it's got a spell on it. He couldn't get to it."

Luttazzi didn't say anything for a few moments, then said, "There's a back entrance to the hotel. I'll send Barbara. No one will suspect her; she wanders around at night all the time. Insomnia or something."

"Thank you," I said.

I hung up and dialed the number Liesl had given me. Brown answered. "Yeah?"

"It's Vaughan," I said. "Houser's in Chicago. He just tried to kill me. I'm leaving town."

Brown said a bad word in the ancient language and then said, "Thanks. We could use your help moving Kader."

"No," I said. Yes, I wanted to help, I really did. "Houser knows I'm here. You can't take the chance of me getting close to Kader again."

"You're right," he said, and there was almost admiration in his voice, mixed with the disappointment. I found myself hoping he'd communicate the admiration to Liesl.

"Good luck," I said, not knowing what else to say, and hung up.

***

Barbara did let me in the back door, through the kitchen, and up the service elevator. She was smarter than I first gave her credit for.

I packed enough clothes to get by and grabbed my money. I thought briefly about going to give some to Liesl, but realized I couldn't risk it.

Luttazzi came to my room before I could leave. "Our men control the lobby. You'll be safe there."

"Yes, but I'm sure they are watching the building."

"Them and the FBI," Luttazzi joked.

"How's Momo taking it?" I asked.

"He's not happy. But I told him you left because you saw one of Houser's muscle and knew Houser was here. He calmed down after that."

I looked at him and smiled. He'd lied to Giancana to protect me. "Thank you."

He shrugged his shoulders. "Joe Kennedy's gonna be here tomorrow to discuss the '60 presidential election and Momo wanted you to make sure he didn't lie."

"Who's Joe Kennedy?" I asked. The name was familiar.

"Father of the next President of the United States," Luttazzi sneered. "If Momo can deliver the union vote, and maybe make sure Joe Junior gets plenty of votes no matter who votes for who."

I shrugged my shoulders—didn't really concern me. "Tell Momo I'm sorry. He obviously can't protect me. I have to protect myself."

"I think he understands. He hasn't ordered you killed."

"That's reassuring," I laughed bitterly.

Luttazzi stepped into the hall and I walked out of my room. He handed me a wad of bills. "This week's pay."

I looked at him. "Thanks. I didn't do much to earn it."

He laughed. "Don't remind me—I might take it back."

I shook the mobster's hand. Yes, I could feel his evil, but at that moment I felt he was a friend.

***

I took the service elevator back down to the kitchen, then slipped out the back door into the alley next to the smelly trash cans. I walked away from the building going north. I was wearing a heavy coat I'd bought in December during the coldest winter on record, so I was plenty warm. I found a taxi and had the driver take me to the airport.

The drive to O'Hare was long enough to give me time to think. I wondered how Houser had gotten to Chicago. Had an adept loyal to him sensed my aborted attack on Castro, as Liesl did, and reported to Houser? But if Houser was in San Francisco, how did he get to Chicago so fast? There wasn't yet jet service between the cities—O'Hare's runways needed lengthening, according to an article I'd seen in the paper—and I couldn't believe a "prop job" could make the trip in less than six hours. I started attempting the rune about eight in the morning. If an adept loyal to Houser sensed it, and if he immediately called Houser and if Houser could get a flight immediately, he might have been able to be at the Ambassador at maybe four in the afternoon, assuming an hour of travel time to and from each airport. I'd been attacked just after five. So I supposed it was possible, but not likely. Meta methods, such as flying carpets, clouds, or pterodactyl, were slower than air travel. (I guess meta methods were much more common before commercial air travel became widespread.) Plus, how would the adept know it was me? Yes, Liesl had known me, been with me when I used meta, and she would be able to tell it was me. But not a stranger or an adept I hardly knew. It just didn't make sense for Houser to be there because of my attempted rune against Castro. There must have been some other explanation.

When I arrived at the airport I wasn't sure where I wanted to go. But, I decided, somewhere warmer. I'd heard people in Havana talk about the Fontainebleau Hotel on Miami Beach. However, I was afraid Houser might have the Miami airport watched, since that was one of the few ways to get into Cuba—or would be if airline service to the island resumed. Looking at a map, I formulated a plan.

I was low on cash so I flew to Houston. From there I flew to Mobile, Alabama. I used different names for each leg.

In Mobile, I took a taxi into town to a dry goods store, where I purchased a cheap rug. Then I had a taxi deliver me to the edge of town, with a stop on the way at a service station. The driver thought I was nuts to want to be let out near the bay just as the sun was going down. I smiled at him and told him not to worry as I paid my fare.

The spell took a few moments to invoke, but soon the rug was hovering over the ground about two feet up. I sat on it, placed my suitcase next to me, and got out the road map I'd been given at the service station. My plan was to follow the coastline until I got to Tampa and then follow roads until I got to Miami. I needed to fly low, even though I wasn't too worried about radar, but I was worried about airplanes. I also needed to go at night. My speed was limited because if I got going too fast, even my heavy dress coat couldn't keep me warm. I ended up stopping at daylight, not far from Tampa. I checked into a roadside motel and slept. The proprietors must have thought it strange when I showed up at their door early in the morning with a rolled-up rug under my arm, looking for a room.

I had paid for the night in advance, so they didn't care that I actually left at sundown. I got to the outskirts of Miami before morning following car lights on the roads and occasionally swooping down to read road signs. The only thing I had to do was find a taxi. I found a phone booth, looked up taxi companies in the Yellow Pages, and about a half hour later one stopped in front of the phone booth and the driver stuck his head out the window: "You the guy who called for a taxi, bub?"

"That's me," I replied and got in.

"Where to?"

"Fontainebleau."

He looked at me as if trying to figure out whether I was joking. "Miami Beach?"

"Yes, please."

He spent a few moments still looking at me, then shrugged, and said, "Okay, Mac."

The Fontainebleau was only a few years old. It was built in an arc, the inside facing the ocean. It was on a narrow strip of a barrier island between Miami and the sea. I checked in as Andrew Stewart of Kansas City, Missouri. Again, a name I'd never used, a place I'd never been. The Fontainebleau was expensive and I'd need to find some money soon. But it was almost as nice as Havana. Not quite as risqué, but almost as nice.

***

Traveling the two prior days I'd missed the news from Cuba. Castro and his "designated" temporary president, Judge Manuel Urrutia, entered Havana with 6,000 rebel troops. Seemed to me the revolution had grown since it had become a success. The next day it was reported that Castro and Urrutia were actually still 350 miles from Havana, stopping at each town to receive a "hysterical welcome from screaming crowds." The good news was Castro disavowed any association with Communists. Nothing would screw up a good thing, I thought, like Cuba going Commie.

Castro also said he would subordinate himself completely to civilian rule and would take no rank higher than major for himself. He even said, "Power does not interest me and I will not take it." Well, if Cuba did become a democracy, the people would probably vote to keep their jobs at the nightclubs and casinos, I decided.

Life at the Fontainebleau, meanwhile, was good. It was right on white-sand beaches but the water was a bit cold to swim in. It had a huge pool surrounded on one side by manicured gardens and on three sides by two levels of cabanas with red and white canopies. There was a high-diving platform on the pool's deep end. It even had a swim-up bar in one corner of the shallow end, which I thought silly, but it sure did a lot of business. I could swim, sit by the pool and ogle the women, eat in the fine restaurants, or take a taxi to someplace recommended by the concierge. Life was good again. It took only about a week to find a poker game with some retired New Yorkers who seemed to have plenty of money. The game was even at a nightclub where I was able to resume my "womanizing" ways, as one of my poker buddies called it (he caught me one night leaving with a zaftig redhead).

I decided unless I was forced to by circumstances, I'd stay here for as long as I could. I even stopped worrying so much about Cuba. I barely noticed when Castro declared martial law.

I discovered a few days later that Gomez was also staying there, which seemed out of the price range for an exiled Major Domo. I saw him sitting at a table by the pool holding a deck of cards. A fat man with a hearing aid joined him. I used a spell to listen in.

"Morning, Gomez, ready for our little game?"

"Sure I'm ready. When you're ten grand in the hole you're ready for anything."

Ten grand? I thought. Where did Gomez get 10,000 dollars to lose playing cards?

"Could I have my usual seat?" the fat man asked.

"You and your suntan," Gomez said, switching chairs so his back was toward the building.

"Same stakes?"

"Let's double it: five dollars a point."

I watched for a while and Gomez seemed to be losing and getting very frustrated about it. He kept trying to quit, but the fat man kept insisting on one more hand.

I walked over and tapped Gomez on the shoulder.

"There you are. I've been looking for you," I said in my most peevish tone.

He looked at me and blinked. Then realization curled his lips as he said, "I'm sorry, I got caught up in my game." He turned to his opponent. "I guess we have to end it here. I'm sorry."

The man looked frustrated, but nodded. Gomez left him with a short stack of twenties to cover his loses and walked away with me.

"*Gracias*," he said, once out of earshot of the other man. "I hope he doesn't think we're faggots."

I laughed. I didn't think I looked very homosexual, but it did fit the stereotype of a young man and an older, well-to-do gentleman.

"I don't know how he wins so consistently," Gomez continued. "I'd think he was cheating if I could figure out how."

"What are you doing here?" I asked. I took him to another table and we sat under the umbrella.

"Had to leave Cuba," he said simply.

I decided not to press the issue. "The Tropicana must have paid better than I thought."

He smiled slyly. "I have connections."

"I bet," I said.

He looked at me. "What are you doing here? Last I heard you left Cuba in early December."

I found it interesting he knew about my leaving Cuba. "Had business," I said. I got the feeling neither of us wanted to talk much about what we'd been doing.

"Well, Castro won his revolution," Gomez growled angrily.

"He's promising elections," I commented, having read it in the paper.

"Baw!" he spat. "The man's a Commie, through and through. I told them that."

"Told who?"

He just looked at me. "Look, he's killed at least 240 people without trials, declared martial law, dissolved the congress, declared he's going to rule by decree, and is disarming civilians blaming 'counter-revolutionaries.' He's just consolidating his power before taking over."

"He says he's not a Communist," I tried, "and isn't interested in power."

"Then how do you explain the executions?"

"Maybe it's fanatics and he doesn't approve," I tried. I didn't know why I was defending Castro, but Gomez's enmity for the man seemed extreme.

"His brother Raul witnessed the mass killing of 71 people," he said.

"Still doesn't make him a Red." I was eyeing some pretty, young things that were walking by.

Gomez swore in Spanish, gaining my full attention. "He's a Commie and he's always been a Commie. And that Argentinean lieutenant of his, Guevara, do you know about him?"

I shook my head, "Seen the name in some stories about Cuba."

"Well, his parents were anti-Peronists," he said, as if that explained everything. "In '53 he was in Guatemala." He looked at me as if that was very significant, also.

"You didn't answer my question," I said, hoping to change the subject. "Why are you here?"

"It's a nice hotel," he answered, waving his hand at the white arc of the building.

"No," I said, "I meant in the States."

He looked at me as if considering how to answer. "I got a chance to get the hell out of Cuba and I took it. I'm not living under that commie bastard."

"Do you have a job? How are you supporting yourself?"

Again he just looked at me. Then his tone changed. "Well, thanks for rescuing me. Hope to see you around." He stood and walked away.

I watched and wondered. Something didn't make sense. I had always thought there was more to the old Cuban than just a doorman at the Tropicana.

I shrugged my shoulders—I really didn't care—and returned to watching the girls.

CHAPTER NINE
Miami, February 6, 1959

Things went well for me for almost a month. I found a couple more poker games so I could increase my income, I found plenty of willing and affectionate women, and I was living by the blue ocean, which grew warmer every day.

It was a Friday night and I was going to visit a favorite club in the Art Deco district. I jumped out of the taxi, and as I approached the glass and neon entrance, a young man walking down the sidewalk bumped into me.

"Excuse me," he mumbled and kept on walking.

I'd felt something. I put my hand in my pocket and found my money clip was gone. When I turned, he was dissolving into the crowd. I gave chase. I didn't get a very good look at him other than his khaki pants, white shirt, and dark hair. That description fit a thousand other guys on the sidewalk.

I decided there was only one way to get him to identify himself.

"Hey!" I yelled, "that guy took my money clip!" and I ran in the direction he'd gone.

Sure enough, he turned around, saw me coming, looked scared, and ran.

We both snaked and dodged our way through the crowd and the sidewalk cafés. He was younger and in better shape, but I had one advantage. I ran a spell on myself and my speed increased. It was like running as a child, when it feels as if you're going as fast as the wind and could run forever.

He made another error, turning up a side street that wasn't nearly as crowded. I was able to catch up to him very quickly then.

He turned and saw me coming and I could see the fear in his eyes. He tried to dodge me at the last moment, but I grabbed his shirt and pushed him into an alley and up against a wall, knocking over a triad of trash cans. The speed spell made me incredibly fast and he didn't have time to react with violence.

"What?" he exclaimed, as if surprised and hurt.

He wasn't more than 18, I decided, maybe younger. "You took my money clip," I said calmly. "Please give it back."

He looked at me as if to figure out whether I was serious. "I didn't—"

I pointed my finger at him. "Son, you don't know what you are dealing with here."

He tried the bravado of youth. "What?" He tried to move and found he couldn't. Then I saw fear twist his face, about the only part of his body I'd left under his control.

"Listen," I said, keeping my voice even, "if you're going to pick pockets, at least do a decent job of it." I went through his clothes as I talked and, sure enough, found my money clip and a few wallets I was sure didn't belong to him. "And whatever you do, don't pick the pocket of an adept."

Now his eyes grew wide and his mouth hung open. "I'm s-s-s-sorry," he stammered.

I smiled at him. "If I had the time, I'd teach you to do it right."

He looked astounded.

I smiled and shoved the stolen wallets into his shirt. "And if you were really good, you'd know who to leave alone."

"Yes, s-s-s-sir."

I released the spell and he almost collapsed before regaining control of his body.

"Remember," I said, "no adepts."

"How," he breathed as if he'd just run a marathon, "will I know?"

"When you get good enough, you'll know."

He nodded his head. I decided he wasn't an apprentice. My master would have had me practicing for days and nights straight if I'd messed up a simple lift. And I'd have to have satisfied him before I tried it on the street.

"Get out of here," I told him.

He nodded and ran away.

I didn't think any more about the incident, figuring I'd done the boy a favor. What do I care if a few careless lessers lose some cash? But there were adepts that would kill a clumsy pickpocket just for the object lesson in it for other petty thieves: don't mess with adepts. But, I found out later he was not just a pickpocket.

***

I came out of the ocean and grabbed a towel. The water was still chilly, but I found it bracing. I was worn out from my swim and breathing hard. I'd purposely fought waves and swum out as far as I dared and back again. Chasing the pickpocket a week ago had convinced me I needed to get back in shape. Too much Italian food in Chicago, I decided.

I heard footsteps in the sand on the beach behind me — the whoosh whoosh sound of feet in soft sand — but didn't give them much thought. The beach was sometimes crowded. Then something cold and metallic pressed against my bare back.

"Keep your hands in sight," someone said. That it was a man speaking was all I knew. "And don't try any meta; I'll kill you where you stand."

There wasn't much meta I could try, as worn out as I was. I nodded and kept my hands from my body. My right hand was grabbed roughly and a handcuff slapped on it.

"Ow," I snapped.

"Walk," the man behind me said, pressing what I assumed was the barrel of a gun into my back. "Go south."

I obeyed. It was a little awkward as my right arm was being pulled behind me. He must have stepped back a bit because I didn't feel the metal against my flesh any longer, but it felt as if my right arm was going to be ripped out at the socket. I slowed down experimentally.

"Keep moving," he said from right behind me and pushed the gun into me again.

"Okay," I said.

My talisman was in a small pocket in my swimming trunks. It was zipped shut so I wouldn't lose it while swimming, but now getting to it would take too long. Someone must have been watching me, known when I was most vulnerable. And I'd gotten complacent. Should never have swum like that without a warrior guarding me. But I was a rogue; I didn't have any warriors.

"Turn here," the man behind me said. I realized I had no idea what he looked like. I imagined something like

Giancana's goons: big, dressed in a suit, and a permanent stupid look on his face.

We were headed for the street. It was a long walk and by the time we got there I'd pretty much dried off. My shoulder was burning with pain. I wondered if anyone would notice my predicament and call the police.

A car very similar to Luttazzi's Cadillac, except white, stopped at the curb. I knew what was coming next, I thought.

The man with the gun said, "Get in."

I opened the door with my free hand and sat down, looking back at the man that belonged to the gun. He looked rather ordinary and was dressed in the light clothes that seemed the uniform for young men in Miami. He had the gun under a folded newspaper, which he discarded, then indicated I should scoot over with a wave of the weapon. The other end of the handcuffs was around his left wrist. I slid over and he sat beside me, shutting his door. I gave my door handle a quick tug with my left hand, but the fact that it moved too easily and nothing happened led me to suspect the mechanism had been disconnected. But it wouldn't have helped, as I couldn't drag the man along with me. That also prevented teleportation.

Trapped, I looked around the car. The pickpocket was in the front seat gazing at me, smiling, and looking quite satisfied with himself. The man from the beach was still sitting next to me looking very serious, and pointing a black gun at me. I could see only the back of the driver's head.

"That him?" the man with the gun asked.

"Yes," the pickpocket replied.

"Let's go," the gunman said. The car moved away. "Keep your other hand where I can see it," he said to me.

I nodded and looked at the pickpocket. He grinned malevolently back at me. I tried to give him a confident look but he didn't react.

After about an hour of driving during which I got thoroughly lost, the car stopped in front of a small but nice house not far outside of Miami. I was surprised. I half expected to be taken out to the Everglades, shot, and the body left for the alligators to dispose of the evidence.

Gun—as I'd taken to calling him—opened his door and said, "Come on," tugging on the handcuffs. He slid out and I had little choice but to follow him. I felt a little strange on the sidewalk in my swimming trunks handcuffed to another man. He strode across the narrow concrete walk that cut through the lawn. He seemed to be in a hurry to get our little vignette out of sight.

I heard a car door close behind us; the apprentice had gotten out and was following. The driver had turned off the engine and was smoking a cigarette, still sitting in the car.

The apprentice cut around us and opened the door of the house with a key. Apparently he wasn't yet able to manipulate a secure spell. The three of us walked in. It was a pleasant little house, furnished in modern metal and vinyl and chrome. Gun led me to a chair while the apprentice disappeared into the back of the house.

"Sit," Gun barked, pointing at a chair. I did, the vinyl cool on my bare legs. Gun unlocked the cuffs from his wrist and snapped them to the metal arm of the chair. I thought that silly. I could certainly teleport and just take the chair with me. Then I noticed the legs of the chair had been nailed to the blond hardwood floor. I thought for a moment it was a pity to damage both the chair and the floor.

Gun stepped away, but still kept his pistol aimed at me. My back was to the door we'd come in and I was facing a living room with sparse furniture.

High heels make a distinctive sound on hardwood. I looked up as the click-clack echoed around the room. Followed at a respectful distance by the apprentice was the adept who apparently lived here. She was tall, with long and luxurious chestnut hair. Her dress was the modern style, a nice cream color that demurely showed just a bit of ankle. The string of pearls around her neck was tasteful to the point of being almost clichéd.

"This him, Roger?" she asked of the man I was calling "Gun."

"Yes, ma'am, according to him." He indicated the apprentice.

She looked at the apprentice. "Is that right, Danny?"

Danny nodded. "That's him. That's the adept, Teacher."

She walked closer to me, giving me a chance to admire her legs. "What's your name?" she asked.

"Stewart," I said. "Andy. Well, Andrew, but only my mother calls me that."

Her lips, a nice red color, curled up into an amused smirk. "Yes, that's the name you checked into the Fontainebleau under." She looked to see if her knowing that surprised me. It didn't. They'd obviously been watching me for a while. I gave up all pretense.

"Your apprentice," I said. "Not very good."

"He's new," she explained. "But good enough to know to report an unknown adept to me."

The apprentice made a face at me the way a child would. I almost expected him to stick out his tongue. He didn't seem to be a good choice for an apprenticeship in meta.

Maybe he was doing more for the female adept than cleaning her bathroom, I mused.

"So," the woman was saying. "What is your guild?"

"North American," I tried.

She laughed—a deep, throaty laugh of one too cynical to really know true joy. "Try again," she stated.

"AMA," I said. Well, it was almost the truth.

She gave me a smile as if I were a misbehaving child. "No, I think not. We'll know soon enough." She looked at her wristwatch. "Won't be too long now."

She left the room and Danny followed. Roger sat down in a chair just like mine, except not nailed to the floor, and watched me, the gun pointed in my general direction.

I tried to talk to him a bit but he only waved the gun and told me to "Shaddup."

An interminable time later, maybe as much as an hour, the doorbell chimed.

"Get the door, Danny," I heard the woman's voice call out.

"Yes, Teacher."

They both walked out of the back of the house, Danny first, hurrying to the door.

"I think our very important guest has arrived," she cooed at me.

I heard voices from the door and then multiple footsteps on the floor. Houser walked in in front of me. Two warriors were with him. One that I recognized from Chicago—that had locked the revolving door-was to my right. They were holding strange weapons that were somewhat boxy with short barrels. If they were half as deadly as they looked I knew I didn't want to risk being shot at with them.

"Mike," Houser greeted me as if I were his oldest and dearest friend.

I just looked at him.

He turned to the woman and kissed her on the cheek. "Very good, Isabelle. I'll remember this."

"Thank you, Teacher," she said and almost seemed to beam with pride.

Houser sat on the low, chunky black couch and looked at me.

"Can you believe?" he asked, still looking at me. "Five hours from San Francisco. I think I love jets. What an age we are in. Did you see the Russians launched a rocket to the sun? I don't know how or why anyone would do that, but it's amazing. What will be next, I wonder?"

I just looked at him, not sure where he was going.

"Mike," he said in a friendly tone, "I'm going to give you one chance and only one chance."

"Really?" I asked sarcastically. When Houser walked in I figured I was dead, and that gave me a lousy attitude.

"Really," he repeated. "You may come back to the AMA — all will be forgiven."

I tried to tell from his face whether he was serious. "What's the catch?"

He leaned forward and looked at me intently. "Where's Louis?"

"Louis?" I asked, as if I didn't know the name.

Houser was controlling his temper. "Louis Brown, Kader's number one lieutenant."

"Oh," I said, as if I realized what he meant. "That Louis."

I didn't say anything and he looked at me intently. "Yes, *that* Louis, where is he?"

I threw it out as if I didn't care. "I have no idea." This was the truth as I assumed they were no longer in Chicago. I figured I'd better be as honest as I dared. I doubted I could bald-face lie my way out of this, but it was worth a try.

"You don't?"

Shaking my head, I said, "Last I saw him was, oh, late November. In Havana." Here come the lies.

"And," Houser probed, "you haven't seen him since?"

I shook my head and frowned as if thinking hard. "Noooo."

"Would you be willing to let me put a truth spell on you?" Houser asked.

I chuckled at that. "And risk you asking my name? No thanks." A strong enough spell and I'd tell them anything, whether I wanted to or not.

Houser stared at me as if deciding what to do. "Mike, you just don't see the big picture here," he finally said.

"The big picture?" I asked. At that moment I was thinking killing me would be more merciful.

Houser leaned forward, his face intense. "Kader built this guild from almost nothing, and for that he deserves our respect and admiration."

"Is that why you deposed him?" I sneered.

Houser was too caught up in his explanation to notice. "He made one crucial error. He decentralized power in the guild. That left factions to operate as they wished. He built the greatest guild ever and then let it go rudderless."

I thought he'd allowed the members freedom. After all, how was Kader, in San Francisco, supposed to know how adepts in Alabama are going to want to run their regional guild?

"Without that leadership, direct leadership, in the hands of one man, who has the power to move the entire guild and the will to do so, we are weak.

"But now," he said, slamming his fist into his palm, "we're powerful. We'll take over the other guilds, the North American, then the European, and finally the Asian, African, and South American guilds."

"Today the AMA, tomorrow the world," I said without irony.

"Yes!" he hissed. "And I will control it all for the good of all adepts."

"You're not in this for you, it's for all the adepts," I added.

"Yes!" he said, his clenched fist pounding his thigh. "And you can be part of it, Vaughan, or you can die here, now. What do you say?"

I think he thought he'd talked me into it.

I looked at him. It was power for power's sake, yet justified by being for the good of those who were suffering under the power. He justified his means by his supposed outcome. I wanted no part of it. "You're insane."

He blinked. I don't think that was the answer he was looking for. His face turned red and his jaw moved as he fought back the anger. He stood up and glared at me for what must have been a full minute. He turned to Isabelle. "Kill him; I don't care how," he ordered, his voice tight with barely controlled anger.

"Yes, Teacher," she said as if he'd told her to get him a beer.

Houser hurriedly left, heading for the front door behind me, his quick footsteps trailing off. The warrior I'd seen in Chicago gave me a malicious grin and followed. When Houser and his men were gone I looked at Isabelle, wondering what she was going to do.

"Allow me," Roger said, moving closer and pointing the gun at my head.

"No, too messy," Isabelle said.

Roger looked disappointed, but backed away.

The easiest way to kill someone is to take their air away. You die pretty fast. An adept can resist, but I knew without my talisman, still zipped securely inside my swimming trunks, I'd probably lose that contest. I'd felt her power and she was at least an even match for me.

"I don't suppose I could talk you out of this?" I asked her, trying to sound casual.

"No," she stated simply. She pointed at me. I felt my ears pop. That was what she was going to do.

I used my free left hand to claw at the zipper on the pocket, but it was on my right hip and the fabric moved without the zipper opening. I could feel the air moving away from me. I gave up on the zipper and pulled air toward myself but she was still pulling it away faster. I pointed at her with my left hand and tried an airbolt, but without my talisman, and without much air, it was feeble and barely ruffled her hair. My breathing accelerated as my body automatically reacted to the lack of oxygen. My sight was going gray. I tried for the zipper again but my fingers didn't want to work correctly.

I heard a crash and a lot of yelling: "DOWN! DOWN! DOWN!" by men used to being obeyed. Almost instinctively I doubled over putting my nose almost on my knees.

Suddenly air was on my face and I could breathe. I heard a clap as atmosphere suddenly rushed in to fill a void. Gunfire rang out so close to me my ears screamed afterwards. More shots were fired and I heard something heavy fall. I heard "GET UP, NOW! AGAINST THE WALL!" The voices were loud and forceful. I had trouble not complying myself.

When my sight returned there were four or five men in dark clothing like uniforms holding short rifle-looking weapons. Two were standing over Roger's body. His blood was spreading on the blond hardwood floor, following the cracks between the boards. The apprentice, Danny, was up against the wall, being frisked by one of the men. I couldn't see Isabella. That clap I heard must have been her teleporting out.

The door behind me opened and I again heard footsteps.

"Mike!" Gomez said from behind me.

I craned my neck to look at him. The old Cuban was dressed as a civilian in a gray suit, but was holding a snub-nosed revolver. He was with two other men, dressed like the ones in the room, only they were holding pistols like Roger had.

"Gomez?" I asked. "What the hell is this?" By now he'd walked in front of me.

"CIA," Gomez said. "A little quick reaction force we just happen to have in Miami."

I glared at him. "You're CIA?" I wasn't very surprised — it explained a lot, I thought.

Meanwhile, two of the men who'd come in with Gomez were talking to the men with rifles. "This one's dead, sir," one said, indicating Roger.

"And him?" one of what I was presuming to be the leaders asked, pointing at Danny.

"He cowered behind the couch."

"Anyone else?"

"A woman. She disappeared when we came in."

"What, out the back?"

"No, disappeared. Into thin air."

"Just like the guy out front," the second guy with the pistol said.

"Metas," the other said as if it were a dirty word.

"Yeah," his cohort agreed.

Gomez had sat down on the couch just about where Houser had, holding his little gun rather casually.

"Sure am," he said, answering my question. "And a funny thing happened today." He was really enjoying this.

"What?" I asked, deciding I had to play his game.

"I was sitting in a chair watching the waves roll onto the beach—and the girls sunning themselves," he added with a leer, "when my good friend, Mike Vaughan, was kidnapped. Right in front of me, can you believe it? It was amazing."

"Amazing," I said, playing along.

"So I got a taxi and said 'Follow that car!'" He laughed at that. "And it came to this house and my friend was taken inside, in handcuffs, even.

"So I go find a pay phone and call the Miami office of the CIA. Of course, we're Federal Officers; we can't allow a crime like that, a federal crime no less, to happen right here on our soil."

"Of course," I said.

"So we raid the house. But first we stop a car that tries to leave. We catch two men with illegal firearms. But the other got away."

One of the leaders came over and talked to Gomez. "This him?"

"Yes, sir," Gomez replied. "My friend, the adept."

The man looked at me as if trying to decide whether I was worth his trouble. "Are you hurt, sir?" he asked with all the compassion of a cop writing a ticket.

"No," I said. "I wouldn't mind having these handcuffs off, though. I think he—" I used my foot to point at Roger's body "—has the key."

The man pulled out a key from his own pocket and it undid the handcuffs. I decided the keys must be standardized.

I rubbed my wrist. "Thank you."

Gomez let me leave with him a few minutes later. The leader of the men came with us. He introduced himself as "Major Stein." Outside, the house was surrounded by police cars with their revolving red lights on top flashing. I saw Houser's two warriors sitting in the back of separate, plain, unmarked sedans with a man in a suit sitting next to each of them, and another man behind the wheel. Gomez took me to a similar car that was empty, but let me sit in the front seat. The vinyl was hot against my bare legs. He got in the back and Stein sat behind the wheel. Gomez leaned forward and grinned at me.

"Not bad, eh?"

"Thank you," I said sincerely.

"Listen," Gomez began, "I have an idea."

I looked at him, listening. "What?"

He turned to Stein.

"Why don't you join us?" Stein asked.

"Us?"

"The CIA," Gomez exclaimed. "Your powers would be useful."

I looked at both of them. "I don't think so."

Gomez leaned forward and looked serious. "You owe me, Vaughan. I convinced them to rescue you just because I said you could be recruited."

"I didn't ask you to rescue me," I stated. It was a weak bargaining position, I know.

"Listen," Stein said. "We know you're a rogue adept. The AMA is trying to kill you. The woman that owns that house is an adept. The man we almost captured is high up in the new AMA leadership according to our intelligence. You need the CIA as much as we need you. We can protect you. You'll be paid so you won't have to cheat at poker with retired haberdashers anymore."

I was amazed at how much they knew about my life and the guilds. It never occurred to me the government might spy on adepts. "I don't know, Stein."

"How many times has the AMA tried to kill you since Kader was killed?"

Well, at least he didn't have everything right. "Twice."

"If you're CIA, the AMA will be reluctant to mess with you."

I wasn't sure that was true.

"You have to leave, don't you," Stein said. "Go back to the Fontainebleau, get your cash and clothes. How do you know they won't be waiting for you there? And where are you going to run to, now? Aren't you tired of running?"

He had me there. I'd been kidnapped because I'd gotten complacent. I was complacent because I was comfortable. And I liked being comfortable.

"We can give you protection while you go gather your things," Stein was saying. "At least, come to D.C. with me and meet Bissell."

"Who's that?" I asked.

"The DD/P," Stein stated, as if surprised I didn't know.

"Dee dee pee?" I asked, this being my introduction to the government's fetish for acronyms.

"Deputy Director for Plans," Stein explained with exaggerated patience.

I looked at Gomez. He'd gotten awfully quiet. "So the only reason you saved me was to, you hoped, recruit me into the CIA?"

Gomez shrugged, trying to look innocent.

"Okay," I whispered. I thought, what would it hurt? And at least I'd get out of Miami with "protection." Almost like being in a guild and having warriors.

***

Two men in dark suits with narrow ties, armed I assumed, accompanied me back to the Fontainebleau. I changed out of my swim trunks into a suit, gathered all my things, no jettisoning everything but necessities this time, checked out, and they took me to the airport. They put me on a Pan Am flight to National Airport. Being in Miami, I'd forgotten it was the middle of February. Walking off the plane, I about froze before I got to the bottom of the stairs and inside the terminal. A young man standing just inside the door apparently recognized me, as he asked, "Mr. Vaughan?"

"Yes," I said and he politely asked me to come with him. He led me outside to a waiting car. It was one of those plain, nondescript cars like I'd seen outside the house in Miami. He opened the back door for me, so I got in. He then sat behind the steering wheel and drove. He left the airport and crossed a wide river, the Potomac I assumed. It was wider than the Snake River at Idaho Falls. After the bridge we passed the Lincoln Memorial and a few blocks past that stopped in front of an office building made of the same granite it seemed most everything in the city was made of. On the left side of the door was a sign with a scroll on a blue field and the words "North Building" in gold letters on the scroll. On the other side of the door was a plaque with the circular blue symbol of the CIA on it and the street address, as if it were a business. The symbol included the words "Central Intelligence Agency" and I realize up into that moment I hadn't known what "CIA" stood for. I thought it seemed strange for a spy organization to have a sign on its building announcing its presence.

"I'll just be a second," the driver said. "Wait here, please."

"Okay," I said, not knowing what to expect.

He got out of the car and ran inside the building. I felt a little conspicuous sitting in the car like that. And with the engine off it was starting to get cold.

He returned in a few minutes. "Sorry, needed to confirm this CI one-forty-two."

"Excuse me?" I asked.

"Form CI-142: authorization form for commercial residential billeting and voucher."

And that was my introduction to government paperwork.

"I wanted to confirm it. Says you're supposed to stay at the Hays-Adams. They must think a lot of you."

He started the car and we drove around the White House to a very nice-looking hotel. He came in with me and handled the registration and the CI-142, for which I was grateful. He even tipped the bellhop who brought up my bags. I had a nice room overlooking the president's home and the Washington Monument. The man said he'd pick me up at nine for my meeting.

I thanked him and closed the door. I didn't know if the CIA had someone watching me or not. My high-profile trip didn't make me feel very safe. I placed alarm spells on the door and windows before I went to sleep.

***

The phone rang in my room at ten to nine the next morning. It was my driver; he was waiting in the lobby for me.

I dressed in my best suit and met him downstairs. I was glad I still had my dress wool coat from Chicago, as it was still quite cold out.

We didn't go back to the CIA building by the same route, as there are a lot of one-way streets in Washington, DC. But we got there long before my 9:30 appointment with the "Deputy Director for Plans," or "DD/P," Mr. Richard Bissell. I was taken to a nicely if sparsely appointed antechamber and told to wait. The walls looked like expensive paneling and the furniture was solid if plain. The room had a desk, and behind it sat a severe-looking middle-aged woman who glanced at me and returned to her typing.

About ten, the phone on the woman's desk rang. She answered it, "Yes, sir?" She listened a few moments, then hung up and looked to me. "I'm sorry, Mr. Bissell is unavoidably delayed. He'll be with you as soon as possible."

"Thank you," I said, not knowing what else to say.

It was close to noon when the woman let me into the next room and shut the door behind me. Someone later told me a phrase to describe this kind of government action: "Hurry up and wait."

The office was classically appointed with a large carved desk, leather chairs, and a leather couch and cocktail table against one wall. There were paintings evocative of historical moments in U.S. history and what I would later learn was the ubiquitous photograph of President Eisenhower.

Bissell was sitting behind the large desk. He was in a white button-down shirt with a narrow tie and wore round horn-rimmed glasses on his large nose. He stood when I came in and extended his hand. "Thank you for waiting, Mr. Vaughan," he said, clasping my hand. "This Cuba thing has us all working overtime." He ran his hand through dark thinning hair and sat down. "Castro had the audacity to depose Batista on my watch," he said with a smile. He pointed at a chair in front of his desk and I sat. I didn't know what he meant by "on his watch" but I did get an interesting mental picture of two miniature men, Castro and Batista, battling on the face of a pocket watch until Batista is thrown off.

Bissell picked up a dark brown folder on his desk, set it before him, and opened it. I couldn't see what the contents were, other than normal-sized typewriter paper, some of it yellowed with age. He started reading: "Michael Vaughn, A/K/A Steve Wendell, A/K/A Andrew Stewart. Real name: unknown. Birthplace: unknown but suspected to be northwest U.S. by his accent. Age: Unknown, appears to be early to mid-thirties.

"First contact Salt Lake City, Utah, as an apprentice."

I sat and listened. Apparently, the information in that file was about me. I wasn't going to tell him whether anything he said was correct. I felt a little uncomfortable knowing they had been watching me for that long and I wasn't aware of it.

He looked at me. "So, Mr. Vaughan, you were a member of the American Meta Association, correct?"

"Yes," I said simply.

He looked back at the file. "You used to spend a lot of time in Havana. That could be useful." He looked back up at me. "Tell me, did you have any contact with revolutionary elements when there?"

"Not that I know of," I replied, deciding that was the safest answer.

"You spent time in Chicago where you were seen with known members of OC," he stated further, again looking at the papers on his desk.

"OC?" I asked.

"Organized Crime," he explained.

I thought about joking about falling in with a bad crowd, but decided against it.

"In fact," he stated, "you were known to associate with members of OC in Havana." He looked at me, seemingly without blinking, as if expecting an explanation.

"Havana was full of mobsters. I tried to avoid them, but since I like to gamble and the mob owns the casinos, it was difficult."

"Yes, I imagine," he said, scratching one of his large ears. "You earned your living in Havana gambling."

"Yes," I confirmed. Having never interviewed for a job before, I didn't know if this treatment was normal.

He closed the folder and tapped the top. "The FBI was gracious enough to send this over this morning."

"The FBI?"

"Yes, they keep track of metas. They have a file on most of them."

I must have looked surprised, because he laughed. "Don't worry. I think if Hoover had his way, he'd have a file on everyone in the country."

That didn't make me feel better.

"What can you do?" he asked.

"I don't do parlor tricks, if that's what you mean." Come to think of it, I had had a job interview before, and it was almost as bizarre as this one.

Bissell was about to ask another question when the intercom on his desk buzzed. He pressed a button on it. "Yes, Mrs. Franklin?"

"Mr. Dulles here to see Mr. Vaughan and you, sir."

"Send him in, please."

Bissell's composure cracked for just a moment as a worried look crossed his face. The door opened and Bissell stood up. I decided I should, also.

Dulles was a tall, thin man with white hair and a white mustache. He had wire-rimmed glasses. He was dressed in a dark suit that seemed too large for him, as if he was so thin they didn't make suits that small. He walked to me and extended his hand. I took it and shook it as he said, "Allen Dulles, DCI."

"Excuse me," I said looking up at him, surprised by how tall he was. "DCI?"

He looked at Bissell for a moment, then smiled at me. "Director of Central Intelligence." He picked out one of the chairs in front of Bissell's desk and sat down. Bissell followed, so I also sat down.

"I'm sorry," I said. "I don't follow politics much." Not at all, actually, other than what you can't help but absorb. "I thought you were the Secretary of State."

Dulles chuckled. "People often make that mistake. That's my brother, John Dulles."

"I see," I said, feeling foolish. "And what is a 'Director of Central Intelligence'?"

"The head of the CIA," Bissell explained, "among other things."

Dulles looked at me as if trying to figure me out. He turned to Bissell. "This is the adept?"

"Yes," Bissell answered. "We're running late, so I just started the interview."

I loved the "we" in that statement.

"What are you thinking?" Dulles asked.

"An access agent?"

"A raven?" Dulles looked at me. "He's got the looks, but considering his talents, that might be a waste."

I loved how they were talking about me as if I weren't there. I found out later that a "raven" was a man whose job it was to seduce women, usually lonely, unattractive women, who were in positions to get secret information, into spying for the CIA.

"Then an operative, NOC," Bissell said. "It'll take longer to get him trained."

"Excuse me," I interjected, "knock?"

"En-oh-See. Non-official cover," Bissell explained. "Means that if you get caught we will disavow any knowledge of your existence."

I felt my eyebrows rise on that statement.

"It can be very dangerous," Dulles added. "However, we have many that volunteer."

"Then why do you need me?"

"Not many make it through the training," Bissell said with a tinge of frustration in his voice. "But with your abilities, maybe you can."

Dulles suddenly stood. "Get him to Isolation. If he makes it, put him in the field as NOC. Otherwise, make him an access agent." He turned to me. "Can you speak Russian or German?"

"I can speak anything you want," I replied. I wasn't going to explain translation spells, however.

Dulles looked surprised. "You are talented." He turned to Bissell. "Have a good day, Richard." Then he looked at me. "Mr. Vaughan." He walked out the door. Mrs. Franklin got up from her desk and closed it after he left.

"Isolation?" I asked.

"Our training facility in Virginia; you'll enjoy it, I think."

Somehow I doubted that.

CHAPTER TEN
Camp Peary, Virginia, February 15, 1959

"Isolation" was the code name for Camp Peary, a wooded area outside Williamsburg, Virginia. Most everyone called it "The Farm."

When I arrived I was given a pseudonym, Richard Jackson, and a "billet," and it was explained that for the first part of my training I would live in the camp in a barracks. Later I'd be allowed to live "on the economy." I imagined this time living on the Farm was much like the basic training for the Army I'd avoided by becoming an adept. I was called a JOT, or junior officer trainee, and told I would be taking a modified version of the "Ops Course." Modified for my special talents, I was told but frankly, it seemed about the same as what all the other JOTs were put through.

The government started paying me with checks. I also had to get a social security number in order to be paid. They wanted a birth certificate in order to issue one. I had to use a very strong persuasion spell to get the battle-axe clerk to ignore that requirement. I got the number under the "Jackson" name because I couldn't think of any other name to use.

I had to take my paychecks to a bank to cash. There was a bank in the camp, which was convenient, because JOTs in their early training couldn't leave the camp. I had to store the cash in my foot locker. When during an inspection my training officer found the cash, yet found he couldn't touch it because of my secure spell, he strongly recommended I get a bank account. That, too, was a new experience for me.

The training consisted of rising before dawn and exercising, regardless of the weather. In March it was not very warm and often raining and occasionally snowing. I used spells to keep me warm and to have the strength needed. After exercise we'd eat breakfast in a communal facility with the other "trainees." Then came classes. Lunch was in the same facility, then more classes or learning exercises in the afternoon. A late dinner back in the "mess hall" and we were dismissed to our barracks to read course materials, clean our equipment, and eventually get to sleep late.

First they taught me about guns. I was given various weapons, from Russian AK-47s to American M-14s. I didn't know why almost all the weapons were named some combination of letters and numbers. Two exceptions were the Browning Automatic Rifle—although its official name was "M1918A2" and the instructors called it "B.A.R."—and the British "Sterling" submachine gun. I was learning a whole new vocabulary.

I was taught how to shoot many of the weapons, which was a lot more complicated than I ever thought it could be. I was a lousy shot. We were on the pistol range and I was firing an "M1911" which someone jokingly called a "Handgun Howitzer." A howitzer, I understood, was a very big gun. This was a lot like the gun Roger had pulled on me in Miami—might have been the same type of weapon.

I fired at a paper silhouette shaped like the upper torso of a person. I emptied the seven-round magazine at the target—each shot like slamming my hand in a door—which was about 25 yards away, and only two bullets hit the silhouette and none were in the "kill zone." One of the instructors noticed and turned on me in a loud, commanding voice: "Mr. Jackson, I believe the safest place to be when you are firing a weapon is in front of the gun! How the hell do you expect to kill your enemy before they kill you?"

I silently put down the gun on the table, put my left hand in my pocket with my talisman, and pointed the palm of my right hand toward the silhouette. The airbolt shredded the paper target.

"Like that."

The instructor looked at me, looked at the target, and said disparaging remarks about his own mother.

I also was taught how to "field strip", clean, and reassemble the weapons. A contest was held for a one-day pass—that is, permission to leave the Farm—for the JOT who could strip and reassemble an M1A1—another American rifle—the fastest, blindfolded. I used far-seeing to see through the blindfold and, naturally, won.

Another class was "Locks and Picks." I aced it, already knowing how to pick locks from my apprenticeship. When the final exam was to pass through a series of locked doors, I used far-seeing to see the other side and teleported through each. The instructors were impressed, but seemed frustrated that it was too easy for me.

"Flaps and Seals" was also "too easy." We were supposed to learn to open envelopes, examine the contents, and replace it all and reseal them so the intrusion was undetected.

In class the JOTs were handed regular business envelopes and told to tell the instructor the contents after returning the sealed envelope to him. They gave us all a few minutes to work. As my classmates struggled to open the envelopes without tearing the paper using their self-made ivory tools and steam, I used far-seeing.

The instructors returned and they walked down the aisle inspecting the resealing job and asking each JOT the contents. When my instructor came to me he looked at the still-sealed envelope.

"Did you even open this, Mr. Jackson?"

"No," I said.

The other students around me turned to watch the exchange.

"Then how do you know what's inside?" he demanded.

"It's a playing card, king of clubs. The back is red checks, like a picnic blanket."

The instructor spent a moment calming down, then said, "That's right," through clenched teeth. "Now, I want a photograph of it."

I learned how to open envelopes with steam and ivory tools that I had to make myself as they were not provided.

There were ersatz border crossings on the camp, complete with watchful "guards,"— actually the instructors—machine gun nests, towers, barbed wire, alarms, and German Shepherd dogs that seemed to have a taste for JOT flesh. Each JOT had three hours to get through. I went invisible, walked to the fence, teleported past, and did it all in about five minutes. I could tell I was frustrating the instructors when they told me to do it again. It took me about four minutes that time.

We spent a week on an Army base in North Carolina, sleeping in tents, if we were lucky, or usually wherever we could find a place to sit and close our eyes. We were denied food and rest and ran through drills and evaluations. I held up better than the others, using spells to keep me going. It was here they taught us what was called a "command voice." It was being loud without yelling, forceful without being shrill. The secret was to project from the diaphragm and open the mouth wide.

One bitterly cold day on the base we threw grenades, small metal spheres that made an astonishingly big explosion. We were taught how to pull the pin, hold the grenade so the safety lever, or spoons, didn't come off and start the fuse, throw them, and then duck under cover so that the shrapnel didn't hit us. Using grenades seemed almost more dangerous for the attacker than the target and I was glad that day was over and I wouldn't have to have anything more to do with grenades.

After that week they let us move "off post" to live "on the economy."

There was even a class on hugging. Since in many foreign cultures men often hug, they explained, this was a skill needed to blend in. After a period of initial awkwardness, we learned to hug men at least without showing our embarrassment.

They took a bunch of us JOTs into Richmond, Virginia, a city about 45 minutes from the Farm. Richmond was a charming city; the parts of it near the James River still had narrow cobblestone streets and antebellum architecture. I was placed in a team of four others and we were told that we were in Moscow, Russia. We were to lose the other team and, once we'd lost them, make a "drop." That was, we'd exchange a package, in this case a manila envelope full of blank paper, with an instructor at a set location. The other team was to keep us under surveillance without being detected and try to prevent the drop.

I convinced my team to let me do the drop. They'd seen me operate and knew my talents, so they readily agreed. I turned down an alley, went invisible, back-tracked, walked past the "enemy" team member following me, and few minutes later made the "drop" on the shores of the river near the Nickel Bridge.

I was living in a small "studio" apartment (and writing checks to pay for rent, which was new to me). There was a kitchenette and a Murphy bed and the only separate room was the bathroom. I had progressed enough in my training to be allowed the privilege of living "off base."

One night the alarm spell I'd set on the door went off. It sounded in my head only, but a bright light formed near the door. I sat up in the bed, scooped my talisman off the nightstand, and looked at the door to see what had set off the alarm.

Three large men were standing in the open doorway, dazzled by the light in their eyes. The door was open, unharmed it seemed; perhaps the lock had been picked.

I pointed my finger at the men, adrenaline and the power from my talisman bringing me instantly awake. One of them saw my hand and put his up. "No!" he screamed. They scrambled out of the portal just as the flame shot across the room.

"Damn it!" one of them called from the hall. "It's a training exercise!"

I stopped the fire, but already the carpet in the hall and the wallpaper were burning.

"Get an extinguisher!" another of the men called from the hall.

I stood up and walked to the door. The hall was filling with orange flame and black smoke. I pointed at the fire and cool water from the air smothered it. Then I pointed at the three men, two to my right, one to my left. "Get on the floor, now!" I yelled, using my "command voice."

They did, flinching away from my finger. They were dressed all in black like the men who rescued me in Miami.

"Who's in charge here?" I demanded.

The one that had yelled "No" identified himself as the leader.

I pointed at him and gave him a truth spell. "What is this?"

"A training exercise; all JOTs go through it."

I let out a long breath and lowered my hand. "Next time, warn me."

"That's the point," the leader explained from his position on the floor, "surprise."

"Get up," I said. They did and looked at me, looking afraid. "I almost killed you all."

"Yes, sir," the leader said. I smiled at that. I'd been called many things through my training, but not "sir."

A week later I was back in Bissell's office.

"I think you've graduated," he said. "At least the commandant of the facility asked me to get you out of there. Did you really almost kill three instructors?"

"They surprised me," I said. "Luckily, they move fast."

Bissell smiled. "They're well trained. Some of our JOTs are ex-military."

He looked at me. "Well, time for your first assignment, I think."

***

I found a nice apartment in the Georgetown section of Washington D.C. and reported to the North Building on E

Street every morning at nine, wearing a dark suit with a narrow tie just like a working stiff. I wondered if they had a bowling league I could join. (I learned later that yes, they did, several in fact.)

I had spent nearly six months at the Farm, and I had to admit that that was the longest period without an assassination attempt by Houser since he'd taken over the AMA. It looked as if maybe joining the CIA, other than the obvious downside—being a government employee—was going to work out. I was a "GS-11," making $587.84 a month plus $86.00 "locality pay" to make up for the cost of living in the Washington-Baltimore area. When I hinted to Bissell I'd like a little more money, he told me regulations stated junior officers were GS-11s and GS-11s in their first year made $587.84 a month plus $86.00 locality pay. I could be raised to GS-12 but to make GS-13 I'd have to be a supervisor, he explained.

(I later asked Gomez how he could afford the Fontainebleau on what the CIA paid. He responded that he was an independent contractor, as if that explained everything.)

He also strongly discouraged me from making money using my "powers." I ended up going to the movies a lot for entertainment. It was cheap and I'd gotten in the habit at the Farm, when movies shown at the camp's movie house were about the only available distraction. One of the other JOTs dragged me to see *North by Northwest* and I enjoyed it much more than I had planned.

The Directorate for Planning was housed on one half of the third floor of the North Building. I didn't see Bissell much at first, except when he addressed a group of the "officers," as we were called. We worked in white short-sleeved shirts with ties, our suit jackets hung up neatly on a steel rack, reading a lot of dispatches, history books, and newspapers. Documents moved through pneumatic tubes in cylindrical containers that clanked as they came to corners on their journeys. There was something satisfying about shoving a container into one of the tubes and having it sucked away with a gush of air.

While I'd been training at Camp Peary, the situation in Cuba had deteriorated. Castro, who'd said in January he wasn't interested in power, declared himself Prime Minister of the Revolutionary Government. He claimed this was "temporary" until the "crisis" was over. In May he put into place "Agrarian Reform" which, according to the analysts in the Directorate of Intelligence (DI), meant he was nationalizing and collectivizing the farms. Most distressing, at least to American businesses, was that the law forbade foreign, i.e., non-Cuban, ownership of land.

In June, according to DI reports I read, Ernesto "Che" Guevara started making overtures to the Soviet Union. I was learning that at the CIA anything having to do with the U.S.S.R. pretty much put the whole place in a panic.

And Cuba wasn't the only situation the CIA was keeping an eye on. For my first NOC mission, I was flown to West Berlin to gather intelligence on Soviet and East German intentions toward the city.

The Chief of Operations of Clandestine Services, who worked for Bissell, briefed me before I left. Apparently, some 40,000 East Berliners worked in West Berlin because the economy was much better. The East Germans were publicly stating that the "border crossers" were engaged in "illegal currency manipulation," and probably smuggling. Bissell's deputy said sarcastically that they were probably smuggling in decent food.

I was set up in an apartment and had a notional job at an American company. I spent my free time wandering about the city, as any expatriate might. I was amazed at the difference between West Berlin, the "free" part of the city, and East Berlin, the part under Communist control. West Berlin, the American, French, and English occupation zones after the War, was prosperous, vibrant, and rebuilding the devastation from Allied bombing and the house-to-house fighting of the invading Soviet army. East Berlin looked like a bad dream. It was dark, dreary, and the repairs were slow if at all.

I spent almost three months, October through December 1959, openly traveling back and forth between the two cities, talking to border crossers—translation spells allowing me to speak German—and other people.

It was there I met Maria Gonzalez again—except she wasn't using that name and was passing herself off as an Argentinean actress. I didn't know if our meeting was coincidence or planned but I was in a West Berlin coffee shop and in she walked. I recognized her from Havana, of course, when she was lunching with Vinnie Scarpelli and lounging by the pool.

She looked at me as if trying to figure out who I was when suddenly a look of recognition crossed her face. She strode over to me, allowing me to admire her tall lean form and lovely dark skin. In Havana I had noticed her eyes but here they seemed even lovelier.

"Mr. Vaughn?" she asked getting close enough for conversation.

I stood and extended my hand, "Miss Gonzalez," I stated.

She put her finger over her lips and looked at me conspiratorially. "I haven't used that name since leaving Havana."

"Neither have I," I clarified for her.

We both sat.

"And what brings you to Berlin, Mister, uhm?"

"Jackson," I offered. "And I'm working for an American company, Morrison-Knutson. Perhaps you've heard of it, Miss…?"

"Never have," she stated tossing her hand in a dismissive manner. "And Fernandez. Do you mind?" She reached into her purse and pulled out a pack of cigarettes, and deftly extracted one and lit it.

"No, not at all," I stated. "And why are you in Berlin, Miss Fernandez?"

She laughed, a very pretty sound I thought. Her personality was completely different from that she had displayed in Havana. "I'm an actress, Mr. Jackson; I go where there's work."

"Oh, so you're working here. In a play, perhaps, maybe one I could attend?"

She smiled dismissively again. "Television, darling."

I was startled by her use of that word but she seemed to be affecting a flamboyant personality and perhaps that was part of the affect.

"Oh, something I could perhaps see on T.V., then?"

She laughed again. "If you like dull German productions about the war."

I noticed she didn't say East or West German and I couldn't quite figure how an Argentinean actress would have a part in something about World War II. At least I assumed that was the war she meant. While she didn't come out and say it I got the idea we were in the same business, although I wasn't sure which side she was on.

"Have you been in Berlin long?" I asked.

She leaned forward and almost whispered, "Ages, darling, ages."

"Care to show me around the sights?"

She laughed again. "Sure, I'll show you the boring buildings where the Nazis did something boring."

I couldn't help but laugh at that.

"A cup of coffee first, perhaps?" I offered.

"Please!" she chimed. "I would denounce capitalism for a cup of coffee."

I waved over the waiter and ordered two cups. She smiled as I spoke German (translation spell).

"What do you do for, what did you call the company you work for?"

"Morrison-Knutson," I reiterated. "Construction. There's been a lot of that since the war, of course."

"Of course," she said, again with a dismissive wave of her cigarette. I got the feeling she didn't believe that I worked in construction.

"Have you been back to Cuba, darling?" she asked.

I shook my head. "No, of course not. There is nothing there for me, now."

"Oh, too bad," she almost pouted. "It's still a wonderful place."

I had to look at her. If she was praising Castro's Cuba, she had to be at least sympathetic to the other side's cause. Of course, I wasn't really on a side, I was just working for the side that kept me safe and paid me.

"How long are you in Berlin, darling?" she said, again effectively changing the subject.

"A few months," was all I answered.

She reached over and placed her free hand on mine. "I, too, am here a few months."

We were also both away from home and lonely. And I hadn't been with a woman for ages. I was pretty sure my apartment was clean of bugs—the electronic kind—so we went there.

When I woke in the morning she was gone. But the next night she showed up at my door with a bottle of wine and her eyes smoldering. I pulled her in, wrapped my arms around her, and kissed her hard before the door was even shut.

***

I didn't tell Maria anything. I didn't even tell her when I was leaving to return to Washington nor that I moved out of my apartment into a hotel the night before.

That night, I used invisibility and teleportation to enter the KGB's *Rezidentura* at the Karlshorst compound east of East Berlin in what was called a "black bag job." It wasn't easy. The Karlshorst was the *Kommandatura* of the Sovs' Berlin Garrison. It was surrounded by a tall, barbed wire-topped fence and guarded by "elite" elements of the East German Ministry of State Security, also called the "Stasi." The *Rezidentura* was inside this fenced and guarded compound with its own special fence and KGB-controlled guards. The biggest problem was my footprints in the snow. I'd try to walk either in cleared paths or where there were already multiple footprints. If that didn't work, I'd randomly teleport to break up the trail.

Once inside I had to pick locks on the file cabinets, and then use translation spells to figure out what documents where important. I burned through three rolls of film for a special camera that was small enough to fit in the palm of my hand, but also could take pictures in the dark.

I escaped just as the sun was coming up. To avoid the risk of being searched as I went through the Brandenburg Gate, I crossed the border my way and returned to the hotel.

During the flight back to Washington I worried what would happen when Maria discovered I was gone. If she truly knew what I did, she'd understand. If she didn't, I might never see her again.

Bissell was happy with my work in Berlin and said he'd be looking for more assignments needing my "special talents." I got the feeling they were starting me out slowly. Most NOC agents were deep inside enemy countries and never, if ever, showed their faces at the North Building.

***

It appeared Castro was going to break his word and not only rule the country, but turn it Communist. Revolutionary hero but non-Communist Huber Matose was arrested and sentenced to 20 years in prison for "treason." Camilo Cienfuego, another hero of the revolution but a reluctant Communist, was mysteriously killed when his plane disappeared over the ocean.

In February 1960, Soviet Deputy Prime Minister Mikoyan visited Havana, resulting publicly with a trade agreement and covertly cementing Cuba's place in the "Soviet sphere of influence."

On Friday, March 18th, Bissell called a meeting of all DP operatives currently on station. We gathered in a large conference room on the fourth floor. Bissell walked in carrying a sheaf of papers covered by a red-bordered coversheet. Dulles walked in after him. The DCI stood aside, almost in a corner, as Bissell called us to order. "This briefing is classified Top Secret," he said before opening his notes.

"As you all know," he began, "the situation in Cuba is becoming critical. Castro has broken his promises not to turn the country socialist. He has made overtures to the Soviets, nationalized or expropriated American property, and executed or imprisoned anyone he feels can threaten his power. His pal Che Guevara has personally supervised the summary executions of an estimated to 2,000 quote 'enemies of the revolution.'

"This situation," he continued, "has become untenable. We cannot allow a communist dictatorship 90 miles off our southern shore to export revolution in our hemisphere.

"Yesterday, National Command Authority—" (I had learned that meant the president) "— approved and authorized this department's plans outlined in the paper titled 'A Program of Covert Action against the Castro Regime.' In addition to the program outlined in the paper, there will be overt actions taken against the growing communist threat in Cuba. The overt measures are an end to all sugar purchases, an oil embargo, and a continuation of the 1958 arms embargo."

I remembered the '58 embargo against Batista was an attempt by the U.S. to appear neutral, after giving him a million dollars in military assistance earlier in the year.

"Now, not everyone worked on the paper that Eisenhower approved."

I hadn't; this was the first I'd heard of it.

"So," Bissell continued, "I'll describe the broad outlines of the plan. There are four components to the program." He read these from his notes. "A: Formation of a Cuban exile organization to attract Cuban loyalists, to direct opposition activities, and to provide cover for Agency operations. B: A propaganda offensive in the name of the opposition. C: Creation inside Cuba of a clandestine intelligence collection and action apparatus to be responsive to direction of the exile operation. And D: Development outside of Cuba of a small paramilitary force to be introduced into Cuba to organize, train, and lead resistance groups."

He looked up at us and smiled. "Congratulations, men, we're going after that bearded commie bastard."

The room broke into cheers. Dulles even smiled after that.

"This briefing," Bissell concluded, "is classified Top Secret." He walked out and Dulles followed, giving him a congratulatory slap on the back.

***

So we started to work. Since I had "experience with Cuba," in April I was sent to Miami to help find prospective paramilitary recruits. We worked out of the Zenith Technological Enterprises office in Coral Gables. Volunteers were interrogated and polygraphed, I ran a truth spell on them, and even then their backgrounds were checked. We didn't want Batista supporters, and really didn't want pro-Castro agents.

Gomez got together with fellow exiles and "reputable" anti-Castro groups—but none connected to Batista—and formed the *Frente Revolucionario Democratico* or "FRD," in May. The FRD was theoretically in charge of the operation but it was all a CIA front. Money ran through my fingers like water as I recruited exiles.

From the beginning there were conflicts. The FRD wanted control of the paramilitary group. The CIA and the State Department wanted the FRD to move to Mexico. The Mexican government didn't want anything to do with the whole mess. The training base in Panama was compromised by a lack of "operational security." You could probably go to a cantina nearby and hear the entire plan. A defecting Cuban naval officer described to the CIA how there were "too many Americans running around with too much money." That

Castro knew something was happening didn't deter anyone in the least.

In August I was visited in Miami by a technician from Camp Peary. He gave me a box of cigars.

"Castro's favorites," he said.

"And what do you want me to do with them?"

"Get them to Castro."

"The CIA is giving Castro a box of cigars?"

The man looked exasperated at my apparent ignorance. "He must not know they came from us. One of them is poisoned."

"You're kidding?" I asked.

The man shook his head. "Get them to Castro."

I wasn't about to go back to Havana and present them to Castro. I knew we were infiltrating operatives on a regular basis into Cuba. I gave the cigars to one group that was going into Havana. I never heard what happened to the box of cigars, but Castro didn't die, so the mission must have failed.

By the end of 1960, when I visited the Panama training base, there were over 700 "paramilitaries," including pilots and naval personnel.

Gomez met me coming off the airplane, an uncomfortable, CIA-owned, metal contraption called a "C-123."

"Have you ever seen such a royal screw-up?" he asked.

I about fell over from the heat, even in early November. I was sweating instantly. "What?"

"They are planning a full scale invasion with five to six hundred men."

I took off my hat and fanned myself with it. We were walking toward an ancient car with all the windows rolled down or missing.

"So?" I asked. The original concept had been an infiltration followed by guerilla war with local support.

"They're loco."

"Who?"

"The FRD. They want an invasion rather than a guerilla war and resistance. They plan to take some ground, set up a government there, and ask the U.S. for recognition and help, which they are assuming they'll get. And Bissell and Dulles and the Joint Chiefs have agreed to it."

We climbed inside the car. I was guessing it predated the war. The seats had springs protruding from them, so you had to watch where you sat. Once it started crawling down the dirt road the heavy, hot air combined with road dust coming in the open windows made it a little less comfortable than I imagine standing in front of a blast furnace would be.

"We shut down recruitment in Miami," I told Gomez, "although we're still getting volunteers through word of mouth and the FRD."

Gomez ground the gears as he shifted the ancient vehicle. "I know; I saw the reports." He steered around a donkey pulling a cart. "We don't have enough forces to take on Castro's army, even with American support, assuming we get it."

That was the second time he'd said that. I decided he must have been worried about the election. "We will," I said, not at all as sure as I tried to sound. If Nixon won the election we would probably get all the support we needed. The vice-president's support of the operation was well known. But Senator Kennedy was an unknown. Everyone talked tough on Communism; you had to if you expected to get elected. Kennedy had even accused Eisenhower of not doing enough about Castro, but that could have been just political rhetoric. How he'd act in office could be another matter.

He looked at me. "Why are you here?"

"Bissell's talking about having me go into Cuba with the strike force," I said, hoping my voice communicated my disdain for that idea.

"You could be useful," Gomez mumbled, distracted by guiding what appeared to be a recalcitrant vehicle down a narrow dirt road.

That wasn't what I was hoping he'd say. "I'd just be in the way. I have no military training other than what I got at the Farm. I'm nearly worthless with a gun."

"Yes, but your other talents. I'll think about it. We'll have to keep it quiet from the FRD."

"Why?"

He smiled at me. "You're classified, *mi amigo*."

I knew that. I was "compartmentalized." Reports on my activities were stamped with the codeword "HOUDINI," which I was told was chosen randomly but found insulting nevertheless. Only those deemed to have a "need to know" could know anything about HOUDINI. You'd think a codeword could be paid better than a GS-11.

I spent the day at the training facility observing training—as if I understood the purpose of crawling under barbed wire in mud—and the next day flew back to D.C. to report to Bissell.

The election was the day after I got back from Panama, the eighth of November. Kennedy won, although the outcome wasn't certain until the next day. A large number of Chicago precincts reported late and then all came in at once and all heavily for JPK. I thought about Luttazzi telling me about Giancana "delivering" the union vote and making sure there were plenty of votes for Kennedy, no matter who voted for him. Kennedy ended up winning Illinois by nine thousand votes, and that gave him the electoral college votes necessary to win the election (I remembered how all that worked from my high school civics class).

Despite Eisenhower's enthusiasm for the program, the operation slowed down until the inauguration of the new president. No one knew if JPK would continue it. But in a meeting the day after the inauguration, Joe Jr. gave the go-ahead.

Up until the invasion, small groups were landed in Cuba to run sabotage and harassing operations. All were exfiltrated successfully, except those that were intended to stay to help build a resistance and spy network.

On April twelfth, five days before the planned invasion, Bissell came into the briefing room. His large ears were tinged red; he was obviously controlling his anger.

"President Kennedy has announced that there will be no overt U.S. action taken in support of the Cuban operations, including U.S. air support."

Everyone present sat in stunned silence for a moment. The invasion force had some World War II vintage bombers, but without U.S. air support the invasion force would be sitting ducks. And Bissell had just decided to send me with that force.

***

I ran my hand down Maria's thigh. My other hand was flopped on her unused pillow as her head rested on my shoulder. I kissed her forehead. April weather was perfect and with the window of my apartment open a cool breeze rolled over us.

"How long will you be gone?" she asked.

"I don't know," I answered honestly.

"Where are you going?"

I just looked at her and she smiled sheepishly.

"Where did you just come from?" I asked.

She gave me the same look.

"Will it be dangerous?" she asked.

"Naw," I said probably too forcefully, "same boring surveillance work." To be honest fear was tightening around my heart like a cold fist and Maria's unexpected arrival in D.C. was the tension release I needed.

We didn't promise each other anything other than mutual access to bodies and skin and tenderness whenever together. After Berlin we happened to meet in Washington. It seemed like a happy coincidence but I always wondered if she was keeping an eye on me for...for whomever she worked for.

But I didn't care. I had always said I couldn't love a lesser (and if she were an adept I'd know it). But I felt I was falling in love with her and I didn't even know her name—her real name. And she didn't know my real name, either.

"I'll be gone a while, too," she whispered.

I nodded. We'd seen each other when we could, almost always in Washington. She always had some excuse: a play, a television program, a commercial. She was always the actress and I was the CIA officer. I liked to believe that was true.

I never told her anything. Anyone watching me could know as much as I told her about my comings and goings. I didn't trust her yet I thought I was falling in love with her.

I kissed the tip of her nose, eliciting a soft giggle, and snuggled up closer. I had to get up early in the morning and while sleep was not my primary concern, it needed to be.

During my thoughts she'd nuzzled her face against my neck and melded her body to mine.

Maybe it was the trip I was about to take. But I felt the need to say it.

"Maria?"

She hummed a reply.

"I'm in love with you."

I felt her body react and she lifted her head.

"No you aren't, silly."

I smiled at her.

"You're right, I'm not. Good night, lover," I whispered.

"Good night, *mi amor*."

***

I flew to Nicaragua, from where the invasion was to be launched, on the thirteenth of April. Well, at least that might be lucky, I thought. It would have been even better if it was Friday and not Thursday.

I was attached to an intelligence-reconnaissance company, "company" being a unit of about 50 men. I was introduced to the commander of the unit as "Major Jackson." He wasn't happy to see me, mumbling something in Spanish about not needing a spy in his unit.

The fifteenth was a new moon, and on the sixteenth when we launched there was very little moon to show. We were loaded in a U.S. Navy "LCD," which basically was a ship that carried and could launch smaller "landing craft." We rode that across the Gulf of Mexico to within a few miles of Cuba. Then the "command element" and one "platoon" of my company were loaded on a LCVP—don't ask me what that means—which was a short boat with a flat front and high sides. One of the American sailors referred to it as a "Higgens Boat." When I happened to touch the side, I realized the boat was made out of wood. That did not make me feel any better.

The men were armed with various "sanitized" weapons, that is, weapons that couldn't be traced back to the United States. Most were AK-47s and I recognized a BAR and some M1s. I was given an M1911 ("handgun howitzer") and wore it in a holster at my hip. I had no intention of firing it.

We were all also wearing sanitized uniforms, mostly solid greens without identifying tags. In addition to that I had a web belt to hold my holster. Even underwear, socks, and boots were issued to assure that nothing could be traced back to the U.S., including our boot prints.

About two A.M. on the seventeenth we were a few hundred yards off Zapata Peninsula, deep inside the Bay of Pigs, with Cuba on three sides of us, east, west, and north. We held position near what had been code-named "Red Beach." It was almost pitch black in the boat, but the men whose faces I could see were tight with emotion. I realized most of these men had been civilians less than a year ago. I saw fear and determination cross their visages. The inside of the boat was thick with tension, as if the men were really a tightly wound spring about to break.

The early morning hours were unbelievably cold but no one complained. For some reason when the boat wasn't moving, the diesel exhaust from the engine seemed to fill its interior, making the inside even more claustrophobic. The smell and the rocking of the sea nearly made me sick and some men did vomit, adding that odor to the cacophony of smells my queasy stomach had to deal with. A quick spell of healing settled my stomach but my nose still registered its dissatisfaction.

There was gunfire coming from the beach and the tension level increased exponentially.

"UD teams," the commander said after talking into his radio. "Preparing the beachhead. They are meeting light resistance."

The phrase "light resistance" seemed to ease everyone's fears. Except mine, I decided. Wasn't this why I'd become an adept, to avoid "hitting the beach" in a "hail of gunfire"?

CHAPTER ELEVEN
Off the Bay of Pigs, April 17, 1961

We heard boat engines moving off toward the beach. We were to be one of the last units to go ashore, so we waited. I could see that the commander was growing nervous. He kept looking at his watch. Finally he got on the radio, holding the handset like a phone. "What's the holdup?"

We didn't hear the reply but heard his exclamation: "Coral! They said it was seaweed!" He put the radio down. "They are running into coral—it's slowing down the landing."

"Sir," one of the other officers said, "it's going to be daylight soon."

"I know," the commander growled in reply. I wasn't sure what the problem with daylight was.

The commander gave me a look of disgust. "CIA said it was seaweed."

We continued to hear bursts of gunfire from the beach. As the sky started to lighten, the commander looked at it with a scowl. "We're sitting ducks out here without air support."

"Maybe our air strikes took out their aircraft," one of the men said.

What none of us in that little boat floating off Cuba's coast knew was that those air strikes had been canceled.

I knew there were eleven World War II vintage B-26 bombers to support the invasion. They were easy to spot. They were the big propeller-driven planes going down in flames around us. There were these jets with pods at the end of their wings, buzzing around the larger slower B-26s like mosquitoes around water buffalos. We were finally headed for the beach when a single-engine prop plane with Cuban markings flew over us so low that the throb of the engine seemed to vibrate the air around us, reverberating off the wooden sides of the boat. I could read the number on the side: 541. The plane was green, but the tail was painted like the Cuban flag—ironically red, white, and blue. I watched it turn in an almost lazily slow manner, and come back, heading straight at us. Instinctively I ducked, which probably saved my life. The plane opened fire, spraying bullets into the boat. I heard the boat's hull snap with the sound of breaking wood and was pelted by flying splinters. Men screamed as they were shot and the smell of scorched metal, shattered wood, spilt blood, and burning flesh filled the air.

The boat jarred hard and the commander screamed, "We're beached on coral, everyone, get to shore, get under the trees!"

The plane had turned and again was coming right at us. I knew going invisible would do nothing, as the bullets were going to hit where they were going to hit.

The front of the boat dropped open, splashing into the sea with a fountain of white foam, and men scrambled out. I could see the beach. It was a long way for a teleport, but I decided that was the only way to save myself. I heard bullets perforating the hull of the LCVP as I gauged the distance and worked the spell.

I missed, materializing over the surf and falling in. A wave pushed me painfully into the sea bottom. Involuntarily I screamed as my skin was ripped by the sharp coral, but my scream was nothing but bubbles. I realized I didn't dare to inhale or I'd drown. Before the next wave hit I scrambled onto the beach and dove behind a berm someone had dug. I looked out in time to see the LCVP sink, men still swimming away from it. It didn't disappear completely, apparently hitting bottom.

I hid behind the berm until a young Cuban approached me. I recognized him as one of the officers on the LCVP. He was wet and his uniform was ripped. He was bleeding from his arm.

"Sir," he said.

I looked at him but didn't respond.

"Major Jackson?" he asked.

"Yes."

"The commander's dead. As ranking officer, you should take command of the company, sir."

I looked up at him, wondering if I looked like a commander cowering behind a mound of Cuban sand. "I'm just a CIA spy," I told him. "Find someone else."

He hesitated, looking worried. I think the "someone else" was him. "Yes, sir," he said and walked away. He moved toward the men on the beach and tried to organize them.

About then the first attack from Castro's forces came.

***

The invaders moved into the jungle and were hurriedly digging foxholes when the first of Castro's militias attacked with "small arms." They simply drove up in open trucks waving guns and were easily repelled with no loss on our side and large losses among the unorganized militias.

But Castro's air force was slicing up our supply ships.

Suddenly a huge mushroom cloud boiled over the ocean. The noise and shockwave washed over me and it seemed I could feel the heat of it on my face.

"My god," someone called out from a nearby foxhole, "does Castro have the A-bomb?"

We found out later that was when the *Rio Escondido*—one of our munitions supply ships—had been hit. There was enough ammunition and explosive on board that the ship disappeared in that fireball.

That spooked the rest of our supply ships and they all took off for the open ocean, leaving the landing force with no supplies, including ammunition.

The Cuban militias fell back, wisely waiting for some heavy support. I found a foxhole between two trees and stayed there the rest of the day. I watched what was left of our airplanes bomb some tanks and huge, towed guns, basically stopping a Communist assault.

I left my hiding spot about sundown during a break in the fighting to try to find the leader. His name was Ramon and he was easy to find: he was yelling into a radio.

"We need resupply! Our ammunition is running very low. We have inflicted heavy casualties on the enemy but we need resupply."

He listened and then growled, "Understood, out," before turning to his men. "We can't be resupplied from the sea without air superiority. They're afraid the Sea Furies will sink their precious ships. They are going to try an airdrop."

Then Ramon noticed me. "Who the hell are you?"

"Major Jackson."

He glared at me and spat on the ground. "CIA," he snarled, as if it were a dirty word.

Darkness ended both the air and ground attacks. An attempted resupply drop landed in the ocean. The commander sent men out to retrieve it but they just got cut up in the coral.

By morning it was decided that "Red Beach" should be abandoned, as "Blue Beach," further to the east, was more defensible. Mercifully, we weren't attacked while moving to Blue Beach. The forces there had "dug in" in the jungle, which gave us cover and concealment.

There were small skirmishes fought that day, and that night we were again resupplied by air. Blue Beach had better luck and ammunition was handed out, but I noticed many of the soldiers grumbling at the scarcity of it.

Castro's forces attacked us the morning of the eighteenth, the third day of the invasion, from three directions. The last of our airplanes stopped one column before Castro's jets — Ramon was calling them T-33s — shot it down.

Ramon was livid. But even with the last of our air support gone and ammunition running low, and the sun going down, he refused to leave, even when ordered by the command ship to do so.

"CIA!" he called to me.

"Yes?"

He glared at me. "What the hell can you do to help this situation?"

I almost said, "Nothing." But I decided if I didn't start to contribute to the fight, I'd probably die there in this hot miserable jungle. I took a chance. "Do you know the codeword HOUDINI?"

He stared at me. "Yes."

"I'm him."

He looked at me, eyes wide, and said some Spanish swear words I'd never heard before.

"I need to know where the enemy is," he said. "The recon company has been nearly wiped out. What can you do?"

I had to think for a second. "I can find them. I need a map."

He gave me one. It had brownish stains on it that I hoped were coffee. He pointed to three lines on the map. "These are the probable roads they'll use. They won't come through this swamp here. I need you back in —" he looked at his watch " — one hour."

"Okay," I said in English. I walked north through the trees going invisible as I did. I used a spell to move quickly and another to see in the dark. I found the first road empty and traveled away from the beach on it. Then I cut east to the second road. I didn't even have to approach it. I smelled cigarette smoke and diesel exhaust overwhelming the smell of the jungle. I moved in close and could see trucks and tanks, along with men standing around.

Still invisible, I got through the column and found the third road the commander had pointed out to me. There was also a force there, larger and better equipped. No one was smoking but there were guards posted — I nearly stepped on one that was lying in a shallow foxhole. I decided the first group was militia, the second Castro's regular army.

I got back just as the sky was starting to glow orange, signaling the coming dawn. When I told Ramon what I'd seen, his face fell for a moment. Then he stood up straight. "They'll attack at dawn, most likely. Thanks, CIA," he said to me. I think he meant it.

Ramon positioned his men to defend our position from the two roads. He separated a small group and had them attack the militia. They didn't return by the time the main force attacked.

Castro's forces attacked and with almost no ammunition, the invasion brigade fell back to the beach. I watched a young exile panic and run just to be shot in the back. Those that fought as they fell back fared much better.

The commander was sending messages for help and more ammunition. He wasn't happy with what he was being told.

I pulled my pistol from its holster and jerked the slide back. It didn't slam forward as I remembered it should. I had to push the slide back into position. I aimed the weapon at the tree line. There were seven rounds in it and, I decided, I might hit something. I pulled the trigger and the gun jammed after one shot fired.

A soldier next to me swore. "It's full of sand," he barked. "Didn't you clean it after getting it wet?"

Damn, I thought. They'd taught me how at the Farm; I was just too preoccupied and convinced I wouldn't need it to do so.

Then I saw huge shapes coming down the road: tanks. The lead one was spitting rapid fire at the beach. I dove for the sand and covered my head with my hands.

I could hear Ramon yelling into the radio: "Tanks closing in on Blue Beach from north and east. They are firing directly at us. Fighting on beach. Send all available aircraft now!"

Of course, aircraft never came.

Ramon ordered all equipment and communications destroyed. I could see Castro's men in the tree line and the tanks had stopped but were still spewing death from their machine guns. Castro's men had stopped firing because our group had stopped shooting at them shortly after my aborted attempt to fire my weapon.

Ramon sent one last radio message: "I can't wait any longer. I am destroying my radio now." And then he smashed the green box.

Finished with that he cried, "To the trees! Hide! Try to stay in sight of the beach in case of rescue."

The men of the brigade scattered. A helicopter flew over and a man leaned out, shooting at the fleeing invaders with an AK-47.

I went invisible and headed for the water. My plan was to swim as far as I could and then invoke a cloud spell, ride it about an hour due south to get past the Isle of Youth, then west until I hit land probably on Mexico's Yucatan Peninsula. Then I'd find the nearest American consulate and introduce myself. But before I could do that, I was resting on a small coastal island and found by U.S. frogmen. Only 27 men, including me, of the original 1,300-strong invasion force escaped. Most of the rest were captured.

***

The invasion was a fiasco. When it hit the news, Kennedy impressed me by taking full responsibility. Gomez grumbled that he would have impressed him more by providing American air support. He resigned from the CIA in disgust. It was obvious from his lifestyle that the old Cuban had squirreled away some money over the years and I was sure he wouldn't be hurting in retirement.

As best as we could figure, there were 114 men killed and 1,189 captured. Castro put on show trials for the captured Cubans, sentencing them en masse to 20-year prison terms. After the revolution, they hadn't bothered with trials but this was a chance to rub the United States' nose in it. Surprisingly, he didn't execute them. Most were later released in exchange for $60 million in food and medicine.

The day after the invasion ended, Castro declared the revolution was socialist and executed ten "counterrevolutionaries" for "treason." On May first, May Day, he referred to Cuba as a "socialist country" in a speech.

Kennedy publicly set up a commission to investigate the "Bay of Pigs" as it was now being called. In private his displeasure at our failing him and making him look bad was felt all the way down to the GS-11 level. It was known that there were to be no screw-ups. I kept my head down and followed my assignments as best I could. Bissell sent me back to Europe and to the Middle East on some rather mundane operations. I got the feeling he wanted me out of town. I spent a lot of time on planes, which gave me time to think. I was wondering why I hadn't gone invisible and headed for Mexico the minute the shooting started. Did I feel some obligation, some duty to the CIA? To the U.S.? I hoped not. Perhaps it was just my hatred of Castro for ruining my playground.

***

Returning to D.C. I was called in to Bissell's office. He returned my greeting with a scowl.

I sat down in front of his desk as he pulled a manila envelope out.

He laid out four 8 x 10 black and white glossies of Maria and me in public. In one of them we were kissing.

"Do you know who this woman is?" he asked.

"I'm not sure," I stated honestly. I decided to state my suspicions. "She either works for Castro or the Sovs."

Bissell looked at me seeming to determine if I was joking. "She's a sparrow for the KGB."

An access agent, used to seduce men into giving up secrets. My stomach turned at that. And that was the first confirmation I had of my suspicions.

It didn't matter; my feelings for her were too strong. If she was a Soviet spy, it didn't change a thing for me.

"What is she doing with you?" Bissell demanded.

"Not her job," I stated, surprised how defensive I sounded.

Bissell just looked at me.

"We're lovers," I stated softly, "nothing more."

Bissell let out a long breath. "There are some that say that Castro knew we were coming. That's why Bay of Pigs was such a fiasco."

"Kennedy cut off our air support," I barked back. "That's why it was a fiasco. Not that it was a very good plan to start with. But we were holding the beaches, we inflicted numerous casualties on Castro's troops. If we'd had air support and air superiority we might have succeeded." I wasn't sure why I was so defensive about what happened on that beach; it hadn't been my plan.

"I know, I know," Bissell said holding up his hands. "But people are looking for a scapegoat and an officer who knew all about it talking to a KGB agent the day before he leaves to join the invasion looks pretty tempting."

"You've been watching me?" I asked slowly, anger rising in my gut.

"We've been watching her."

"Oh." That made sense. I don't know why I hadn't thought of that possibility.

"You need to stop seeing her," Bissell said.

I shook my head. "I'm not going to do it."

"We can put you in jail," Bissell said low and soft.

I chuckled. "You can try."

Bissell looked at me, realizing he was losing that argument. "What did you tell her?"

"Nothing. We don't talk 'shop.'" I thought that wasn't quite true. I did tell her I was going away but I often told her that. Just when we were both in Washington we met. She gave me a number to call. If she answered, she was here. I gave her my apartment phone number. If she was in town she called it. If I answered, I was here.

Bissell pulled a small reel-to-reel tape player from a drawer in his desk. He turned it on.

"Can I see you?" It was my voice but changed as it would sound on a telephone.

"When?" Maria's voice.

"Tonight. I'm going out of town tomorrow." I recognized the conversation, it was the one we'd had on the phone the night before I left.

"Yes, I'll be at your apartment in an hour, okay?"

"Yes."

Bissell turned off the recorder.

"I tell her I'm going out of town all the time," I explained. "She's never burned any previous operation of mine because she doesn't know what I'm doing.

"How would she know where I'm going and even that I'm part of any invasion force? Hell, that there even is an invasion force. If Castro knew anything it was due to the poor operational security the whole mess had."

Bissell shook his head. "You should understand by now how intelligence works. Perhaps Castro did know there was going to be an invasion. Perhaps he or the Soviets knew you were involved. You tell her you're leaving town, they put two and two together. That's why we have an entire analyst section: to put two and two together. So does the KGB and you can bet Raul Castro does, too."

I had no answer for that. Had she told the KGB my schedule? Had they figured out that the invasion was eminent because of it? I didn't know but I did know the thought I'd burned the operation was twisting my insides. I was at some level amazed I cared.

Bissell sighed. "I'm going to burn this tape. It's the only copy. It's not damning but someone could twist it as easily as I just did. But you must stop seeing her."

I shook my head. "No. You can't take that away from me."

"We'll fire you."

That took me aback. If I was fired would I be in danger of Houser trying to kill me? Since joining the CIA there had been no assassination attempts. I didn't know why and didn't care.

"You're going to explain to Dulles how you let a man with my talents get away?"

"He agrees with me."

I shrugged. "Then fire me."

Bissell looked at me for a long time. I could tell he was debating doing just that. Finally he stated, "Damn it, you're too valuable an asset.

"Just be careful what you tell her."

"I always am."

***

Dulles left the CIA in November of 1961. No one would confirm if he resigned or was fired. He was replaced by John A. McCone, Chairman of the Atomic Energy Commission and, Maria said, a war profiteer. Bissell followed in February of '62. My new boss was Richard Helms, who'd been with the CIA since the OSS days of World War II.

On Monday, May 21st, I showed up for work at nine. I'd just gotten back from Berlin the week before on a counter-intelligence mission looking for the person in the Berlin consulate that was giving intel to the Stasi. It turned out to be a homely American secretary who had been seduced by a handsome East German spy. It was a sordid business and it made me happy Dulles had not made me an "access agent." It also made me worry about what Maria did to accomplish her job for the KGB.

As usual when in the office, I hung up my suit coat in the metal coat rack and headed for my temporary desk. There was a cylinder from the pneumatic system on my desk. I opened it by twisting the end and pulled out a neatly typed note ordering me to report to Helms.

Mrs. Franklin, who'd stayed on after Bissell left (civil servant), let me right in, without even warning Helms. The DD/P was standing behind his desk when I walked in. He looked at me with his piercing dark eyes and said, "Get your coat; we're going to the Pentagon."

I felt my eyes get wide. "The Pentagon?"

"Yes," he confirmed flatly, straightening his already straight tie. He looked right at me. "The AG will be there."

"AG?" I still hadn't learned all the acronyms.

He looked frustrated. "Attorney General Kennedy."

"Oh," I said. Even I knew that JPK had put his kid brother in his cabinet.

Helms accompanied me outside to an idling sedan. We both got in the back and it drove south. The driver piloted the car around the Tidal Basin and the Jefferson Memorial and onto a bridge crossing the Potomac. We pulled up to a door on the east side of the Pentagon and a soldier in a dress uniform opened the door for Helms. I jumped out before he could open the door for me.

Inside the Pentagon we crossed the highly polished floor to an elevator. We took the elevator to the next story. The doors opened on a wide hallway as highly polished as the first. There were uniformed men and civilians walking along on various tasks, each looking serious and in a hurry.

Helms led me toward a dark oak door. I followed him in and found I was in a conference room with a long dark wood table and chairs arranged around it. There were four men already sitting: a pudgy, baldpate man with a double chin, a man in a blue military uniform with a single star on each epaulette, an older man I didn't recognize in civilian attire, and Robert Kennedy. The AG was ten years younger than the president, with thick wavy hair that so many of the secretaries swooned over.

"Thank you for coming," the pudgy man said, pointing us to seats. "Officially, this meeting never took place." I noticed he emitted an aura of alcohol as if he'd been drinking even at this hour.

I looked at the man in his tired-looking eyes, then at Helms. I didn't like how this was starting.

Kennedy, for his part, looked at me for a long moment, then turned to Helms. "This Houdini?" In his New England accent it sounded like "Thas Howdanah?" and I wasn't quite sure what he'd said.

"Yes," Helms said simply, "this is the operative codenamed HOUDINI."

The AG turned and looked at me, giving me a toothy smile. "Mr. Vaughan, I've been reading about you. I think you can help us."

I looked at him. "Yes?" I didn't know what to expect.

"You have connections with Chicago organized crime," Kennedy said, as if it were a fact.

"Yes," I replied. This was really getting my curiosity up. I remembered Luttazzi's complaining that Bobby Kennedy was after Momo. And a central piece of the Kennedy administration was prosecuting organized crime.

"Good," he said. He looked around, his eyes landing on the fourth man, who had remained quiet throughout this exchange. "This is FBI Special Agent in Charge of the Chicago field office, Heston."

Heston leaned forward. "What I am about to tell you is classified Secret Codeword. The codeword is COCOTTE." Heston was older than the other FBI agents I'd run across in my time working for the government. I suspected he was close to or past retirement age. Probably working a desk job, I mused.

"The FBI has an agent very close to the head of the Chicago OC hierarchy. I can't reveal the agent's identity to you, and simply revealing this person's existence to anyone in the Chicago Mafia would greatly endanger the agent's life.

"I have a report here on your activities, Mr. Vaughan, with the Chicago crime syndicate in December 1958 and January 1959. Apparently you became close to one Teo Luttazzi, lieutenant and muscle for Giancana."

I couldn't see any reason to deny it. "Yes."

Heston looked at Kennedy and Kennedy looked at the military man. "This is General Lansdale," he said as introduction.

Lansdale grimaced broadly, which caused his eyes to squint and, it seem, his short-cropped black hair to stand up straight. "Since the Bay of Pigs, the situation in Cuba has deteriorated. We now know that the Soviet Union has shipped at least 30,000 tons of arms to Castro. There are Russian and Czech military advisors in Cuba right now and Cubans are traveling to the Soviet block for military training, including combat flying.

"Last summer U-2 surveillance pictures showed indications of Soviet-supplied MiG-15, 17, and 19s on the island."

I knew what a U-2 was—working at the CIA one couldn't help but know about the high-flying spy plane. Besides, Gary Powers got shot down almost two years ago over Russia. But, "What's a mig?" I asked.

Lansdale looked at me as if he didn't know whether I was serious. "Soviet fighter jets," he said finally.

"Okay," I replied, not quite seeing the seriousness of it.

"And," Lansdale went on, "in December Castro announced he's a Marxist-Leninist and always has been. This while maintaining, with Soviet and Communist Bloc assistance, the largest army in the Western Hemisphere outside our own."

He paused to let that sink in. When I didn't respond he said, "Cuba is obviously a major Communist threat in this hemisphere and it's right on our doorstep.

"Therefore, President Kennedy has authorized a new operation against the Communist regime in Cuba. It's called 'Operation Mongoose.'"

I felt my stomach tighten. I had a bad feeling this meant another trip for me to Cuba to be shot at—and eventually, it did.

"It is being run by a 'Special Group,'" Lansdale continued, "consisting of military and CIA operatives. One of the objectives of the operation is to eliminate Castro."

I'd learned long ago that "eliminate" was a CIA euphemism for kill.

Then Heston spoke. I wondered why all three of them were needed to explain this and what the pudgy man was doing there, just watching, listening and looking bored. "We know the Chicago mob lost millions in revenue because of the revolution. Castro's nationalized all businesses and shut down their casinos. If there is any prostitution going on in Havana, Castro must be keeping the money himself." He smiled at his joke.

The pudgy man leaned forward. "Let me introduce myself. I'm William Harvey. I'm in charge of Operation Mongoose. The former DCI, Mr. Dulles, authorized the CIA to work with the Chicago syndicate in efforts to eliminate Castro." I hadn't heard anything about that, but I wasn't surprised; I didn't have a "need to know." Harvey continued, "AG Kennedy has ordered it stopped."

Then what was this about? I wondered.

"Officially all contact between the CIA and the Chicago syndicate has been ended," Kennedy clarified. "However, we'd still like to continue the contacts through back channels."

"What we'd like you to do," Lansdale began explaining, "is be liaison between the Special Group and the Chicago mob."

"To have them continue to try to kill Castro?" I asked. Back channels meaning me, apparently.

"Yes."

I blinked and looked at him to make sure he was serious. He gave no reaction that indicated he was joking.

"Deniability," Harvey explained. "If the plot is exposed, it'll look like revenge for costing them millions of dollars. And AG Kennedy has his official order for it to stop to protect the CIA and the President."

I looked at Kennedy. "I'm sure you are not Giancana's favorite politician. He might not want to protect you."

"Don't worry about that," the AG said, indicating he was disinclined to elaborate.

Heston looked at me. "I dealt with metas during the war. I know what you are capable of."

I wondered what he meant by that. I had wondered why Giancana had helped the brother of the man who had called him before the McClellan Committee become president. What exactly was the connection between the Kennedy family and the Chicago Mafia? I had no idea, but it worried me. Giancana had acted as if the president's father was his vassal. And Luttazzi had acted as if Giancana was going to give Joe Jr. the presidency. But in exchange for what? I wondered. Something the senior Kennedy had said came back to me. When asked why the election was so close he said he was a frugal man and refused to pay for a landslide. What did the Kennedy family owe the mobster?

"All you have to do," Lansdale explained, pulling me out of my thoughts, "is act as liaison between the special group and Giancana."

"And," Kennedy added, "do it quietly enough that my order to end it looks like what is actually happening."

"And as NOC I'm deniable?"

"Exactly," Harvey said.

Kennedy looked at me. "What are we paying you, Vaughan?"

I returned his gaze, wondering why he was asking this. "I'm a GS-12," I said simply. "Step one."

Kennedy looked confused and looked at Helms. "What does a GS-12 dash one make?"

"He was just increased from GS-11 dash five," Helms stated defensively.

"Around seven-ten a month, plus locality pay," I said, answering the question and earning an angry glance from Helms.

Kennedy shook his head. "A man of his talents requires compensation commensurate with his value. I want him paid GS-15 dash ten."

"Sir," Helms started, "regulations—"

Kennedy cut him off. "Mr. Vaughan is not a regular General Services employee. He's to be GS-15 step ten by the end of the week. The president will authorize it."

"Yes, sir," Helms said softly. I could tell he was feeling chastised.

"And give him an unlimited expense account."

Helms was about to protest, then thought better of it. "Yes, sir," he repeated.

I tried hard to suppress a smile. When I got back to my desk I looked it up in the General Services Handbook. A GS-15 dash ten made the handsome sum of fifteen hundred a month with $250 "locality pay" for the D.C. area. This was going to improve my lifestyle significantly.

"One last thing," Harvey said, his second chin wagging, "as far as the DCI is concerned, this operation is not happening. Helms will give you a cover assignment. Do you understand?"

I looked at Harvey. "I'm supposed to not tell my boss about this?"

"Exactly," Harvey stated.

Lansdale was nodding in agreement. I looked at Helms.

"McCone has moral objections to this operation. Your orders come directly from the Special Group which works out of the White House," he explained but the tightness in his voice indicated he wasn't happy about it.

"Okay," I agreed reluctantly, looking at the men in the room.

So the next week, as liaison between the "Special Group" and the mob, I was back living in Chicago and visiting the Ambassador Hotel, after calling ahead and talking to Luttazzi.

It was a nice spring day when I stepped out of my taxi in front of the Ambassador Hotel. I decided Chicago was much more pleasant when it was warmer. I looked at the revolving door with trepidation. It had, of course, been repaired so the bullet holes were missing, but I felt claustrophobic going through it.

I didn't recognize the goons in the lobby. They eyed me and apparently didn't consider me a threat. I took the elevator to Luttazzi's floor. He was still living in the same suite and Frankie let me in, after giving me a funny look.

"Mike!" Luttazzi called out, walking across the room and embracing me. After the CIA training I was able to give him a proper hug back.

Barbara was still there, sitting on a divan, looking at me with her empty blue eyes that would have been lovely if there'd been some life to them. But as our eyes locked, there suddenly was a moment as if she'd come out from behind the wall she built up for herself. But it was just a flicker, and then it was gone. But I saw acres of pain and an abyss of sorrow in that moment.

"So, Mike," Luttazzi said, "Welcome back. You're looking good. I guess working for the CIA agrees with you."

I stared at him and he laughed. "Yes, we know. They doing a better job protecting you?"

"No assassination attempts since joining them," I said.

"That's good. Where you staying?"

"The Bismarck," I replied.

Luttazzi made a face. "Not the high-class joint it used to be."

"CIA likes to save money," I explained. Actually, I could have afforded somewhere nicer, with my new unlimited expense account, but I wanted to keep a lower profile.

Luttazzi laughed at my CIA comment and then looked at his watch. "We'd better get going; Momo doesn't like to be kept waiting."

As we walked out of the room I glanced back at Barbara, but nothing of what I'd seen before showed in her eyes.

Momo was in the same room I'd interviewed in more than three years ago. It had changed slightly: the phone was new, the carpet was now blue not red, and some plants were different. There were still large men arrayed around the room.

Giancana glared at me from behind his desk. "I don't like people who cut and run at the first sign of trouble," he growled at me.

This wasn't the greeting I was expecting and I didn't know how to answer.

Luttazzi spoke up. "Momo, we agreed it was dangerous to have him around. When they tried to kill him, two of our people were killed instead."

Giancana looked me over. "So, what do you want?"

"You've been working with the CIA to try to kill Castro," I said. I felt foolish standing in front of his desk, but none of the chairs in the room were occupied except Giancana's.

"Yeah, and we were just told to stop," Giancana grumbled.

"Kennedy has a plan to overthrow the Castro regime."

Giancana laughed. "Like the Bay of Pigs?"

"No," I said. "This one is better, more thought out. And the first step is to kill Castro."

Giancana leaned forward and looked at me. "Then why the hell did they tell us to stop?" he yelled.

"Political cover for JPK," I said. "But unofficially, they'd like you to continue the efforts. And the CIA will pay you for it."

It took him a moment to realize what I'd said. "The CIA is reinstating the contract on Castro?"

"Yes," I said. "We want your organization to do the job."

Giancana laughed. "That damn hypocritical Catholic bastard Kennedy." I didn't know which one he meant, Joe, Joe Jr., or Bobby.

He chuckled for a moment, a sound coming from him that was more evil than mirthful. "Fine, we'll do it. Live by the sword, die by the sword, I say."

The meeting went longer as there were details to work out. Giancana and Luttazzi were both given clandestine methods to contact me. Funding had to be arranged carefully and clandestinely, as CIA funds transferred to a known organized crime figure had to be covered — laundered they called it — carefully.

Giancana told Luttazzi to work with me on the "contract."

I lived in Chicago in the Bismarck for a week, working with Luttazzi. Coming out of my hotel on a rainy day, I asked the doorman to get me a taxi. He was facing away from me, and when he turned I saw the gun in his hand. I realized he was wearing only the jacket and the hat of the doorman's uniform, and neither fit very well.

Before I could react he fired and I almost doubled over with pain, but I knew if I fell down I'd die. The world took on a slow-motion effect. I shoved my hand against him and pushed him back. He staggered into the street. I landed face-down on the hard sidewalk. I put my hand in my pocket and gripped my talisman. I could see the gunman had recovered and was walking purposefully toward me, aiming his gun at my head. I shot an airbolt at him that knocked him into the street again. Tires hissed and grumbled on wet pavement and a car hit him with a snap of breaking bone and a crack of shattering glass. He was thrown down the street and landed on the asphalt with a wet thud before sliding along the rough surface.

The driver of the car, a woman, got out and started screaming hysterically. I put my hand where the bullet had entered me, ignoring the wet warmth, and ran a healing spell until I passed out from the effort.

I came to in a hospital. There was a large man in a light gray suit sitting in a wooden chair reading a comic book. He saw me move and asked, "How are ya?"

"Who are you?" I asked drowsily.

"Luttazzi asked me to keep an eye on ya. I gotta make a call." He walked out, leaving his comic book on the chair.

I pulled back the covers and pulled up my hospital gown to examine my injury. I'd been operated on, to remove the bullet I assumed, and sewn up. I used a healing spell to finish the job and fell back asleep.

"Vaughan," I heard. I opened my eyes to see Luttazzi standing over me looking concerned.

"Who?" I asked.

"Contract killer. We've used him ourselves. No idea who paid him."

"Houser," I whispered, not having the energy for more.

"Maybe," Luttazzi said, shrugging his shoulders.

"Dead?"

"Yeah, car finished the job for you."

I shook my head. "I got lucky."

***

I was out of the hospital a few days later. The doctors, after noticing my "miracle" healing, removed the stitches and let me sleep.

I first went to see Luttazzi.

"Where's Scarpelli?" I demanded.

He looked at me curiously. "Tahoe, why?"

"Listen," I said. "The first attempt on my life was in Havana in '58. The SIM. I thought maybe it was Rosenberg."

"Yes, I remember you asking me about that. I guarantee you it wasn't Rosenberg or the Genovese family."

"So that leaves Scarpelli."

"Or this Houser who runs your guild now."

I didn't correct him; unfortunately, it wasn't my guild anymore.

"Or Scarpelli working for Houser," I said.

He thought about that.

"The next attempt I'm in Chicago. How did Houser know I was here? Did Scarpelli know?"

Luttazzi thought about that. "He was in town then. He was in trouble over the Rosenberg trouble in Havana. We asked him about you, as you suggested. So, yes, he knew you were here."

"The next attempt was Miami in February, '59, but I know how Houser found me there."

Luttazzi listened thoughtfully.

"Then," I continued, "Nothing until now, and less than a week after having contact with Giancana, who Scarpelli works for, a hit-man tries to kill me."

Luttazzi still looked thoughtful, then asked with controlled anger, "You're not accusing Momo?"

"No," I explained. "But Scarpelli could have heard I was in town."

He looked around the room as he contemplated that. Finally he reached for the phone and dialed four digits. "Tell Momo I need to talk to him," he ordered whoever answered.

Hanging up, he looked at me. "We'll take care of Scarpelli for ya."

"Thank you," I said, and I meant it. I didn't care that "take care of" quite probably meant "kill."

***

Operation Mongoose proceeded apace. My part was fairly simple. Giancana's men suggested various ways of killing Castro and I'd pass them to Helms, who'd usually approve. They would be tried and all of them failed, usually because the methods were so convoluted and silly. Even so, none was as silly as the idea of poisoning a cigar and presenting it to him in a box of his favorites.

Luttazzi told me a few weeks into the project that Scarpelli had disappeared and no one knew where he was. I hoped sleeping with the fishes somewhere, but felt I was probably wrong.

Then, in October, some U-2 photographs changed everything. McCone was on his honeymoon in Seattle, the only continental U.S. city the nuclear missiles in Cuba couldn't reach. I was recalled back to the North Building to stand by on the sixteenth. On the twenty-second Kennedy went public with the news that the Reds had nuclear missiles in Cuba. Two days later a piece in the *New York Times* questioned the existence of the missiles. Meanwhile, U-2 photos of Cuba showed Soviet-made "medium range" bombers capable of carrying atomic weapons.

I started wondering if this was a good time to visit, oh, Australia.

CHAPTER TWELVE
Washington D.C., October 26, 1962

Maria looked at me across the restaurant table. Her meal was growing cold as she ignored it. Even though it was dark in the room I could see the burning anger in her eyes. "This is going to get us all killed," she growled at me. She was puffing on her cigarette manically, putting all her anger into it.

"Don't tell me, love," I said around a mouthful of cannelloni. "Tell your bosses."

She ignored that and spat out a swear word in Spanish. "This will be World War III. Does Kennedy know that?" She was waving the cigarette around, the glowing tip bright in the dim light.

The president had gone public on Monday night. It was Friday. "Yes, he must. Does Khrushchev?"

She ignored that, too. It was the second time I'd hinted that I knew she worked for the *Komitet Gosudarstvennoy Bezopasnosti* but she wasn't reacting to it.

"My bosses don't like you," she said, surprising me. Perhaps she thought with the end of the world seeming eminent she might as well drop the charade.

I didn't mention that my bosses didn't like her, either. But, with the president thinking I was his magical James Bond, I had even less to worry about. I'd seen *From Russia with Love*. It looked as if seducing enemy agents was part of the job.

"What don't they like?" I asked.

"That you're CIA, of course."

"And?"

"They ordered me to never see you again."

I smiled. "Yet, here you are."

She took a drag on her cigarette. "I told myself this was to tell you goodbye."

"And?"

She shook her head. "I cannot—especially not now. We could die tomorrow and I'm supposed to give up the one thing in my life that brings me joy."

I couldn't help but grin at her words.

"Will they punish you?" I asked, worry in my voice. I'd heard the KGB could be brutal in its discipline, a nine-millimeter bullet behind the ear being most common.

"Not after we are all radioactive ash."

Her fatalism was starting to depress me a bit.

"There's no guarantee of that. No one wants atomic war."

"Don't be so sure, *mi amor*."

I don't know what she meant by that.

"Let's get out of here," I said waving for the check and ignoring my half-eaten meal.

She nodded. We both knew where we were going.

***

October 27th was a Saturday. When the phone rang in my apartment I disentangled myself from Maria's arms and legs and scent and warmth and wandered to my apartment's kitchen where the phone was.

"Hello?"

"This is Helms," came the answer. "There will be a car to pick you up in front of your apartment in ten minutes. Be outside dressed in a suit and bring your ID." The line clicked and went dead.

I didn't know why the DD/P was calling me at—I looked at a clock, was it really almost two?—to order me to wear a suit and bring my CIA ID. As NOC I rarely used it and it was at that moment in my safe.

I hurried to the bedroom and started to dress—no time for a shower. Maria looked at me sleepily.

"What is it?" she asked, the white sheets contrasting with her dark skin.

"I have to go."

"Go, where?"

I gave her the look.

"Oh," she said softly. "Are we about to be bombed?"

"Doubt they'd care if I wore a suit for that," I stated, finding my dark narrow tie. It seemed *de rigueur* at the CIA.

"The White House," Maria gasped. "They are taking you to the White House. Why else wear a tie on Saturday?"

I laughed. "I doubt it."

I finished dressing, kissed her goodbye, and went downstairs to the street where a typical government nondescript sedan was waiting. What I didn't realize was I wouldn't see her again for over a year.

The car headed south and I was sure it was going to the North Building. But it continued south to Pennsylvania Avenue. I wondered if it was my imagination but there seemed to be more military on the streets than usual.

The car pulled up to a guard shack at the east entrance to the White House. Both the driver's and my ID's were checked and compared to a list on a clipboard before the armed guard let us through.

I caught a glimpse of protesters outside the White House fence. Some held signs demanding an invasion of Cuba. Others signs called for peace as if we were already at war.

The car pulled up to a door in the stone side of the building.

"If you'll accompany me, sir," the driver stated, exiting the car.

There was another guard at the door and the same ritual of showing ID's.

I was taken down a hall with marble floors, wainscoting on the wall, chandeliers hanging from the high ceiling, and the occasional painting. It was more luxurious than the Ambassador Hotel in Chicago.

I was shown an office with a light blue motif. AG Kennedy and Director of Central Intelligence McCone were there seated on plush chairs around a dark oak cocktail table.

The men were short with the pleasantries. The AG simply handed me two pieces of paper.

"These are photocopies of two telegraphs we received from Premier Khrushchev," Kennedy said, still in his heavy New England accent. "Please read them. We received this one, first." He pointed to the top photocopy.

I read the letters. The first one they received was passionate, angry, insisting the U.S. remove missiles from Turkey before they—the Russians—would remove missiles from Cuba. The other, more consolatory letter, only asked that the U.S. agree not to invade Cuba.

I looked at Kennedy. "What do you want from me?"

"I want to know," the AG ordered, "which letter is genuine."

"Genuine?"

"Yes," he spat angrily. "We think one is from Khrushchev, the other from someone else in the Kremlin. We need to know which one came from the Premier. Can you do that?"

I looked at him and then said, "Give me a moment."

"Please hurry," McCone stated.

"A quiet moment," I clarified, managing to shut up my boss and the president's brother.

I picked up the demanding letter, the one that wanted missiles removed from Turkey. I concentrated on it, ran a spell of far seeing. I tried to determine who wrote it and what they really meant. It was difficult. And I found myself blocked by a spell of protection—a spell that had to be placed by an adept working for Khrushchev.

I set the letter on the table. "This one was very likely written by Khrushchev himself."

"How do you know?" McCone asked.

I just looked at him. "I just know."

I picked up the more consolatory letter. It felt completely different. The writer had no protection spell around him, as he was a Kremlin official writing on behalf of a drunk and worried Khrushchev. The writer was worried too but about being put against the wall for not writing this letter as Khrushchev wanted and for what would happen to him if Khrushchev lost power and was replaced by someone more hard-line than Nikita.

I looked at Kenney and McCone. "Both letters came from the Soviet Premier, but only one was written when he was sober."

"Which?" Kennedy demanded leaning forward.

I pointed to the demanding one. "This one—the first one to arrive. Someone else wrote the second one for him when he was drinking."

"Damn," the AG spat.

The he spent a long moment in thought. "Khrushchev will have to acknowledge the second letter. He can't admit he was drunk and didn't even write it himself. If we ignore the first letter then that old Commie will have to admit the second letter came from him."

I realized they were going to ignore the first angry letter and just acknowledge the second consolatory one.

Kennedy looked at me. "Thanks, HOUDINI."

He probably didn't realize how much he'd just insulted me.

Kennedy stood. "Gentlemen, I need to get to EX-COMM," he said. He placed the letters in a briefcase and left nearly without a word.

I had no idea what "EX-COMM" was.

The AG strode out of the room, closing the door.

McCone looked at me. "God help us all."

***

Khrushchev pulled the missiles out of Cuba, and Kennedy pulled missiles out of Turkey that were supposedly obsolete, anyway. I didn't quite understand why the missiles were pulled if they ignored the letter demanding that.

Operation Mongoose was halted October 30th, 1962. Kennedy had agreed publicly not to invade or take further overt or covert action against Cuba. I still worked for the CIA and knew that wasn't true.

I took on a couple more assignments, one to South Vietnam—the heat and the humidity made summer in D.C. feel chilly- one to Egypt (at least it was a dry heat), and spent over six months in Finland posing as a geologist for an American oil company. Helms wanted an "on the ground" assessment of Finnish neutrality after the end of what came to be called the "Note Crisis" where the Soviets tried to assert dominance over Helsinki for the second time since World War II. Finnish president Kekkonen was, in Helms' words, "licking the black off of the Sov's boots" to prove Finland was not on the side of the West while claiming neutrality in the cold war. Kekkonen had increased trade and "cultural" contacts between the countries while pushing the West for peace including pushing for a "Nordic Nuclear-Weapons-Free Zone."

I spent the time talking to politicians, bureaucrats, men on the street, using translation spells and truth spells if needed to get to the truth.

And I thought Chicago was cold.

On November 14th, 1963, Helms ordered me to his office. Bobby Kennedy was there; they were seated in chairs around a cocktail table away from the desk.

"Vaughan," Helms stated as I walked in. "Mr. Kennedy would like a word with you."

I looked at Kennedy as I sat down in a chair opposite McCone. He'd aged in the year since I'd last seen him during what came to be called the Cuban Missile Crisis. Stress of the job, I speculated.

"Giancana has failed us, as I'm sure you know," Kennedy stated.

I nodded. Castro's security hadn't been the third-world Keystone Cops brigade the CIA had expected. They'd probably had Soviet help was the consensus. I wondered if perhaps they just were that good on their own.

"The president, of course, knows about you and your talents. He'd like you to utilize them to kill Castro, and, if possible, Raul."

I looked at him. "The president wants this?"

"He's ordering it," Kennedy clarified. "He's tired of this burr under his saddle."

"Here," Helms said, handing me a piece of paper.

I read it and blinked. It was signed at the bottom by Joseph P. Kennedy, Jr., President of the United States, and it ordered me, Michael Vaughan (assumed alias), to "eliminate" Fidel Castro Ruz, Prime Minister of Cuba, and if possible, Raul Castro Ruz, Minister of Armed Forces of Cuba.

"When?" I asked.

"As soon as possible," Kennedy said. "But the president is making a trip to Dallas next week, the twenty-second, so please not before that. We don't want any distractions."

"I understand," I said, amazed that I did. In the four years of working for the government I had come to a pretty good understanding of politics, office, bureaucratic, and elective. JPK was not doing very well in the opinion polls—some said he caved on the missile crisis—and needed to start working on his re-election. Speculation was Nixon would run again, and he'd almost beaten him last time—some say he actually did. The news of Castro's death would overshadow any good publicity the trip would generate.

"Okay," I said, taking the paper and putting it in my pocket.

"You can't take that," Helms said. "We'll keep it safe for you."

Kennedy looked like he wanted to stop me but I just glared at him trying to look dangerous. I hadn't used my power on my bosses ever. But this was a good time to start. I didn't want them to have "deniability" were I caught.

I smiled. "I'll keep it safe."

They let me take it, I guess sensing that they'd eventually lose that argument.

I left the "order" in my safe in my Georgetown apartment with a secure spell on it that should have lasted a couple weeks for such a small space. I traveled to Florida to prepare for infiltration of Cuba…and to enjoy some of that unlimited expense account.

***

And that's how I ended up with the leader of the Cuban Guild waiting for darkness to infiltrate the villa occupied by Castro's adept.

We drove up into the hills southwest of the city. The cab stopped along a narrow road that ran along a high wall.

"His house is behind this wall. It was the home of a sugar plantation owner. The entrance is down the road a short distance. There are always armed guards present."

I looked at the wall. I guessed it was about a foot thick and nine feet high. "Thank you. You'd better leave before we arouse suspicion." I opened the car door and stepped out. I ran a quick spell of far-seeing. On the other side of the wall was a manicured lawn with occasional trees. The house was a good hundred feet from the fence. It was built in the style of a Spanish villa. I could see men in uniform with AK-47s slung over their shoulders. There were some French doors not far from my position. I could get into the house there. I ran an invisibility spell and teleported to the other side of the wall. I walked toward the doors, trying to stay out of the moonlight for fear of casting a shadow however faint. I hoped my footprints in the grass were not obvious. Suddenly an alarm sounded. The men with the weapons ripped them from their shoulders and held them at their hips while surveying the lawn. I didn't know what caused the alarm, but I tried to hide next to a tree trunk just in case. My hand ran into something smooth and cold on the bole. I looked at it. It was a round lens about the size of a rukhkh's eye, about three inches in diameter. It had a wire that ran down the trunk of the tree into the ground. Rukhkhs could see in the dark and see you when invisible. Also, at the CIA someone had once explained how infrared radiation, the heat from my body, could be detected, but I didn't understand them. This device, this technology, must have spotted me where human eyes couldn't.

I heard dogs barking. Damn. Dogs could smell me, but they were easily fooled. I sprinted for the French doors, arriving just as three big dogs pulling a guard by their leashes came around a corner of the villa. The dogs made a beeline for me. I had no choice: I pointed my finger at them and then at the guard holding them. They turned and attacked the guard. He screamed and went down under their assault. Dogs were so easy to fool.

I looked in the windows and saw what looked like a study: books on the wall, leather chairs, a fireplace. I teleported into the room. I felt reasonably safe for the moment, so I sat in a wing-back chair and rested. I let the invisibility spell naturally dissipate. Any guard who looked in could easily see me, but they were too busy looking for me in the yard and would probably think I belonged there as they wouldn't know how I got inside otherwise. The screams of the man attacked by the dogs grew less until I heard some shots. Either they shot the dogs or the man or both.

Rested, I went to the room's door, which was closed. I opened it and saw that it led to a long hall. If there was a powerful adept nearby I should feel it unless he was masking (I couldn't mask because I was using spells, so I knew that he knew I was there). I did feel him and felt that he was to my left. I started walking in that direction. Occasionally I heard shouted orders from outside. They were still looking for me, apparently.

The hall opened up into a large room. I approached it warily; the adept was near. I readied a powerful spell to attack him with. If I could catch him off guard I might manage to disable him before he could retaliate (yes, he knew I was in the area, but not exactly where, and I lacked the same knowledge about him, so surprise was going to be a big factor in this conflict). Since I didn't know his name, I couldn't cast a spell that affected him but only cast spells the effect of which hurt him. The spell I chose caused the oxygen in the air to vibrate very fast, and when oxygen gets hot, it will burn almost anything. Unfortunately, I couldn't cast it while invisible so I would be vulnerable during my attack. I felt he was very near and I had the spell ready. Since the area affected by the spell was small (about three feet in diameter), and the closer I was to him the more powerful it would be (inverse square law), I had to step into the room and see him before the attack. I went in fast and saw, standing and (strangely) smiling, the adept that had been at the house where I was arrested. I noticed he was wearing a military dress uniform that was khaki in color and had many superfluous ornaments. I was about to cast my spell when a pain in my abdomen caused me to double over. What, an attack of appendicitis now? I wondered.

I looked up at the adept with tear-filled eyes. He was just looking down on me as if I were some sort of pitiful animal. Then he was joined by another man, also wearing a uniform but with more ornamentation. It was the cab driver/guild leader that had brought me here.

"Too easy," he said, shaking his head.

"What?" I managed to gasp.

"To lure you here and—" he held up a piece of paper, unfolded "—to learn your name," and he said my name, my given and family name that gave him the power to attack me directly. Then he pointed at me and I collapsed in pain again. I tasted blood in my mouth. Then suddenly, I felt fine although I could still taste the blood. I tried to teleport away but he must have had some kind of holding spell on me. He could do that, knowing my name.

"Bring her in," he ordered the younger adept, who nodded and left the room.

"Her?" I wondered. I hoped he didn't mean Mrs. Salinas.

He didn't.

The young adept lead Maria in by her arm. Her hands were bound behind her back and she had a gag in her mouth. She looked at me and the shock and pity on her face was immediately apparent despite her situation.

I doubled over at that moment in pain, crying out involuntarily. My guts were twisting as if there was a knife being turned in them. I felt as if I were about to vomit and bile taste joined the lingering aftertaste of blood in my mouth.

Then suddenly I was fine again.

"I can do this forever, you know," the sham cab driver said, putting the paper with my name on a small table by a chair. He was addressing Maria. "Damage him and repair him. He can live in excruciating pain as long as I please." And he punctuated the point with another round of internal organ-twisting. He could have simply hit me with a truth spell, and if it were strong enough I'd tell him anything. But he must have been enjoying my agony and Maria's anguish. Knowing this didn't make it any more pleasant. Sparing her the pain of watching this became more important to me than stopping the pain.

"What do you want?" I asked, spraying reddish spittle on the carpet.

"Simple. Everything you know about the CIA's network in Cuba. You think we don't know about the CIA's adept, codename HOUDINI?" He gave me another jolt of pain and then I felt better again. "Let's start with the name of your contact."

"You arrested him before I got to his house," I said.

Pain made me see red as I squirmed on the floor. I heard Maria stifle a sob behind her gag.

"Your second contact. Where did you get those clothes? Someone had to help you."

I nodded. "I don't know his name."

"Where does he live?"

I felt almost well as he healed me again, but the memory of pain still lingered like a cold finger probing my brain. I told them the apartment building.

"Which apartment?"

I gave the block captain's apartment number.

Maria couldn't look at me. I hoped it was because of the pain and not because my weakness.

"That seemed too easy," the young adept said, speaking for the first time.

"Yes, it did," the cab driver/guild leader/Communist adept said. "We'll check it out and if he lied," he pointed at me and my left little finger bent back—my own muscles causing it to happen—to touch my wrist with a bone-snapping quickness, "he'll regret it."

"No," a voice said and a third man came into the room. I recognized him from the news and CIA briefings. It was Ernesto "Che" Guevara, the Cuban Minister for Industry and co-revolutionary with Fidel who had volunteered to keep order in the ranks through executions he reveled in carrying out himself. He was shorter than I expected, but, of course, he still had the scruffy beard. He had a scar running from his chin to his temple that reportedly — according to the Cubans — was from a bullet he got during the Bay of Pigs invasion — except CIA reports were that he wasn't there. He was not, at that moment, wearing a beret. He was wearing plain green fatigues of the type Castro was always pictured in. He had a Russian-made Makarov pistol in a holster on his hip. It was one of the weapons I trained on at the Farm. I knew it was a Soviet rip-off of the Walther *Polizei Pistole*, had an eight-round magazine, fired the Russian 9 x 18 millimeter cartridge, and was a pretty reliable weapon for something made by the Reds.

"No," Che said. "He is lying, but I can make him talk and then we'll find the *contrarrevolucionario* soon enough."

Che drew his weapon and pointed at Maria. I tried to react but couldn't. He didn't fire but only spoke, "Put the traitor on her knees."

The adepts forced Maria to her knees in front of me. We locked eyes. I wondered about the word "traitor." What had she done? Was this simply because she'd slept with me? If I were the cause of this I would hate myself for it.

Che put the muzzle of the pistol to the back of Maria's head.

"Tell me all you know, or I will execute her."

I was desperate; I said the first thing that came into my head. "You can't execute her without a trial!" I tried. "The Bay of Pigs invaders got trials."

Che grimaced at me. "To send her or anyone to the firing squad, judicial proof is unnecessary. Trials are an archaic bourgeois detail. This is a revolution! And a revolutionary must become a cold killing machine."

"No," I spat out. "I could give you the entire CIA network in Cuba if you let her live." I only knew about my two contacts, one they'd already captured and probably executed. I knew the CIA had operatives in Cuba, but so did they. In reality, they probably knew more than I did.

Maria was crying quietly, tears streaming down her face.

"You're lying," Che said, not moving the gun from its position.

"I'm an adept: I have no loyalty to the CIA, or the United States. Hell, I don't even have a guild to be loyal to." All of which was basically true except somehow I'd grown loyalty to the CIA and by extension the United States. But it was Maria that mattered most to me at that moment.

"He could be telling the truth," the cabbie/adept said.

"Let her live, let us live, and I'll tell you everything I know about CIA operations in Cuba," I said.

"And Bolivia, Africa, and Argentina?" Che asked.

I decided Maria's life—and probably mine—hung in the balance here and I'd better sound credible. "I don't know much about Africa or Argentina, but Bolivia I know a lot." I knew nothing. I was stalling for time and it seemed to be working. I hadn't been bleeding internally for some time now. If I could get the three of them within a 3-foot diameter—without Maria near—we might survive this.

"What about Bolivia?"

I got to my knees and sat on my ankles. "It's a house of cards. The government is barely hanging on with help from the CIA. One strong shove and the whole place will fall apart." I was making this up.

"I didn't realize," Che said softly.

"Yeah, the U.S. government is covering it up but the place is ready to go any day now."

Che looked at me sharply. I worried I'd gone too far.

"He's lying," the younger adept said.

"Maybe," Che admitted. "But if he isn't..." His voice trailed off.

By now I was feeling pretty healthy (with the exception of my little finger, which was dangling like a broken branch from my hand). "Why would I lie?"

"Because he's a CIA pig," the younger adept spat at me.

"Look at you," I said, "working for the Commies."

"Communism is only a means to an end," the old cabby adept said. "We have grander plans."

I looked at Che. Everything I'd heard about him said he was a true believer in Marxism. "How do you feel about that?" I asked him.

"Only through armed revolution will the socialist utopia be established," Che said. "My nostrils dilate while savoring the acrid odor of gunpowder and blood. With the deaths of my enemies I prepare my being for the sacred fight and join the triumphant proletariat. To that end, these hero adepts have developed a way to speed the downfall of bourgeois capitalism."

I think Che liked to hear himself talk. And what he was saying was scary. This man was a sadistic ideologue. But as long as he talked I was still alive.

"What?" I asked.

"We don't have to tell him," the younger adept said. "Just kill them both."

I could tell the older adept wanted to tell me. He was probably dying to tell someone, especially another adept who could appreciate his brilliance.

"My guild is unique," he said. "We can do things most other guilds cannot. We can give the revolution an army that cannot be defeated."

I thought for a few moments. What power did the Cuban guild have that others didn't? "Zombies," I said.

"Exactly," the older adept confirmed.

I shuddered; Maria gasped behind her gag. Even she understood. It was a terrifying prospect to have red zombie armies. Imagine an army of armed zombies. You can't stop it: you can't kill them. The only way to stop a zombie is to do so much damage to it that it can't move. If you nuke a zombie army all you get, other than the ones at ground zero who are vaporized, are radioactive zombies. You can't even kill them with a spell: they are already dead.

Your troops killed by the zombies become zombies and join your enemies. No one had tried it before, at least not in modern times, because it took the wealth of a nation to arm and equip such an army and few guilds wanted to get in bed with any government.

"A zombie army liberating the oppressed peoples of the world," Che said. "We might even start with Bolivia. Soon we will have the worker's paradise Marx predicted, Lenin and Stalin worked for, and Khrushchev has betrayed."

"And my guild will be the most powerful in the history of the world," the older adept added.

I almost snorted. It was the old ends-justify-the-means argument. Who cares how many people you kill as long as your goals are supposedly laudable? I'm sure Hitler and Stalin felt they were doing good as they murdered millions. "Does Fidel know about this?" I asked.

Che shook his head. "The man no longer has any revolutionary vision. He's little more than a petty dictator, now."

"Even the Soviets don't know about it," the older adept said. "I drive that taxi so I can hit the party officials I carry with truth spells and learn what they know. They are completely in the dark."

"It's a brilliant plan," I said truthfully. It was the most frightening thing I'd ever heard.

There was an uncomfortable pause. I suppose they were ruminating on whether to kill Maria and me.

"And the CIA network in Cuba," Che suddenly demanded.

Oh, no, I realized, he'd called my bluff.

"I know nothing, just my two contacts."

"You're lying," Che screamed, his voice high pitched with anger.

"No," I said, trying to remain calm, "that's all I know."

"You have condemned her to death," Che said simply.

"NOOOOOOOOOOOOO!" I cried and tried to stop him but I was still under the holding spell and could not move. He fired into Maria's skull. Blood splashed on my face as she fell to the floor, more blood spreading from her body. Blood was also on Che's uniform and the look of satisfaction he gave me was almost sexual.

Anger and pain electrified my nerves. I looked at the adepts who were about four feet apart. Che was about ten feet from them still holding the gun with which he'd just killed Maria.

No one noticed when I put my hand in my pocket to touch my talisman. I raised my other hand (with my pinkie finger swinging around loosely) toward the adepts. The older saw my move and my guts twisted. He was trying to kill me. I ignored the pain and hit the space between the adepts with my spell. The air shimmered brightly. My anger and pain made the spell more effective than normal.

Blood washed into my mouth and I felt it squirting out of my anus. I suspected my insides were mush. As soon as blood stopped pumping to my brain I was dead.

The adepts' clothes ignited from the radiant heat. Then their hair. I touched my chest and ran a quick spell of healing on myself while they were distracted. It didn't cure me, but I knew it should keep me alive a few more seconds. Unfortunately, this caused my first spell to dissipate quickly.

A motion to my right caught my eye. Che was raising his pistol. Three bullets ripped through my torso before I was able to bound over Maria's body — the adept must have released me when he lit on fire — put my hand on his leg, and knocked Che out of commission, which was easier than a protection spell for me. He probably had protection from an adept but that didn't matter as physical contact negated that. I didn't kill him — that would take too much time and too much meta — but he was unconscious and crumpled to the floor, dropping his gun near me. The bullet holes he'd put in me just made three more places for what was left of my insides to leak outside.

The adepts quickly dowsed the fires on their bodies. The older one was mumbling words in the ancient tongue. I was sure his next attack would be on my brain itself. It wouldn't be painful, but it would be fatal. And I was getting weaker by the moment.

I scooped up Che's pistol and shot the older adept in the head. At that range it was hard for even me to miss and the move must have surprised him, judging from the look on his face as he fell back quite dead.

Despite my instructor at the farm insisting that that safest place to be when I held a gun was in front of it, I aimed it at the surviving adept.

He was by that time shimmering. He had had time to put a protection spell around himself that would repel bullets. But he couldn't attack me or teleport out or do any other spell while maintaining the protection spell, and he couldn't quit it while I had the gun on him. I ran as strong a healing spell on myself as I could without risking passing out. I stopped bleeding and my heart started pumping blood to my head again. I should live a few more minutes. I smiled grimly at my adversary.

"Do you know my name?" I asked. I knew he'd heard it once, but did he know it well enough to cast spells on me? If so, I had to kill him. And, if so, he was going to be much harder to kill.

"Yes," he said overconfidently. But his eyes darted to the paper on the table.

"Then I have to kill you," I said needlessly. He knew that.

"You may try, but the guards will have heard the gunshots and should be in here any moment to protect Che. You can't fight them off with just that," he indicated the pistol, "and if you try I'll kill you the moment that gun is off of me."

In fact at that moment I could hear shouting and the sounds of boots running.

Keeping the gun in my hand pointed at the adept, I moved to the table and picked up the paper. It ignited and burned. I dropped it.

Five angry men with pistols and AK-47s burst into the room. One was shouting loudly in Spanish. I teleported so that the adept was between them and me. Before they figured out where I had gone, I fired three shots over his shoulder at what looked like the leader. As he dropped to the floor—I must have hit him at least once—the rest of the group turned toward me with their weapons.

"No!" shouted the adept as they opened fire. I ducked down behind him.

The bullets ricocheted off him and into the ceiling and the walls. Some went straight back at the shooters and they screamed in surprise and pain. The survivors just kept firing more intently, not realizing that they themselves were what was killing them.

"¡*Cese el fuego!*" the adept yelled uselessly.

I knew I couldn't stay in this position forever. Eventually they'd come get me. And I was sure reinforcements were coming. Then suddenly the adept fell to the floor. His protection spell must have failed as he grew tired. The last remaining guard stopped shooting. Then he looked at me and started to aim his assault weapon. I fired twice and he joined the pile of bodies on the floor. The slide had locked back on the pistol. That meant it was out of bullets.

I dropped the weapon and rushed to Maria, kneeling beside her. She was obviously dead as a large portion of the back of her head was missing and the puddle of blood around her was about the size of a dinner table. Even a healing spell couldn't fix that. And even that powerful of a spell required knowing her name—her real name—and I didn't. She had never told me.

I blinked back tears and ran my hand down her back. Even then it felt somehow like touching a warm doll. There was no life left in her.

I figured I had little time before more guards would arrive. Fighting back anger and the desire to wail in my pain, I went to the dead leader of the *Gremio Cubano*. I found a talisman in his pocket. It looked African in origin and I could feel its power flow into me. I cured myself again as much as I dared—including my much-suffering little finger—and then went invisible. With this new talisman I could cure myself without passing out more than with my old one.

As more armed guards entered the room I decided it was time to leave. Too bad—I would have liked to have killed Che for all the trouble he caused me and would probably cause the world—and for what he did to Maria. It would only take a moment but I would have to be visible.

With one last look at Maria's bloody body, I sprinted from the room just as the guards came rushing in. I found a closet and hid in it. I put an alarm spell on the door and curled up in a ball and cried. I'd read of the murder of innocents, the summary executions by Fascists, Communists, and simple petty dictators who's only ideology is remaining in power, and it had always been abstract and somewhat unreal to me. But now I suffered due to the cruelty of one man with power.

Houser was a dictator and tried to kill me numerous times. But that bothered me less then Guevara killing Maria. At least Houser had reason to fear me. Guevara killed because he could.

I eventually fell asleep, exhausted from the emotional and meta toll I had suffered.

When I woke up about twelve hours later, the house was deserted. Bloodstained tiles marked where the battle had occurred, but all the bodies were gone. I explored the house. There was a room a lot like an office, with a large ornate desk. There was a wall safe behind a large picture of Castro. I opened it easily, feeling the residual of an alarm spell from the now-dead head adept. Inside it was a collection of talismans, including the one that had been taken from me when I was captured. Also there was a handwritten book. It was written in Spanish and the ancient language. I leafed through it and found some interesting things. And there were documents, letters, and agreements in various languages, including English. One in English was dated 1943 and included the name Brooks and the town of Yuma, Arizona.

I found a small valise to carry all my new treasures. The African talisman went into my pocket.

I set up in the room where Maria had died. The adept was dead; Castro and Che should be vulnerable. Even though in my mind—as I had just decided—I was going to resign from the CIA, I still wanted to finish this mission and kill that Argentinean sadist.

The counter spell blew me back against the wall. It took me a moment to realize my hair and clothes were smoking. I found a bathroom with a shower and doused them before they burst into flame. And I got the hell out of there, knowing they'd be looking for me. I had killed an adept, all right, but apparently neither Castro's nor Che's.

It was night when I left. The house was being guarded for intruders, not for someone leaving. I teleported over the wall and walked back to Havana, masking as best I could. Helicopters flew toward the house, one containing someone very powerful.

I spent the rest of the walk trying to talk myself into going back to the house to try to kill them. I didn't succeed.

***

I tried repeatedly to kill Che with meta (I had to learn his entire name "Ernesto Guevara de la Serna" but with help from friends in the CIA that wasn't hard) but he always had strong protection. When he went to New York to speak at the UN I tried to get close enough to touch him but I could not get to him.

Two years after our encounter, Che left Cuba (rumor was he and Fidel had a falling-out) and tried to start revolutions in the Congo and Bolivia. I wondered if he believed my story. Having lost track of him personally (I'm sure the CIA always knew where he was) it was even more difficult to try to kill him (inverse square law). As my anger and hurt subsided I tried less and less.

Che didn't have zombie armies (apparently that plan died with the head of the *Gremio Cubano*) and was not very successful in his armed revolution to "free the oppressed peoples of the world." In 1967 he was reported killed in a battle with the Bolivian army. A contact in the CIA told me he was actually wounded and captured and, despite a CIA request that he be kept alive at all costs, executed by a Bolivian soldier. He was buried in an unmarked grave. I hoped at a crossroads with a stake through his heart. Last thing the world needs is the ghost of a power-hungry sadistic ideologue like Che haunting it.

***

Bonita and I arrived in Key West about three in the morning. She had slept through the trip after I gave her a sleeping spell. I figured riding a cloud at wave-top level would scare the poor girl (scared me when we almost broadsided an oil tanker). I woke her up on the sidewalk by the sign pointing out this was the southernmost point in the U.S. She looked at me and asked, "*¿Dónde estamos?*"

"U.S.A.," I said, and she wrapped her arms around me and gave me a tight, albeit platonic hug.

CHAPTER THIRTEEN
Washington D.C., December 2, 1963

Upon delivery of his "precious item," Gomez gave me the papers on the leaders of the NAG and a person to contact. I didn't. I had other plans formulated since I opened that safe in Cuba.

I traveled to Washington D.C. and the North Building. I used a persuasion spell on Helms' secretary to get an appointment that day—first time I'd used my power inside the building.

"What is it, Jackson," Helms asked as I walked in.

"I'm resigning," I stated simply, sitting in the same chair I had for my interview with Bissell.

"Just a moment," Helms said and picked up the phone. "HOUDINI is resigning," he said into it and hung up.

I started to speak but Helms held up a hand. "Wait until McCone is here, please."

It only took a few moments for the DCI to enter. Out of habit I stood up and shook his hand before all three of us sat again.

"Problem with the mission?" Helms asked.

"I couldn't accomplish it," I said simply. "Castro's adept is too powerful."

McCone leaned forward. "It was a long shot to begin with and President Johnson has put all covert action against Cuba on hold pending a review.

"Where's your presidential order?" he asked.

I pulled it from my pocket and held it up. It burst into flames.

Both men gasped, never having seen what I could do.

"I was burned," I stated simply.

McCone looked shocked. Helms looked resigned.

"I suspected, "he said. "Johnson was not pleased to hear of your mission. We just missed catching you in Key West. We wondered if the State Department burned you."

"On Johnson's orders," I clarified.

"Yes," McCone said softly. He must have sensed my anger because he added, "I strongly suggest you don't go after the president."

I shook my head. "No, he's not worth it. I would like to kill Guevara, however."

Helms looked at me. "Why?"

I explained what happened to Maria.

They were both sincere in their sympathies.

"We'd appreciate it if you didn't kill Guevara," McCone stated, "at least not until we can interrogate him."

"Don't worry," I replied. "He, too, has a strong adept protecting him." I'd have to touch him to kill him and odds of that seemed slim.

Neither McCone nor Helms was happy to see me leave the CIA but they understood, they said.

I wasn't sure I did. I wondered if I shouldn't stay and fight those like Guevara. If Johnson hadn't burned me perhaps I would have.

But I had other battles to fight.

***

The magic of compounding interest: I had taken my stash—what was left of Sidney's money and my winnings from Miami—and put it in the bank and left it there, untouched. It had grown by almost ten thousand dollars in the four years since I first opened a bank account. That came in handy.

Intercontinental jet flights were now quite common. I flew to Oslo via London. From there I flew to Tromsø on a rickety prop-driven aircraft, asking myself if it would have been better to use a flying carpet and suffer the obvious cold. Tromsø was a smallish city north of the Arctic Circle buried in snow almost up to rooflines of the quaint multi-colored houses. It took a day of exploring the city—a short day as the sun barely got above the horizon and it started getting dark around two in the afternoon. But I found it. It was a small coffee shop that served very strong coffee in small cups. In contrast to the near darkness outside it seemed to radiate warmth and light and the smell of the coffee enveloped me as I entered. The proprietor was a large middle-aged man with long, curly blond hair. He came out from the back and approached me. I fingered my talisman since I couldn't understand Norwegian otherwise.

"What name do you go by?" he demanded. "What is your guild?"

Obviously he'd felt that I was an adept.

"I call myself Mike Vaughan. "I was with the AMA," I told him, "but no more."

He looked at me. "What do you want?"

"I need to talk to Brunhild."

"Why?"

"It has to do with Kader. Tell her that."

He stared at me as if his eyes could discern my motives. "Give me a phone number where I can reach you. I'll let you know."

"Thank you." I gave him the number of my hotel.

I waited at my hotel for three days, not daring to leave lest the call come while I was out. Luckily there was a decent restaurant attached although I learned to stay away from something called "lutefisk."

On the third day I was called to the front desk to answer a call on the hotel's only phone.

"Vaughan?" It was a woman's voice.

"Yes. Who is this?"

"Come to the coffee shop." The line went dead.

I returned to my room, grabbed my satchel, ran downstairs, and got a taxi to the shop. It was dark by the time I got there at three in the afternoon.

Inside the shop I saw her, Brunhild, looking about as she had five years ago in San Francisco. She was sitting at a table looking very much like any well-dressed, handsome middle-aged woman. Except there were two very large men wearing business suits with her. Berserkers, I presumed. I also noticed there were no other patrons in the shop.

I walked over. She looked up at me with blazing blue eyes. "I'm surprised you are alive." She was speaking the ancient language. "How did you manage? Always run?" She said it without malice or anger, which was worse.

I looked at the only vacant chair around the small table. She looked at one of the berserkers. He pointed to my satchel. I gave it to him and he opened it and inspected the contents. Finding nothing that worried him, he handed it back and nodded to her.

She pointed to the chair.

"Usually I ran," I said as I sat down. "But I'm through running."

She looked up from her coffee. "Oh?"

"I've learned some things," I said, "about fighting."

"Such as?"

"There are things worth fighting for, other than your own hide."

She almost smiled at that.

I looked at her. "Is Kader alive?"

"How can I trust you?"

"I saw him in Chicago, alive. But he wasn't doing well. That was January 1959." And here it was December, 1963. Almost five years.

"Yes, I know." She took a deep breath. "He's in a coma. More than four years now. They are keeping him alive medically. They move him regularly. Houser has found them a few times. Luckily, they've managed to escape."

"I thought Houser let Kader go in San Francisco. Why would he be hunting him now?"

"Some are still supporting Kader," she sighed. "So now Houser needs him dead."

"Louis and Liesl?"

She nodded, taking a sip of her coffee. "They are fine — still caring for him. Addleman died the last time Houser found them. Died protecting Kader. They — we — are paying medical doctors to keep him alive." She looked into her coffee cup as if to hide the pain in them. She whispered, "It's all I dare do."

She must have really loved him and this was difficult for her.

"I need to see Kader; I think I know what's wrong with him."

She looked at me, her eyes wide. "How would you know?"

"Houser made a deal with the *Gremio Cubano*." I said that last in Spanish. I pulled papers from my satchel and handed them to her. "Houser bought a spell from them."

"What spell?" she asked.

"Zombification."

She almost dropped her cup. "But he's an adept — they'd need his name."

"They know his name," I said.

She looked at me, hard.

"During the war he apparently gave his name to a Negro guild's leader, someone named Brooks in Yuma, Arizona?"

"Yes," she said. "He had to. But he and Louis killed Brooks."

"Apparently Brooks sold Kader's name to a Mexican adept before they killed him," I explained, "and from there it made its way to Cuba where the *Gremio Cubano* got a hold of it." I pointed at the papers. "It's all in there."

She looked angry. "That man's vileness knew no bounds," she spat.

I shrugged my shoulders; Kader had killed him twenty years ago. "So Houser bought Kader's name and the zombification spell from the *Gremio Cubano*. And that's what he used against Kader."

Happiness dawned on her. "If you know Kader's name and the spell…"

"I can cure him." I was pretty sure I could cure him, at least.

She smiled at me and I realized what a lovely woman she was. And how much she loved him.

"If they knew his name, why not just kill him?"

"I'm not sure," I replied. "But I think it's because if Kader died, there'd be a sudden power struggle and Houser would have no guarantee of coming out on top. With Kader getting sick and looking weak, Houser could recruit others to his side slowly until he had enough to challenge a weakened and sick Kader. But, as you said, now they want him dead, but don't know where he is. And since he's almost a zombie, they can't kill him with a spell."

She nodded. "That makes sense." She looked at me and seemed to come to a decision. "Seattle," she said. "I'll get you the address and phone number."

***

My flight to Seattle stopped in New York. I called the Huntington Hotel in San Francisco from a payphone and asked for room 1313.

"Yeah?"

"This is Mike Vaughan; let me speak to Houser."

It took a few moments, during which I needed to deposit more dimes.

"What do you want, Vaughan."

"You want Kader dead?"

The line was silent for a moment. "Yes."

"I want one million dollars and your name on my survival."

Again he was quiet a few moments before speaking. "Fine."

"Meet me in Seattle," I said, "At the base of the Space Needle. Tomorrow at two P.M."

"Okay," he said.

"And bring Scarpelli," I said. "I want him to deliver the money."

There was a long time when all I could hear was line noise. Then, "Fine."

I hung up, knowing I had guessed right: Scarpelli had run to Houser.

***

Considering it was the day before the winter solstice it was no surprise that the sun had already gone down by the time my plane landed in Seattle. It was also not a huge surprise that it was raining.

As I stepped out the plane's door, I was handed an umbrella by a smiling stewardess. I thought she must be cold in her honey-colored dress with a bright orange scarf, but was still smiling bravely and wishing me a good day.

The rain wasn't hard; it was just incessant. It was still raining by the time I had gotten my luggage and gone to the front of the terminal to catch a taxi. It rained the entire trip into Seattle up Highway 99. Finally the taxi stopped at the hotel the travel agent in Oslo had recommended, the brand new Edgewater Inn. It was readily identifiable by the big neon "E" on top. Upon check-in I was offered a fishing pole so I could fish from my room. I politely turned it down. I only wanted to rest.

In the morning, bright sunshine reflecting off water woke me up. I looked out the window and blinked. The sky was blue and reflected in the blue water of the bay. There were sailboats, freighters, and in the distance large jagged mountains, white with snow, that looked like the rough teeth of some animal. They reminded me of the Tetons of my childhood, but were bigger, taller, more numerous and closer. The sight was so wonderful I stood and watched, entranced. It reminded me of the view from the Hotel Nacional except where that was a warm sunny view, this sight had a cold beauty I seemed to feel to my core.

After a light breakfast I had arrangements to make. I caught a taxi on Alaskan Way.

"Where to, bud?" the driver asked.

***

At a quarter to two I was standing in front of the Space Needle. It was a saucer shape on top of three spindly legs. It looked as if it were about to topple over to me, despite massive nuts screwed onto huge bolts that were anchored in the ground. Three gold elevators ran up and down a central shaft between the white legs. It had been built for the World's Fair the year before and now looked to me to be a permanent white elephant, although there were still people paying the dollar to take the elevator ride to the top.

Near the Space Needle was an amusement park that was shut down for the season. It was strange and somehow sad to have the rides seemingly frozen motionless. The dual concrete monorail tracks curved around the Needle before running down the street to the north, and about every ten minutes one passed by with a whoosh of air moving aside and electric motors.

It was still a cloudless day, but very cold. My breath showed as I exhaled and I had my hands shoved in my coat pockets, the same coat I'd bought in Chicago during the coldest winter on record five years ago. The fingers of my left hand were curled around my new talisman.

I spotted Houser walking toward me from the direction of the street, passing under the monorail tracks. Two large men were on either side of him and Scarpelli was walking a few feet behind him. They were all wearing long overcoats. Houser was wearing a grey snap brim hat and had his hands in the pockets, one of them most likely wrapped around his talisman. Scarpelli's pockets seem to bulge as if he was carrying rocks.

Once Houser had spotted me he didn't take his eyes off mine, but simply walked straight for me, stopping a few feet away.

"Vaughan," he said by way of greeting. His two warriors passed by him and were on either side of me. Scarpelli stood to Houser's right and a foot or so behind him.

"Houser," I said back.

"Where's Kader?"

I laughed. "I'm not going to tell you what country he's in without your name in my hand."

He stared at me with his gray eyes a few minutes, his prominent jaw moving imperceptibly as if he could barely control it.

I looked at Scarpelli. "How the mighty have fallen," I said with a chuckle.

The ex-mobster scowled at me.

"Did you know," I told Houser, "that he used to be a big man in the mob?"

"Shut up, Vaughan," Scarpelli hissed, his dark brows brought together in anger.

"Used to report to Meyer Lansky," I continued, "ran the casino at the Hotel Nacional in Havana before the revolution."

Scarpelli looked around as if searching for an escape.

"And now he's nothing more than a hired gun," I went on, trying to make contempt drip from my voice.

"That's enough, Vaughan," Scarpelli yelled and reached inside his coat.

"No," Houser said simply and directly.

Scarpelli glared at him for a moment, then pulled his hand out, showing both Houser and me that it was empty.

I laughed at his embarrassment. "So, Vinnie," I said, smiling. "You told Houser I was in Chicago in '59?"

"Yes, he did," Houser revealed.

"And Havana in '58?"

"I had Scarpelli keeping an eye on you to see if you'd join with Kader. He told me a Negro adept had asked about you; I knew it had to be Louis Brown."

"So the men that attacked us in Havana?" I asked Scarpelli.

"SIM," he said as if bragging. "Returning a favor."

I didn't ask what. The mob and Batista's secret police were so intertwined as to be often indistinguishable. The Cubans had disposed of a bastard to—unfortunately—replace him with a bigger bastard.

"And you heard I was in Chicago last year."

"That one," Houser said, "he did on his own. I was not happy."

"Neither was Luttazzi," I said. I looked at Scarpelli. "Bad move." I looked at Houser. "And how did you get involved with this criminal?"

"When I learned you were staying at the Hotel Nacional in Havana, I asked my pal Joe Kennedy if he knew someone down there I could trust. He called his pal Sam Giancana and Giancana gave him Scarpelli's name and he gave it to me."

I looked at Scarpelli. "Gee, even Giancana treated you as just another hired gun."

Scarpelli started to reach inside his coat again but thought better of it. He looked at me with hatred etched into the lines on his face.

Houser took a step forward toward me and looked up at the Space Needle.

"Up there," he said.

"What?" I asked, not knowing what he meant.

"Let's talk up there." He pointed to the saucer shape on top of the spindly legs.

I looked at the three other men. "Alone, no goons."

He gave a mirthless laugh. "You've spent too much time with the Mafia."

"Alone," I repeated.

"Scarpelli?" Houser asked.

"Leave him here, for now."

"Fine."

We went to the ticket booth and Houser paid the two dollars for two tickets. We boarded one of the elevators, the one that faced north. Houser and I were the only passengers, but there was an impossibly cheery girl in a blue uniform-like dress who regaled us with facts: "The Space Needle is 605 tall, and is 730 feet, three inches above sea level. It is the tallest building west of the Mississippi River. The observation level where we'll be disembarking is at 520 feet. The elevator trip takes 43 seconds, during which we will travel at a maximum speed of 14 feet per second or ten miles per hour."

I was hardly listening. The elevator doors and walls next to the doors had windows. As soon as the elevator cleared the ticket booth, I could look over a hill, covered with houses and trees, cut through with steep-looking streets. Then a body of water came into view east of the hill, and as the elevator rose, a range of mountains. They weren't as steep and pointed as the ones to the west I'd seen from my hotel room, but seemed more rugged and primitive. I might just have been because they were closer. Snow accentuated the rocky peaks. Finally, a snow-covered mountain in the distance became visible, the more so the higher the car climbed.

"From here," the girl continued, "you can see Queen Anne Hill, Lake Union, the Cascade Mountains, and in the distance, Mount Baker, 80 miles away."

I almost forgot Houser, looking at that mountain.

"We're fortunate today as Mount Baker is not always as visible as it is today," the girl continued.

"And when on the observation deck, be sure to look southeast to see Mount Rainier, the tallest mountain in the state," she finished just as the elevator came to a stop. "Thank you for being such good listeners, gentlemen."

The elevator opened in the center of a circular room. The exterior walls contained large plate-glass windows. Some people, tourists probably not wanting to face the cold, were milling around inside. There were more outside on the deck, also. The outside deck was a few feet lower than the interior floor allowing those inside to see over the heads of those outside.

I followed Houser to a door that was almost directly in front of the elevator. We had to go down about four steps to get to the door. Wordlessly I followed him out the portal. It was cold with a light breeze, which made it very chilly. There were still puddles on the deck from the rain the night before. There was a short wall, maybe three feet high, and above that glass panels about four feet long and maybe two more feet up so it hit me about chest level. There was a red metal ring around the outside of the deck extending maybe ten feet beyond the glass. There were smaller rings, made of steel rods, running between the spars holding it. I wondered if its purpose was not just decorative but to also make it harder to commit suicide by jumping.

I kept my hands in my pockets, still touching the talisman.

Houser started walking around, ignoring the other people who were mostly pointing out things on the ground and admiring the view. Mount Baker was even more impressive from out here. As we faced east I saw more of what must have been the Cascades, and was taken aback by their beauty. I had never realized there was a place such as this in the world. If I was about to die, I could almost be happy having seen this.

Houser kept silently walking. I wondered if he was going to walk around the full circle and whether perhaps he was stalling for some reason, maybe for his warriors to make the 43-second trip up the elevator.

I gasped when I saw the mountain to the southeast—Mount Rainier, apparently. It was rounded and white with snow. It was absolutely huge—the biggest mountain I'd ever seen. It towered over the Cascades and the hills of the city and the buildings. I could see all of it, from foothills to the top.

I took a deep breath. I could feel the power of the mountain, yet not as much as I'd expected. It must have been farther away than I thought, which was another testament to its size. The sun was lighting up its western flanks, showing its crags and glaciers. I stood staring at it, knowing my mouth was hanging open.

"Kader," Houser said, interrupting my admiration of the mountain.

I reluctantly turned and looked at him. "I have three requirements, as I told you on the phone. The money, Scarpelli, and your name."

He looked annoyed. "You think I'm going to give you my name?"

"If you want Kader."

I could tell he was holding back his anger with some difficulty. "How do you know where Kader is?"

"Louis Brown has kept in touch."

That interested him. I'd just sweetened the pot.

"And I'm supposed to just trust you?" He wasn't totally convinced. "I don't understand why you didn't just give me Louis and Kader in Miami."

"I would have loved to, but at that time I didn't know where they were. They'd just left Chicago and I didn't know where they'd gone."

"They were in Chicago?"

I nodded. "Same time you were there trying to kill me."

He looked angry, I wasn't sure with whom.

"Listen," I said. "I'm willing to give you my name on this. If I don't come through, kill me."

He looked at me. "You know what I figure?"

I stared at him. "What?"

"There's a reason you wanted to meet in Seattle."

I moved my right arm in the general direction of mountains. "The scenery."

Houser stopped looking at me and was looking south over the bulk of the city's core. "I don't think so. I think Kader's here, in this town."

I had expected him to deduce that. "So, it's a big city."

"Yes, it is," Houser said, still looking south. "But before he died, Addleman told us something very interesting. Do you know what that is?"

I didn't know if he was bluffing. "What?"

"Kader requires medical attention to stay alive." He looked at me. "Already I have adepts and warriors throughout this town talking to doctors, hospitals, medical supply companies. We'll find him."

He turned to look at me. "Sorry."

I laughed; it was probably forced. This was a move I'd expected. "I make a call—meta or Ma Bell—and they are gone."

"I think not," Houser said. "Remember my pterodactyl?"

I stared hard at his face. "How could I forget?" I may have involuntarily shuddered. I hoped the bulk of my coat hid it.

"I've retrofitted it with new equipment," he said with a smile. He looked south again. I followed his gaze. "See?" he said, pointing.

I could see a large bird flying toward us, but that wasn't unusual—there were birds everywhere. But this one was growing larger and headed straight at us. When I realized it was too big to be a bird I turned to Houser.

"Five hundred twenty feet, did she say?"

I realized he was going try to teleport to the ground. I reached out and grabbed his shoulder, hard. He turned and looked at me and tried to pull away. I had the strength spell on full by then and my fingers dug into the flesh of his shoulder. I probably did it harder than needed and I enjoyed his wince of pain.

He turned, looking at the pterodactyl, eyes wide. He moved his hands quickly. He pulled the large talisman I'd seen in San Francisco from his coat pocket and pointed at the horror swooping down on us. At what seemed the last possible moment it screeched and swerved away from us seemingly inches from our faces. It crossed the sun and the light shone through its wings of skin.

I heard the tourists scream, but I ignored it. Houser turned and looked at me, his eyes wide with anger. He swung his hand around and hit me in the chest. He'd gotten his strength spell going, too. I was knocked across the deck, hit the outside wall as it curved around, and fell to the wet floor. Part of his coat was still in my hand. I threw it away and jumped to my feet. Houser was running . . . away. That I didn't expect. I watched him disappear around the curve of the building. I tried to look through the glass, the bottoms of the windows were at about eye level, but the glass was too dark and tilted out at the top. I did see something else.

Through the nearest window I could see a tourist pointing at the sky behind me. I turned fast to see the pterodactyl flying straight at me, opening its mouth. I scrambled back against the outside wall of the building, against the light-green painted metal.

The wall and glass were not high enough to keep the pterodactyl from reaching me. If I didn't want to get eaten, I decided, I'd better get inside. I ran in the direction Houser had gone.

The monster landed on the red metal ring. The whole structure seemed to sway a bit at its weight and I heard metal groaning. I was expecting it to hop over close and scoop me into its maw. But instead I heard air rush into its mouth and felt the heat.

Damn! I swore to myself. It wasn't going to eat me, at least not yet. My left hand was still in my pocket, my grip on my talisman tight with fear. I got the spell up and turned to look at it just as the flames shot from the great beak.

Houser had used a spell to give it fire-breathing. The legends of the fire-breathing dragons were usually based on such pterodactyls, used since the time of Atlantis in wars between the guilds. It was a strong spell that took a long time and the work of more than one adept to invoke, and only lasted a few hours, from what I understood.

The flames washed over me. I felt the heat and nearly screamed with the pain but I was undamaged. I didn't dare breathe, as I'd suck the flames inside. The protection spell protected only my exterior. I was vaguely aware of screams from others, but my eyes were locked on the vortex of fire shooting at me.

The beast flapped away on its long wings, the downdraft fanning the flames. The decking material was burning. The paint on the exterior of the enclosure was scorched and blistered and smoking. The fumes almost knocked me over.

I sprinted after Houser, certain he'd used this opportunity to teleport to the ground.

I saw him, standing still, holding his talisman in both hands. I wondered what he was waiting for when it hit me. Teleporting is not like setting a dial to 520 feet and that's where you go. It's more like throwing a ball; you have to have an idea how far to "throw" yourself. When we were talking calmly he'd had time to prepare for the extremely dangerous spell. But now that I was chasing him, he didn't have enough time. And teleporting without proper preparation would be tantamount to suicide.

He saw me coming and I half expected him to wink out, but instead he turned and ran.

I jumped and caught him, pulling him down to the deck and knocking off his hat which flew over the wall and presumable fell all the way to the ground below. He managed to squirm around under me so that he was facing me, his eyes wide with anger. He hit me, hard, in the jaw, which made me loosen my grip on him. He scurried out from under me and ran a few feet away. He still had his talisman in his hands, still apparently working on the teleportation spell.

I heard the pterodactyl's brain-rattling screech and its shadow passed over me. I hoped it wouldn't attack this close to its master. I shot an airbolt at Houser, hitting him full on the side. He was thrown through the air, his talisman escaping his grip and going over the wall. It clanged on the metal ring before falling. I could imagine its long drop to the ground. Houser was slammed into the wall, breaking a glass panel. He stood, dazed, then slowly looked at me. Terror filled his eyes when he realized his talisman was gone.

The pterodactyl screamed and swooped in. I got the protection spell up in time. Houser couldn't, not without a talisman. He did the next best thing: he was right next to a door to the inside, so he ripped it open and ran through it. The door wasn't completely shut as the fire spurted from the great lizard's beak.

The flames again washed over me, but not as intently, as Houser had been the target. I wondered why it attacked Houser.

When the beast flew away two parts of the Space Needle were on fire, the observation deck and the interior carpet burning in multi-colored flames with black smoke.

I teleported inside, using the windows to see where I was going. The fumes from the burning carpet were almost overwhelming. I used the same spell I'd used in the hall outside my apartment. But the air was dryer here and I only managed to quell the flames slightly.

Crowds were clamoring for the elevator. A young girl in a blue dress like the one the girl in the elevator wore, and obviously ill prepared for this emergency, was trying to calm the crowd and direct them to a set of stairs next to the elevator. Houser was using persuasion spells to get himself to the front of the line for the elevator. Without a talisman, they weren't very good spells, and people were starting to resent him.

"Houser!" I called out in my command voice. Almost everyone looked at me, including Houser.

He stared at me.

"I'll kill you where you stand, Houser, and kill all those nice people next to you if I have to."

Everyone scattered, leaving him exposed, as I'd hoped.

"Call off the pterodactyl!" I ordered, pointing at him.

"I can't," he whimpered. "No talisman."

"Damn," I whispered, realizing the horror of the situation. The talisman Houser had lost was his control of and protection from his monster. Now it was out of control. That's why it had shot fire at him.

The shadow of the pterodactyl was crossing the room. A searing and angry orange light showed it had sprayed fire again—I hoped in frustration, and not at some innocent person caught outside.

I realized I was going to have to kill the pterodactyl and I had no idea how. But Houser was an immediate problem. I decided to kill him. The airbolt hit Houser in the chest and smashed his body through the elevator doors, breaking them apart in the process. Since the elevators operated outside, he fell. I thought I heard him scream until a sickly wet thump indicated he had hit something. I suspected it was the rising elevator.

I turned and looked outside. The pterodactyl was circling, trying to see inside, I suspected.

I sprinted to the girl. "What do these people need to do?

She looked relieved to have help. "Go down the stairs; elevators are too slow and now that one probably won't work." She pointed to the one I'd just broken.

I turned to the crowd. They'd been stunned while Houser and I talked, but now the menacing pterodactyl and the growing flames had them starting to panic again.

"Ladies and gentlemen," I called, again using my command voice. "The elevators are too slow. If you'll please follow this young lady down the stairs, you will all be safe." At the same time I ran a persuasion spell to convince them they'd be fine. I added another spell so they'd listen to the girl.

"Please take small children by the hand," she added to my instructions and looked pleased when all the parents actually did, "and please move quickly but calmly down the stairs."

I knew as long as I stayed there I was going to add to the danger. I needed to draw the pterodactyl away from the innocents.

I could think only of one way. I looked out the window. I couldn't see the pterodactyl, but that didn't reassure me much. I decided if Houser could do it, I could. I went back outside, bending over the wall as much as I could. I could see the ground, but not directly below me. I didn't have time to run a far-seeing spell, as I heard large wingbeats that shook the Space Needle's structure.

I fingered my talisman and worked the spell. A shadow passed over me and I felt heat and hot air. I invoked the spell. I was in mid-air about 20 feet from the saucer at the same altitude. I started falling but was able to see the ground. Quickly I picked out a bare patch of real estate and teleported again. I undershot and ended about five feet over the concrete that surrounded the Space Needle, still falling at the same rate as when I teleported. I smacked the ground hard and had the breath knocked out of me.

I was happy with that, even though hitting the surface hurt. Better that than end up a smoking crater in the ground as I and the soil tried to occupy the same space.

I picked myself off the hard cement, feeling the bruises but happy I had no broken bones, and looked up. The pterodactyl was flying around the saucer, apparently looking for someone to immolate then eat. Smoke was curling into the sky from the observation deck. Frustrated, the animal hovered a few feet from the building and sprayed it with fire. I don't know if the screaming I heard was my imagination or real.

I yelled at the beast, but it must have been too far away to hear me. I was working on a spell to increase my voice when a car roared off the street and squealed to a stop near me. Another squeal answered from above. The pterodactyl was looking at me. It dove, holding its wings close to its body.

That worked, I thought as I jerked the door open and jumped into the back seat. The warrior I'd seen washing dishes in Chicago was behind the wheel. I'd since learned his first name was Zack. Scarpelli was next to him, gagged and his hands bound behind his back. He looked at me with wide eyes.

"Liesl's caught Scarpelli," Zack said, a little too calmly. "Thought you'd want to see him."

"Drive!" I screamed. I'd pulled the beast away from the Space Needle, but now I didn't know how I was going to get rid of it.

The car jerked away just as flames splashed over it.

"Damn!" Zack yelled, but he kept the car going. "What in the hell was that?"

"Flying death," I said, translating a term in the ancient language to English.

Zack turned the car around in a cloud of blue, acrid smoke from the screaming tires and headed back for the street, under the monorail tracks. A shadow passed over us in warning and flames surrounded the car. There was nothing to see out the front of the car but blazing orange. Scarpelli screamed through his gag and fear twisted his face.

Zack kept going from, I guessed, memory. When the flames cleared he was in the street. He turned south, following the monorail tracks. "Maybe the tracks'll give us some protection," he said.

"Maybe," I said. I didn't sound hopeful. "Where did Liesl go?"

"Back to the house."

"Good," I said. Someone needed to be with Kader and Brown in case Houser's minions found them.

"Houser double-cross you?" Zack asked.

"Of course. I expected it, but I didn't expect this."

The pterodactyl screeched just then and I was surprised the car's windows didn't shatter. My insides sure felt like mush.

"Do any good if I shoot it?" Zack asked, looking intently out the windshield as he gripped the steering wheel.

"Maybe get it mad."

"It's not mad now?"

St. George got lucky and got his pike through a pterodactyl's torso as it was running at him for the kill. No one was sure whether it actually was a fire-breathing "dragon" or if that was just an embellishment of the story.

I doubted there were many weapons that could bring the thing down. I'd seen bullets bounce off it in San Francisco. And it could deflect meta attacks. If I was going to kill it I had to find a way past its defenses: a thick hide and meta protection.

"I have three grenades," Zack said interrupting my thoughts. "How about those?"

"Not unless you can get them inside it somehow," I stated watching the pterodactyl out the back window.

The car jerked left and we were going down another street. The monorail tracks had cut over the corner of a garage, and then run down the middle of the street supported on single concrete pillars. There were two lanes of traffic on the left, one on the right. The street was one-way in the direction we were going.

I was watching out the back window. The pterodactyl was flying just above the level of the tracks, between the buildings on either side of the street. I was hoping maybe a train would hit it.

Zack was weaving the car around the pillars, trying to stay under them while simultaneously missing the other cars on the street. We ran a red light, barely dodging a city bus. He swung wide once to miss another car and the pterodactyl swooped down and gave us a blast. There was a loud snapping explosion and the car swerved.

"Blowout!" Zack yelled.

Must have been from the heat, I thought. I could see Zack struggling to keep the car under control. It got sideways on him and we smashed into one of the pillars against the front passenger's side. Metal and glass shattered with a sound that seemed to make the world shake. Scarpelli was thrown against the door that was smashing in at him. I heard a crack and his skull ran into the intruding concrete.

The warrior managed to hang on to the steering wheel and avoid crashing into Scarpelli. I smashed into the back of his seat. When the jostling was over I pulled Scarpelli off the door. He was bleeding from his skull but still breathing.

"You okay?" I asked Zack.

"Yeah, but he doesn't look so good." he indicated the unconscious Scarpelli.

"He's alive," I said, noting the pulsating blood pumping from the wound on his head. At the rate he was bleeding I wondered how long he'd survive.

I looked out the broken back window. The pterodactyl was hovering over the monorail tracks, looking at us and opening its mouth. The car with broken windows was going to give us no protection. I looked for an escape route. The monorail tracks were closer to the right side of the street, but the buildings there had no doors on this side. To my left was a hotel, but I'd have to cross two lanes of traffic and get there before the thing in the sky fried me. And I'd be leaving Zack vulnerable and perhaps give Scarpelli a chance to escape if he regained consciousness. The warrior and I could run in opposite directions but that might just have meant it would pick us off one by one rather than together.

While I was pondering this, a monorail train passed overhead. It startled the beast and it flew higher in the sky, staying there even after the silver train had passed. It must have been trying to decide if it was safe to fly lower. That gave me time to try something, something I'd learned in Cuba. I touched Scarpelli.

"What are you doing?" Zack asked watching.

"Maybe giving you a chance to escape."

The spell took a long time to craft. It would have been faster if Scarpelli were conscious.

"Give me the grenades," I said. The driver, moving frustratingly slowly, pulled the baseball-sized lemon-shaped steel grenades from his pockets. "GRENADE HAND FRAG DELAY M61" was redundantly stenciled on the olive drab exterior. They were the same type of grenade I'd thrown during CIA training.

I pulled the pins and keeping spoons on them, carefully shoved them in Scarpelli's pockets, making sure the spoons wouldn't come off and start the 5-second fuses.

"Maybe we'll get lucky," I breathed. "In any case, he should distract the pterodactyl long enough for you to escape."

"What about you?" the driver asked his voice tight with fear.

"I have to try to kill that thing." I didn't think I'd have much luck but no need for both of us to die.

I felt the downdraft of the pterodactyl's wings coming in the broken windows by the time I was finished with the grenades. It had come lower and was again just above the tracks. I knew the car would give us no protection from its next blast, but at this point running wasn't an option. Even with a speed spell I'd never make it to the hotel and the warrior would have even less of a chance. Our only chance was Scarpelli distracting it.

Scarpelli's body moved. He sat up, his head still bleeding but slower.

"Run!" I screamed at it. Zombies are notoriously hard of hearing.

Scarpelli climbed out the shattered window in his door and fell to the pavement. He picked himself up and ran down the street away from the car.

The beast took off after him, wings spread. Pedestrians were scattering in front of the running zombie and the fire-breathing pterodactyl swooping down on it. It blasted Scarpelli with fire and then seemed confused when the zombie kept running, its clothes and hair burning.

"What the hell?" the warrior exclaimed. He didn't know what I did to Scarpelli.

"Run!" I screamed at him but he didn't move and instead watched Scarpelli in horrid fascination.

The beast dove toward the street and Scarpelli was scooped up in one snap of the pterodactyl's beak. The monster landed, its claws digging into the asphalt, and turned back to look at us, the smoking zombie hanging from its mouth. It sucked what was left of Scarpelli in and I saw the skin on its throat move as it swallowed. Then it started walking back toward me, each step ripping up more pavement. I could almost believe it was smiling at me malevolently.

That's when it exploded, one blast followed by two more followed by the release of the meta power it carried inside. Red flesh and violet blood splattered the walls of the buildings surrounding the street and splashed on the asphalt. A mushroom cloud of smoke and flame boiled into the blue sky. Car tires screeched and people screamed. The head was blown down the street and landed near the car, facing me.

I looked at it. "Poison cigar zombie," I said to Zack. "Didn't work with Castro; glad it did with that." I indicated the head of the pterodactyl.

S. EVAN TOWNSEND

EPILOGUE
Seattle, December 22, 1963

I resisted the urge to get out of the car and kick the pterodactyl's head. I did get out of the car and realized how much I hurt. Zack got out beside me and lit a cigarette nervously. He was moving as if he was sore from the accident, also.

"How?" he asked.

"Zombie spell to get him running. Then the grenades must have slipped out of his pockets when the pterodactyl turned him upside down. Spoons popped off and..." The rest was inevitable.

The warrior nodded. "Lucky that."

"Where did you get grenades," I asked him, still breathing hard.

"Scarpelli had them. Liesl took them from him when she captured him."

It would be easy for her, a holding spell like I used on that pickpocket in Miami.

I healed myself enough that I could move with minimal pain. I looked back at the Space Needle. The top had smoke pouring out of it as if it were an industrial smokestack. I hoped everyone got out alive. Sirens warbled through the air, coming closer.

I sat back down in the car and rested while Zack paced back and forth puffing on the cigarette and eyeing the pterodactyl's head as if worried it would come back to life. That's how the police found us. I convinced one of them to drive the warrior and me to a house on Queen Anne Hill. Persuasion spells are so nice sometimes.

***

Kader put his hand on his head and turned to me. "What year is it again?"

"It's December, 1963, Teacher." We were in the house where Louis and Liesl had been watching over him. He'd woken up after I'd applied the correct incantations to reverse the zombie spell.

He shook his head. "Damn," he whispered. "Five years." He looked at Liesl. "Where's Brunhild?"

"Valhalla," the Valkyrie said. "But as soon as she gets word you're okay…"

Kader smiled, but then looked suddenly tired as if he was about to pass out.

"Teacher!" Louis called and rushed over to support him. I grabbed his other arm and we helped him to the couch.

"I'm fine," he insisted.

"You're still weak, Teacher," I said. "It'll take a while for you to regain your strength."

"Yes, I suppose," he said wearily.

"You'll be running the guild again in no time," Louis said.

Kader shook his head. "No."

We both looked at him, surprised.

"I'm too old and too worn out. Not strong enough. Besides, I'm too vulnerable. Who knows who else has my name?" He looked at Brown and me. "You have to do it."

I looked at Brown and Brown looked at me. We weren't sure which one he meant. "Who, Teacher?" Louis asked.

"You," Kader repeated slowly as if fighting to get out each word. "Both of you. It's going to be hard to get the factions back under control. But I know you two can do it." He laid his head back and started breathing deeply and slowly as if asleep.

I looked at Louis and he looked at me. I think each was as surprised as the other.

"Can we do this?" I asked.

Louis slowly started to smile grimly. "I think we can because we have to."

I nodded my agreement.

***

I stepped outside into the chilly evening air. With a clear sky, it was going to be a cold night. The house was on the south side of Queen Anne Hill and I could look at the Space Needle, its saucer part seeming almost at eye level up here. The sun had gone down, but the twilight was bright enough to still see the tower. Smoke was no longer wafting from it, so the fires must have been put out. Part of the gold roof was blackened and there were no lights on inside. It seemed to be made mostly of steel, so it probably couldn't have burned down, I thought.

Liesl walked out and looked at me.

"What?" I asked.

She smiled. "You're not the same man I met in Havana."

I shrugged my shoulders. "I know. I've been through a lot since then."

She wrapped her arms around me and I reciprocated. She hummed her pleasure. "You're even a better hugger."

I chuckled. "You can thank the CIA for that."

She looked up at me with her blue eyes full of questions.

"If you really want to know…" I offered.

She shook her head, making blond hair move in lovely undulating waves. She broke the embrace and stepped back. "I need to get in touch with Brunhild. It'll be nice to see Valhalla again." She walked back into the house.

I smiled as I watched her go. At that point I felt I'd never love again, the scar from Maria still fresh upon my heart. It, of course, wasn't true.

But it wasn't Liesl, either.

I returned to staring at the Space Needle and the darkening sky.

***

It took a while to bring the AMA back under our control. In all honesty, Brown was the brains of the team and I was the muscle. Many Houser loyalists tried to join the North American Guild and fight us. With the data I had obtained on the North American Guild's leadership from Gomez, Louis and I were able to keep them from becoming a threat.

My career as a leader of the American Meta Association was long and satisfying. And it was certainly better than working for the CIA.

Except you don't get to save the world from radioactive communist zombies.

AGENT OF ARTIFICE

If you enjoyed Agent of Artifice, you will enjoy the prequel Hammer of Thor, now available from World Castle Publishing.

ABOUT THE AUTHOR

S. Evan Townsend is a writer living in central Washington State. After spending four years in the U.S. Army in the Military Intelligence branch, he returned to civilian life and college to earn a B.S. in Forest Resources from the University of Washington. In his spare time he enjoys reading, driving (sometimes on a racetrack), meeting people, and talking with friends. He is in a 12-step program for Starbucks addiction. Evan lives with his wife and two teenage sons and has a son attending the University of Washington in biology. He enjoys science fiction, fantasy, history, politics, cars, and travel.

Made in the USA
Charleston, SC
29 October 2011